TAILS FROM THE CRYPT

Also by Sarah Fox

The Magical Menagerie Mysteries

MURDER MOST OWL *
DEAD MEN WAG NO TAILS *

The True Confections Mysteries

SIX SWEETS UNDER
BAKING SPIRITS BRIGHT
BOULEVARD OF BROKEN CREAMS

The Literary Pub Mysteries

WINE AND PUNISHMENT
AN ALE OF TWO CITIES
THE MALT IN OUR STARS
CLARET AND PRESENT DANGER
THROUGH THE LIQUOR GLASS

The Pancake House Mysteries

CREPES OF WRATH
FOR WHOM THE BREAD ROLLS
OF SPICE AND MEN
YEAST OF EDEN
CREPE EXPECTATIONS
MUCH ADO ABOUT NUTMEG
A ROOM WITH A ROUX
A WRINKLE IN THYME

The Music Lover's Mysteries

DEAD RINGER
DEATH IN A MAJOR
DEADLY OVERTURES

* available from Severn House

TAILS FROM THE CRYPT

Sarah Fox

SEVERN HOUSE

First world edition published in Great Britain and the USA in 2025
by Severn House, an imprint of Canongate Books Ltd,
14 High Street, Edinburgh EH1 1TE.

severnhouse.com

Copyright © Sarah Fox, 2025

Cover and jacket design by Piers Tilbury

All rights reserved including the right of reproduction in whole or in part in any form. The right of Sarah Fox to be identified as the author of this work has been asserted in accordance with the Copyright, Designs & Patents Act 1988.

British Library Cataloguing-in-Publication Data
A CIP catalogue record for this title is available from the British Library.

ISBN-13: 978-1-4483-1576-5 (cased)
ISBN-13: 978-1-4483-1548-2 (e-book)

This is a work of fiction. Names, characters, places and incidents are either the product of the author's imagination or are used fictitiously. Except where actual historical events and characters are being described for the storyline of this novel, all situations in this publication are fictitious and any resemblance to actual persons, living or dead, business establishments, events or locales is purely coincidental.

No part of this book may be used or reproduced in any manner for the purpose of training artificial intelligence technologies or systems. This work is reserved from text and data mining (Article 4(3) Directive (EU) 2019/790).

All Severn House titles are printed on acid-free paper.

Typeset by Palimpsest Book Production Ltd., Falkirk,
Stirlingshire, Scotland.
Printed and bound in Great Britain by TJ Books,
Padstow, Cornwall.

The manufacturer's authorised representative in the EU for product safety is Authorised Rep Compliance Ltd, 71 Lower Baggot Street, Dublin D02 P593 Ireland (arccompliance.com)

Praise for Sarah Fox

"A charming cozy full of unexpected surprises, romance, magic – and murder"
—*Booklist* on *Dead Men Wag No Tails*

"This delightfully warm and charming series starter is filled with romance, murder, and magic"
—*Booklist* on *Murder Most Owl*

"Cozy fans will find plenty to like"
—*Publishers Weekly* on *Claret and Present Danger*

"[The] charming atmosphere, solid plotting, and several enticing recipes are sure to please cozy fans"
—*Publishers Weekly* on *The Malt in Our Stars*

"Fox offers plenty of plausible suspects and a thrilling confrontation with the killer, along with a dash of decorous romance"
—*Publishers Weekly* on *An Ale of Two Cities*

"Readers will cheer this brisk, literate addition to the world of small-town cozies"
—*Kirkus Reviews* on *Wine and Punishment*

About the author

Sarah Fox was born and raised in Vancouver, British Columbia, where she developed a love for mysteries at a young age. When not writing novels, she is often reading her way through a stack of books or spending time outdoors with her English springer spaniel.

www.authorsarahfox.com

ONE

When I started my day, I didn't expect to end up wrestling with a skeleton. Yet, there I was, with phalanges of the right hand tangled in my hair and toe bones wrapped up in the laces of my left sneaker.

'A-woo,' cried Fancy, my brown-and-white English springer spaniel.

Both of my dogs had followed me up to the attic of the farmhouse. Fancy danced around me while her black-and-white sister, Flossie, grabbed a tibia and tugged at the skeleton.

The bony left hand smacked me in the face. I let out a growl of frustration, but it was mostly drowned out by Fancy's continuing chorus of 'woo-woo'.

'Georgie?' a familiar voice called out.

Fancy fell silent, allowing me to hear footsteps on the attic stairs.

'Up here,' I shouted to my best friend, Tessa Ortiz, even though she was already on her way to the top level of the house.

The dogs abandoned me to my skeletal attacker, running to greet Tessa as she reached the top of the steps. Their tails wagged with excitement as my friend crouched down and showered them with attention. When she finally straightened up and looked my way, I still hadn't managed to extricate myself from the unwanted embrace of the skeleton.

'Is this some sort of new fashion craze?' Tessa asked as she sized me up.

'More like skeletal harassment,' I replied, trying for the umpteenth time to get the finger bones out of my hair.

Tessa took pity on me and crossed the room to join me by the pile of boxes that had drawn me to the attic. She carefully untangled my wavy hair from the hand bones and then removed the toe bones from my laces.

'Thank you,' I said with relief as I set the skeleton down to sit on top of a box. 'Auntie O told me she had some old Halloween decorations up here, but she failed to warn me about this homicidal maniac.'

'I don't know,' Tessa said as she picked up the skeleton. She wrapped one arm around its waist and held its left hand with her right one, as if they were about to dance. 'He's probably been longing for company for years and just got a little too excited.' She twirled around with the skeleton and then held his right hand out toward me. 'How can you possibly hold a grudge against such a handsome fellow?'

'I suppose we can call a truce.' I gave the skeleton's hand a shake. 'Nice to make your acquaintance, Ichabod.'

'Ichabod?' Tessa echoed.

I shrugged. 'I think it fits.'

'A-woo,' Fancy said in agreement.

Tessa sized up the skeleton. 'You're right. Ichabod it is.'

Tessa carried Ichabod down the stairs, the dogs racing off ahead of her, while I followed more slowly with a box of other decorations held in my arms.

My Aunt Olivia ran an animal sanctuary on her farm and we were organizing a fundraising event that would take place the night before Halloween. We were calling it the Trail of Terror. Ticketholders would follow a trail across the fields and through the woods while volunteer actors, dressed up as all manner of creepy creatures, would add to the spooky atmosphere and attempt to scare the attendees. I made my living as a screenwriter, so I'd written a storyline to tie everything together and to hopefully add to the experience.

Although we wouldn't be setting up props and decorations along the trail for another week or so, I wanted to make sure that the farmhouse would be well decorated for the event and the season. It was, after all, the first thing visitors and Trail of Terror ticketholders would see when they arrived on the farm.

Decorating would have to wait, however. Fetching the decorations from the attic had taken longer than I'd anticipated – thanks to Ichabod's antics – and I now had to get ready for a meeting with the volunteer actors for the Trail of Terror. Tessa and I barely had time to sit Ichabod on one of the wicker chairs on the back porch of the yellow-and-white farmhouse before a car pulled into the driveway. Another followed on its tail, with several others arriving over the course of the next few minutes.

My aunt emerged from the carriage house to greet the volunteers. When I moved from Los Angeles to Twilight Cove, Oregon, Auntie O had insisted she reside in the carriage house, while I lived in the

Victorian farmhouse. I didn't need such a large space all for myself, but I shared it with Flossie, Fancy and Stardust, the sweet kitten I'd adopted at the end of the summer.

Stardust sat in the kitchen window, watching Ichabod with curious but wary hazel eyes, while the dogs bounded around the yard, greeting each volunteer as they arrived at the farm. I was glad that Auntie O had shown up at the first sign of people arriving. She knew many of the volunteers far better than I did, and making small talk with strangers or people I didn't know well wasn't one of my strengths. For me, writing words was far easier than speaking them.

Linette Mears was the first volunteer to pull into the driveway. If it could be said that there was a leading role for the Trail of Terror production, it belonged to her. Before heading off along the spooky trail, event attendees would be greeted by Linette, dressed as a terrifying witch who looked like she belonged in a horror movie. She would provide the backstory I'd written for the production, which involved a curse placed on the forest, which then trapped for eternity anyone who ventured too deep among the trees. After telling the brief story, Linette would dare the ticketholders to set off along the marked trail.

Vera Jackson, one of my aunt's friends, arrived right after Linette. Vera and my aunt belonged to a group called Gins and Needles. Members – all of them women – met regularly to work on sewing, knitting, and needlework projects while gossiping and enjoying cocktails. By the time Vera had parked her car, Miles Schmidt had also arrived. Miles was a tall, fair-skinned man with light brown hair that was starting to go gray at the temples. After he said hello to me and Tessa, his gaze landed on Linette. He seemed to steel himself before walking toward her.

'Morning, Linette,' he said as he approached her.

To my surprise, Linette blatantly ignored him, turning away and hurrying over to Vera.

'How are you today, Vera?' she asked in a rush. 'I hear you just got back from a cruise.'

As the two women chatted, I watched Miles. Linette's reaction to his greeting had left him flustered and I couldn't blame him. His cheeks red, he busied himself with looking at his phone, a technique I'd used on many occasions myself when feeling awkward in social situations.

I smiled when the next car pulled into the driveway and my friend

Cindy Yoon climbed out, her black hair gleaming in the afternoon sunlight. Fancy let out a happy howl and she and Flossie raced over to Cindy.

'Somebody's popular,' Tessa remarked with a smile as we approached Cindy, who was now crouched down and hugging the dogs.

'I'm not sure if it's me that's so popular or the fact that they know I usually come bearing treats.' Cindy stood up and reached into the pocket of her jeans, producing two small bone-shaped dog cookies.

Flossie and Fancy immediately sat and gazed up at her with eager anticipation.

'What good girls you are,' Cindy cooed as she fed them.

Flossie and Fancy trotted happily over on to the lawn before lying down to devour the treats.

'They love you *and* the cookies,' I assured Cindy. 'And your store is by far their favorite in Twilight Cove. Or anywhere, for that matter.'

Cindy ran the Pet Palace, a store that sold all manner of pet supplies, including dog snacks.

'And they're two of my favorite customers,' Cindy said with a smile.

Once all of the volunteers had arrived, we had a quick meeting. By the time it drew to a close, everyone had an assigned role for the event. The local theater group had loaned us some of their spookiest costumes and a few volunteers had supplied their own. For those who didn't have a costume, borrowed or otherwise, one would be made for them, either by Tessa, Vera, or Praise Adebayo, who were all excellent sewers. Praise, recently retired, was the newest member of my aunt's Gins and Needles group.

As the meeting – which we held on the sunny patio behind the carriage house – broke up, another car arrived on the farm.

'Isn't that Genevieve Newmont?' I asked Tessa and Cindy as a white woman in her late forties climbed out of the vehicle. She wore a snakeskin-print blazer over a black, lace-trimmed camisole and tight jeans. Her blonde hair had dark roots just starting to show and fell past her shoulders in loose waves. As she shut the car door, I noticed that her high-heeled shoes sported the same snakeskin print as her blazer.

'That's her all right,' Cindy confirmed with an unusual edge to her voice.

'Praise won't be happy to see her,' Tessa said.

Praise Adebayo stood chatting with my aunt near the front of the cute, yellow-and-white carriage house. She was a tall and slender Black woman in her mid-sixties, without a speck of gray in her short afro. She'd emigrated from Nigeria when she was a teenager and spoke with a melodic accent. Although I'd met her just a few times – once at a Gins and Needles meeting held at the carriage house and subsequently at other Trail of Terror volunteer meetings – I'd never known her to be anything but calm and collected.

Now, however, I saw that Tessa was right. When Praise noticed Genevieve strutting along the driveway – or strutting as much as was possible while wearing high heels on a gravel driveway – she frowned and her eyes narrowed. Striding away from Auntie O, Praise intercepted Genevieve and glowered.

'What,' she demanded in a frosty voice, 'are you doing here?'

TWO

'I don't believe that's any of your business, darling,' Genevieve said in a haughty voice.

Praise crossed her arms over her chest. 'Don't "darling" me. You already bulldozed your way into the Pumpkin Glow. Don't think you'll be doing the same here.'

'Last time I checked, you didn't own this farm.' The haughtiness had slipped from Genevieve's voice, replaced with a caustic edge. 'So you have no say in whether I can be here or not.'

With that, Genevieve brushed past Praise. I didn't think for a second that she'd jostled the other woman's shoulder by accident.

'That's my cue to get out of here,' Tessa whispered.

'Same.' Cindy gave me an apologetic smile. 'Sorry, Georgie.'

'Run while you still can,' Tessa advised me before hurrying off to her car.

Despite Tessa's parting advice, I followed Genevieve instead of fleeing to the safety of the farmhouse. I did that partly to prevent my aunt from being left alone with the woman and partly out of good old curiosity. I'd met Genevieve Newmont once, briefly, when I'd registered to take part in the Pumpkin Glow, an annual competition that required each team to build a structure – be it a mermaid or the Eiffel Tower – out of jack-o'-lanterns. At the time, Genevieve had struck me as efficient and slightly brusque, but I didn't know anything more about her. After witnessing her brief interaction with Praise and after Tessa's words of warning, I figured the woman wasn't likely to win the title of Ms Congeniality anytime soon.

I glanced back over my shoulder when I heard a car door slam. Instead of starting the engine, Praise sat in her vehicle, probably fuming. I'd have to ask someone about the bad blood between Praise and Genevieve. At the moment, however, I was more interested in what the latter woman had to say to Auntie O.

'I heard about this little fundraiser of yours and wanted to pitch in,' Genevieve was saying as I joined her and my aunt.

'That's very kind of you,' Olivia said with a smile. She put an arm around my shoulders. 'Have you met my niece?'

'Briefly,' I said. 'At the Pumpkin Glow registration.' When Genevieve gave me a blank look, I added, 'Georgie Johansen.'

Flossie and Fancy appeared and sat on either side of me. They made no move to befriend Genevieve. She ignored the dogs and gave me a brittle and insincere smile before returning her attention to Auntie O.

'As I was saying, I'd like to take part in the fundraiser.' She fingered the locket hanging from a gold chain around her neck. It looked to be enamel and was decorated with a delicate rose. 'I heard you need an actor for the leading role. A witch, isn't it?'

'Oh.' Confusion clouded my aunt's blue eyes. 'That was the first role to be filled, actually. But there's always room for more spooks and ghouls roaming the woods.'

Genevieve pursed her lips, almost like she'd taken a bite out of a lemon. 'I don't think that would suit me. I'm sure we can shift some people around.'

I couldn't quite believe what she was saying.

My aunt's smile faded away. 'I'm afraid that wouldn't be fair. All the speaking roles were awarded based on auditions.'

Genevieve reached into her oversized handbag and pulled out a checkbook and pen. A charm that matched her rose locket hung from a gold bracelet around her wrist. 'I'm sure we can come to an arrangement that will make us all happy. What sort of donation would it take to get me the role?' She held the pen poised above a blank check.

My aunt didn't often get mad, but I could see anger brewing in her eyes. 'That's not how we do things here.'

'Oh, come now. Surely you could use the money for this . . . hobby of yours.'

Her condescending tone stoked my own anger. 'We won't accept any donations that are meant to buy a role in the production.'

Genevieve turned her flinty gray eyes on me. 'Then that's your loss, not mine.'

She dropped her pen and checkbook into her handbag and stalked off in her snakeskin-print high heels.

Praise got out of her car and waited in the middle of the driveway. Genevieve tried to walk past her, but Praise stepped into her path.

My shoulders tensed and my heart rate ticked up. There was no way this was going to be a friendly conversation.

'You move to this town and think you can run it,' Praise seethed, 'but all you'll do is run it into the ground. Do the right thing and step down from the Pumpkin Glow's organizing committee.'

Genevieve's bark of laughter was full of disdain. 'I think everyone in this town knows that the Pumpkin Glow is far better off in my hands than yours.'

'I've organized it for the past three years!'

'And that was three years too long,' Genevieve said. 'Clearly, you weren't committed to the event this year. Otherwise, you wouldn't have left town last week.'

'My aunt was in the hospital and I was only gone for a few days!' Praise fumed.

'And somebody had to take control in your absence.' Genevieve flashed a smug smile. 'You should be thanking me.'

'*Thanking* you?' Praise clenched her fists at her sides. 'You usurped my position. One I *earned*.'

'You dropped the reins. Now you have to face the consequences.' Genevieve flipped her blonde hair over her shoulder. 'That's not my problem.'

She climbed into her gold SUV and slammed the door.

Praise watched, her hands still clenched at her sides, as Genevieve drove off the property. I realized that Auntie O and I weren't the only ones who'd witnessed the unpleasant scene. Linette and Miles stood frozen by their respective vehicles. When I looked over at Miles, his cheeks flushed and he ducked into his car. Linette did the same, though more slowly. Once she was ready to drive off, she waved at us through the window.

Aunt Olivia approached Praise and rested a hand on her shoulder. 'I'm sorry, Praise. I don't understand why the rest of the Pumpkin Glow committee allowed Genevieve to take over.'

'Miles was my second-in-command,' Praise said, shooting a glare at the man across the driveway.

He quickly looked away from us and started his vehicle.

'I left him in charge when I had to rush out of town. He's besotted with that woman. All she had to do was whisper a few sweet nothings in his ear and suddenly he was convincing everyone else to let her take over.'

Miles drove off and Praise kept her eyes on his car until it was out of sight.

'Everyone knows what a good job you've done with the event over the years,' Auntie O said. 'I'm sure by next fall they'll have come to their senses.'

'If that woman is still around, I won't hold my breath.'

With a whine, Fancy trotted over and touched her nose to Praise's left hand. She patted Fancy's head and the ire seemed to drain out of her. She usually had such an elegant, upright posture, but now her shoulders sagged. 'I'm sorry, Olivia. I shouldn't have caused a scene here.'

My aunt put an arm around her. 'Don't you worry about that for a minute. We're so grateful to have you involved with the Trail of Terror.'

That brought a faint smile to Praise's face. 'Thank you, Olivia. I'll see you again soon.' She turned her slight smile my way. 'You too, Georgie.'

'Goodnight, Praise,' I said in return.

My aunt and I stood with Flossie and Fancy, watching until Praise had driven off the farm and on to Larkspur Lane.

'That's not quite how I expected the meeting to end,' I said once we were alone.

'I heard there'd been some drama with the Pumpkin Glow's organizing committee.' My aunt shook her head. 'Poor Praise. She puts her heart into that event. She's the reason it's been so successful in the past.'

'It's too bad Genevieve had to rock the boat,' I said.

'That's for sure.' Auntie O sighed. 'I don't like to speak ill of anyone,' she added, 'but Genevieve Newmont strikes me as nothing but trouble.'

THREE

By the time I'd taken care of my evening farm chores, the sun was sinking below the horizon to the west, suffusing the farm with golden light. Despite the beauty of the moment, I shivered as I approached the house. With the sun's warmth quickly dissipating, the autumn chill was growing more pronounced. I drew in a deep breath of crisp air lightly scented with wood smoke, reveling in how lucky I was to live in Twilight Cove.

Fancy let out one of her characteristic howls, her gaze fixed on something behind me. She and Flossie raced off as I turned around to see what had them so excited.

Like some sort of surreal vision, a horse and rider approached, backlit by the last golden rays of the setting sun. Shadows hid the rider's face, but I would have recognized his silhouette anywhere.

Callum McQuade, the sanctuary's farm manager and my boyfriend, approached at a leisurely pace, riding Sundance, a sorrel Quarter Horse. He wore his usual outfit of jeans, a plaid shirt, and a cowboy hat. Flossie and Fancy had already reached the horse's side and now trotted along beside the large animal.

'Will you ride off into the sunset with me, Georgie?' Callum asked as he brought the horse to a stop in front of me.

'In a heartbeat,' I replied before I had a chance to choose my words.

The slow grin that appeared on his face made me glad I hadn't taken the time to filter my response.

'Mighty glad to hear it,' he said in what I figured was meant to be a Texas twang.

Fancy let out a long 'woo' while Flossie lowered her head and put a paw to her snout.

'Hey,' Callum protested in his normal voice. 'Was my fake cowboy accent that bad?'

'A-woo!' Fancy replied.

I laughed. 'I'm afraid I agree with them, but you've got the hot cowboy look down pat.'

'Yeah?'

My cheeks flushed. Maybe I should have censored out the 'hot' part.

Then again, maybe not.

Callum gazed down at me with such intensity in his green eyes that the air between us practically sizzled. 'Better join me up here so I can keep you warm, then.'

I stroked Sundance's nose. 'Won't two people be too much for her?'

'We're about to head back to the barn. She can handle the two of us for that short distance.'

'And how, exactly, am I supposed to get up there?'

Sundance was a good-sized horse, and Callum was riding with nothing but a bareback pad. No saddle. No stirrups.

'Climb up on the fence,' he said with a nod at the nearest pasture.

Flossie and Fancy seemed to like the suggestion. They charged off in that direction, the white ends of their tails waving like flags in the growing darkness.

I followed after them, with Callum and Sundance keeping pace at my side. Callum drew the horse up to stand parallel to the fence and, when I climbed up on to the second rail, he offered me his hand. I held on to it as I found my balance and then moved my grip to his shoulder as I swung one leg over the horse and managed to slide on to her back, right behind Callum.

I wrapped my arms around him and held on tight. 'I think I'm going to fall.'

'Just hold on to me and you'll be fine.'

He sounded so certain that I relaxed, a little bit at least, but I didn't loosen my grip on him.

'I've never ridden bareback before,' I said, though he'd probably figured that out on his own.

'It takes some getting used to. Ready?'

'Sure?' The word came out sounding decidedly unsure.

I felt, more than heard, Callum's low rumble of laughter. Then he clicked his tongue and Sundance began to walk. I closed my eyes tightly, my fear of falling off the horse making a comeback. After a few strides, I dared to open my eyes. I was still sitting safely on the horse's back, hugging Callum from behind. The dogs wandered along next to Sundance and the sun had dipped below the horizon, leaving the sky streaked with pink and orange.

The beauty of the moment chased away my fear. Most of it,

anyway. I relaxed into Callum and rested my cheek on his broad back.

'You make the best pillow,' I said with a contented sigh.

Another rumble of laughter made me realize I'd spoken out loud. I raised my head. 'Did I really say that?'

'You don't need to censor yourself with me, Georgie.'

'You say that now, but if you knew half the dorky things that run through my head . . .'

'I want to hear them all.' He sounded so sincere and serious that I couldn't stop myself from smiling.

'Be careful what you wish for,' I whispered in his ear.

He turned his head just enough so I could see his grin. It sent butterflies fluttering in my chest, like it always did.

We'd reached the barn, but instead of stopping, Callum guided Sundance around the big yellow building.

'I spoke to my parents earlier,' he said after a moment of comfortable silence.

'How are they doing?' I asked. 'Feeling better?'

His parents had planned to travel to Twilight Cove in September, but they both ended up with a bad case of the flu and had postponed their trip.

'So much better that they're heading out this way in a week or so.'

I tensed, no longer so relaxed.

Callum must have sensed the shift in my hold on him. 'Have you changed your mind about wanting to meet them?'

'No,' I assured him. 'I definitely want to meet them.' I took a moment to figure out what I was feeling. 'I'm just nervous. I want to make a good impression.'

One of his hands rested over mine where they were clasped over his stomach. 'They're going to love you, Georgie.' Callum drew Sundance to a stop at the far end of the barn. 'I can guarantee that.'

I hoped he was right. I knew how important his parents and sister were to him and I wanted desperately to fit in with his family.

'We should have them over for dinner at the farmhouse,' I said as I pushed aside my worries.

I knew his parents planned to stay at the Twilight Inn when they came to town. The inn was housed in a beautiful Victorian mansion with a view of the lighthouse and the Pacific Ocean.

'I'm sure they'd like that,' Callum said.

I released my hold on him and slid off the side of Sundance's back. When my feet hit the ground, I stumbled backward. I lost my balance and ended up sitting in the dirt with all the grace of a hippopotamus.

Flossie and Fancy were on me in an instant, licking my face and wagging their tails.

'I'm OK, girls,' I assured them, ruffling their fur.

Callum dismounted with far more finesse and offered me a hand. Despite the deepening darkness, I could see that he was fighting a grin.

'No laughing,' I warned.

He chuckled as he pulled me to my feet, tugging me right up against him.

'You laughed,' I grumbled, only pretending to be mad.

Keeping hold of Sundance's reins with one hand, Callum slid his other arm around my waist. 'Any chance you'll forgive me?' he asked, his face a mere inch from my own.

I tried not to let his green eyes mesmerize me. 'That depends.'

He brushed his lips against mine for a brief, tantalizing moment. 'On?'

'Are you cooking me dinner?'

He laughed again. 'How about I buy us some pizza? Is that an acceptable apology?'

I traced a finger along his collarbone. 'Almost.'

'Then how about this?'

His lips met mine and I lost myself in the kiss until Sundance nudged us apart with her nose. A few feet away, Fancy flopped on to her side and gave a dramatic sigh.

'All right,' Callum said with a grin. 'We get the message.'

'A-woo!' Fancy said as she jumped back to her feet.

'I'll feed the dogs and order the pizza while you take care of Sundance,' I said.

The spaniels took off toward the farmhouse, clearly in favor of that plan.

Later, while Callum and I were enjoying slices of delicious pizza in the farmhouse kitchen, I told him about the Trail of Terror meeting and how it had ended with Genevieve showing up uninvited.

'I don't think she's happy that she couldn't buy her way into a role for the Trail of Terror,' I said as I wrapped up the tale. 'I hope she's not going to hold it against me if I see her when I'm helping out with the Pumpkin Glow.'

'She probably won't want the whole town to know she tried to bribe you and Olivia,' Callum said, 'so even if she bears a grudge, she might keep it to herself.'

I hoped he was right about that.

'Are we still on to get a load of pumpkins tomorrow?' I asked.

Callum and I had volunteered to help carve pumpkins for the Glow. Artists and other people far more skilled with knives than I ever would be had entered the competition part of the event. They would build sculptures out of jack-o'-lanterns that would be judged before the display opened to the public. However, all the pathways and spaces in between the sculptures would be filled with other carved pumpkins so that Griffin Park – where the event would be held – would be alight with the glow of hundreds of pumpkins. That required a lot of helping hands and a lot of time.

'We're on for the pumpkin patch,' Callum confirmed.

I smiled at that and dug into another slice of pizza.

Even if Genevieve harbored a grudge, I vowed not to let her stop me from enjoying my first ever Pumpkin Glow.

FOUR

I reminded myself of my vow the following morning when I parked my car at the edge of Griffin Park, a large green space in the middle of town where the Pumpkin Glow would be held at the end of the month. In addition to volunteering to carve pumpkins, I'd offered to help decorate the park with orange twinkle lights. They would light up the trees along the park's winding pathways, adding to the magic of the event.

At the moment, the park looked like it always did, except for some orchard ladders, two wheelbarrows and a couple dozen pumpkins sitting on the grass near a covered pavilion where outdoor meetings and other events were often held. I'd heard that another group of volunteers would be gathering at the park that afternoon for a pumpkin carving party of sorts. I figured that must be why the pumpkins were there.

As I let the dogs out of the back seat of my car, I waved to Tessa, who was also helping out that day. She'd arrived before me and stood over by the pavilion along with Genevieve, Catherine Adams – who owned the Twilight Inn with her husband – and Cindy Yoon's brother, Nicholas.

Tessa returned my wave, but not with her usual enthusiasm. That was the first sign that something wasn't quite right. The dogs raced across the grass to greet Tessa while I followed more slowly. As soon as I drew close to the pavilion, I could hear Genevieve's strident voice.

'I was told this town was safe!' She threw up her hands. 'I was told we could leave the pumpkins here without any problems!' She glared at the people gathered around her. 'And now look what's happened!'

I slowed my steps, not eager to get any closer.

Tessa caught my gaze and rolled her eyes. She didn't look like her usual happy self, but considering Genevieve's state, I couldn't blame her.

Genevieve whipped out her cell phone. 'I'm calling the police.' She stomped away with her phone held to her ear.

I sidled up to the others as they watched her retreating form with wary eyes.

'What was all that about?' I asked. 'Or do I even want to know?'

'We've got a pumpkin thief in Twilight Cove,' Tessa replied.

'Either that or Genevieve miscounted when they were delivered yesterday,' Nicholas said.

'Don't let her hear you say that,' Catherine advised. She wore a down vest over a long-sleeved shirt and dark jeans. Her chestnut brown hair was fastened at the back of her head with a claw clip and she had a string of unlit orange twinkle lights hanging around her shoulders like a shawl.

'How many are missing?' I asked.

'Eight,' Nicholas replied. 'No big deal, really.'

'Not according to Ms Queen Bee,' Tessa said as she gathered her long brown hair into a ponytail.

Catherine kept a straight face, but I could see humor dancing in her blue eyes. 'Let's get started. These lights won't string themselves.'

'And *she's* not going to lift a finger,' Nicholas muttered with a dark look at Genevieve's back.

We worked in teams of two, me with Tessa and Nicholas with Catherine. Each pair loaded up a wheelbarrow with boxes of lights before transporting them to one of the ornamental cherry trees lining the park's main pathway. Then we returned to the pavilion to fetch the ladders.

Genevieve seemed even grumpier after her phone call – probably because the police didn't consider a possible pumpkin theft a high priority – and strode up and down the pathway, criticizing our work. Just as Nicholas had predicted, she never once offered to lend a hand. After nearly half an hour of listening to Genevieve bark orders at us, I could tell that Tessa was about ready to explode. I suspected that the rest of us weren't far behind her.

Probably the only thing that prevented all of us volunteers from quitting and walking off the job was the fact that Genevieve eventually retreated to the pavilion, where she paced back and forth, her phone to her ear again.

'I know we're volunteers,' Tessa grumbled once Genevieve was out of earshot, 'but we should be getting hazard pay for working with her.'

'Do you think the rest of the organizing committee regrets letting her take charge?' I asked as I stood halfway up my ladder, weaving a string of lights through branches.

'That's a definite yes,' Catherine replied from the next tree over. 'I've heard plenty of rumblings. There was some talk of trying to get Praise back in control, but I think everyone's scared of Genevieve.'

'Except for Miles,' Tessa said as I tossed her the strand of lights so she could wrap it around her side of the tree. 'He's just obsessed with her.'

Maybe he wasn't the only one.

As I climbed down the ladder so I could shift it to a new position, I let my gaze stray back toward the pavilion. Off to the right of the structure, a man stood among a cluster of evergreen trees. He was a long way off, but I could have sworn that he was watching Genevieve. She whirled around, gesturing with one hand while she spoke on her phone, and that seemed to spook the man. He turned and took off through the trees, quickly disappearing from sight.

A shiver of unease ran through me, but maybe that had partly to do with the wind that had picked up. A particularly strong gust blew my hair away from my face and sent a scattering of dried leaves tumbling along the pathway.

After I moved my ladder and made sure it was steady, my gaze drifted to the pavilion again. Genevieve snatched something off the ground. A piece of paper, it looked like. She studied it for a second and then came marching over.

'Incoming,' Nicholas warned from the top of his ladder.

As Genevieve got closer, he busied himself with the string of lights he was adding to the tree. I was tempted to flee and I suspected that my fellow volunteers felt the same way, but we all stayed put.

'A word, please, Tessa,' Genevieve said, her gray eyes flashing with anger.

Tessa hesitated and shot me a glance, but then climbed down to the ground and followed Genevieve a few paces away from the rest of us. I stopped working and watched from my perch up the ladder.

Even though she tried to make her conversation with Tessa private, Genevieve's words carried to me on the wind.

'Are you trying to humiliate me?' she seethed.

'Sorry?' Tessa asked, at a loss.

Genevieve thrust the paper at her and Tessa barely managed to get hold of it before the wind could whip it away.

'My measurements. You wrote them down and then left them lying around for everybody to see!'

'Actually,' Tessa countered, 'I left this paper folded and sitting under my water bottle in the pavilion.'

I glanced over at the structure and could just make out a pink, insulated water bottle lying on its side on the ground. The wind must have toppled it over.

'I won't tolerate this treatment!' Genevieve said as if she hadn't heard Tessa.

That was the final straw for Tessa.

'You're the one treating us volunteers like dirt!' my friend shot back. 'I didn't even offer to make you a costume for the Glow. You just assumed I'd do whatever you wanted because you think everyone in this town is here to serve you.' She thrust the crumpled piece of paper back at Genevieve. 'Well, guess what? You can make your own costume.'

Tessa stormed off, heading for the pavilion.

'What a little—'

We didn't get to hear what she was going to call Tessa because another gust of wind blew through the park. Catherine's takeout cup of coffee, which she'd set on a rung of her ladder while she untangled more lights, flew off its perch and hit Genevieve square in the chest. The lid popped off on impact and creamy coffee splashed all over Genevieve's white sweater.

She gasped and looked down at herself in horror that quickly transformed into rage.

'Look what you've done!' She screamed the words at Catherine, Nicholas, and me.

'You mean what the wind did?' Catherine said, her blue eyes like ice. I'd never seen her with such a hard expression.

Genevieve let out an angry bellow reminiscent of an irate bull. She stomped off, bypassing the pavilion where Tessa stood watching with her arms crossed over her chest. Genevieve made a beeline for her gold SUV parked by the curb. She climbed in the vehicle, slammed the door, revved the engine, and roared off down the street, all within a matter of seconds.

I glanced at Flossie. She sat next to her sister, looking up at me with a doggy grin on her face.

'Did you . . . ?' I didn't finish the whispered question.

Flossie gave a woof and bounded off to the pavilion, Fancy on her tail.

I glanced at Catherine and Nicholas. Catherine was fighting a smile now, the ice gone from her eyes, and Nicholas was straight-up laughing.

'Talk about a perfectly timed gust of wind,' he said.

The two of them got back to work while I walked over to the pavilion where Tessa was now seated on one of the benches, petting the dogs. I wasn't so sure that the wind had caused the coffee to spill on Genevieve. I didn't think the gust was strong enough to pick up a cup holding that much liquid.

Soon after Flossie and Fancy came into my life – following the death of the human they previously lived with – I discovered that they had unusual abilities. Fancy could emit a blue glow, almost like bioluminescence, and she could camouflage herself in any surroundings. Flossie could open locks with a simple touch of her paw and, a few weeks ago, she'd revealed another talent: the ability to move objects without touching them.

Maybe I was wrong about the wind, but I didn't think so. I strongly suspected that Flossie was responsible for Catherine's coffee splashing all over Genevieve. Thank goodness Catherine and Nicholas didn't seem to think that anything was amiss. I hadn't told anyone about the spaniels' abilities – not even Auntie O or Callum – and I didn't want the secret getting out. I couldn't blame Flossie for what she'd done, but I hoped she wouldn't use her powers so publicly again in the future.

When I joined Tessa in the pavilion, she still had fire in her eyes, even though she was calmly petting the dogs. I sat down next to her and Flossie jumped up on to the bench beside me. She lay down and rested her chin on my leg. Fancy stayed sitting at Tessa's feet.

'What happened to send the she-devil storming off like that?' she asked.

'Catherine's coffee and a well-timed gust of wind, apparently,' I said, wishing – not for the first time – that I could be completely honest with her and share my suspicions.

Tessa smiled. 'I guess I should have stayed over there. I would have liked to witness that.' Her smile faded. 'I'm not making Genevieve's costume.'

'I think that's the right decision,' I said. 'Anyone who treats you like that should be cut out of your life.'

'It wasn't just today. She's been awful the whole time. When she heard I was making costumes for the Trail of Terror, she demanded that I make her one to wear to the Pumpkin Glow. She appointed herself the official greeter for the event. She wants to stand at the park entrance as people arrive. Really, I think she just wants attention. She wants the Pumpkin Glow to be about her, not the competitors.'

'That sounds about right. If she wants a costume, she can buy, borrow, or rent one.'

Tessa ran her hand over Fancy's silky brown head. 'That's what I told her the other day. She seemed disgusted by the thought of wearing something anyone else had worn before her. And she wanted something custom-made to her specifications.'

'The whole process would have been a nightmare.' I had no doubt about that.

'I want nothing more to do with her,' Tessa said, a note of finality in her voice. 'As far as I'm concerned, if she moved away from Twilight Cove tomorrow, that wouldn't be soon enough.'

FIVE

The Pumpkin Glow was the town's event, not Genevieve's, so the four of us continued working away at stringing twinkle lights among the trees. An hour later, another group of volunteers arrived, bringing with them a cherry picker that one man drove into the park. That made it far easier to get the lights around the upper branches of the trees.

After Tessa and I had finished our volunteer shift, I returned to the sanctuary with Flossie and Fancy. We had time for a quick lunch and a brief spell of playtime with Stardust before heading to the pumpkin patch with Callum. The local farm was located on Larkspur Lane, the same road as Auntie O's farm, just a couple of miles to the north. Although we would be donating both our carving time and our jack-o'-lanterns to the Pumpkin Glow, as registered volunteers we would receive a discount on our purchases at the pumpkin patch.

When we arrived, the sun shone brightly from a clear blue sky, providing enough warmth that I left my jacket in Callum's truck. Since dogs weren't allowed in the pumpkin patch, I'd left them at home with Auntie O, so Callum and I wandered around on our own, sizing up pumpkins and choosing the ones we liked the best. Whenever we found one we wanted, we clipped it off the vine and carried it to the truck.

We'd already picked out half a dozen and were on the hunt for more when I noticed two young couples with toddlers nearby. While the two tiny children wandered about unsteadily, patting pumpkins and looking around in wonder, the adults stood in a cluster, talking and looking our way.

I tried to keep my attention on the pumpkins, but I could feel the group's eyes on us. Really, they were probably looking at Callum and hardly knew I was there. As a recently retired major league baseball player, Callum got recognized by fans on a regular basis. It was something I was still getting used to and, even though their attention was likely solely on my boyfriend, I couldn't quite relax.

I moved closer to Callum, who was walking in a slow circle

around a couple of pumpkins, studying them. He hadn't seemed to notice the scrutiny of the other pumpkin seekers.

'Those people are staring,' I whispered with a discreet tip of my head in their direction.

Callum glanced at the four adults, unconcerned. Then he grinned and took my hand, pulling me in close to him. 'How about we give them pumpkin to talk about?'

I laughed. 'That's bad.'

'But you did laugh,' he pointed out.

'Only because it was such a terrible pun.'

'Or because my pumpkin puns are just *so gourd*.'

'Stop. Please,' I begged through more laughter.

His hand pressed against my lower back, the pleasant heat from his touch seeping through the fabric of my shirt. 'So you don't want to give them something to talk about?' he asked.

'Just a little something.' I kissed him briefly and then pointed to the pumpkin at our feet. 'How about this one?'

'It's a keeper,' he said.

It's not the only one, I thought.

We chose several more pumpkins and finished loading them in the truck. A white woman in her late fifties to early sixties had parked her aging, burgundy sedan next to us. She pulled a wagon from the pumpkin patch to her car, four pumpkins loaded on it. She wore a bucket hat over short, curly hair that appeared to be dyed the same shade of burgundy as her car.

'Lovely afternoon, isn't it?' she said with a smile as she opened the trunk of her car.

'Can I give you a hand with those?' Callum offered, already grabbing one of the pumpkins off her wagon.

The woman beamed at him. 'Thank you.' While Callum worked, she spoke to me in a stage whisper. 'It's always nice to have a strong man around to help. Even better when he's handsome.' She gave me a conspiratorial wink.

My cheeks flushed but Callum just grinned as he set the last pumpkin in the trunk.

She thanked him and Callum moved back to his truck to shut the tailgate.

'Hello, Hattie,' Linette Mears called out as she strode over our way. 'And Georgie,' she added when she noticed me.

Callum had stepped away as the two young couples from the

pumpkin patch approached with their toddlers in tow. As I'd suspected, they were baseball fans and had recognized him. While Callum chatted with his fans, I turned my attention back to Hattie and Linette.

'You know Genevieve Newmont, don't you, Linette?' Hattie asked. 'Do you think she'd ever harm a cat?'

The question took me by surprise and it seemed to do the same to Linette.

'Genevieve? Of course not,' she said with certainty. 'She's my best friend and I've known her most of my life. She's allergic to cats and doesn't want them near her, but she'd never hurt one. Why do you ask?'

Hattie unzipped the light jacket she wore. 'I knew the two of you were friends back in Portland, but I didn't know your friendship was that long-lasting.'

Maybe, like me, Hattie was wondering how anyone could manage to be friends with Genevieve for any length of time.

'Oh, yes. We met in middle school. When I decided to move away from the city, it was hard to leave her, but it all worked out because she decided to join me here in Twilight Cove.'

I recalled hearing that Linette had moved to town within the past couple of years. She was already actively involved with the local theater group and she'd eagerly auditioned for a role with the Trail of Terror. She'd impressed Olivia and me, and it was an easy decision for us to cast her in the main speaking part.

'Anyway,' Linette continued, 'I need to pick up some pumpkins to carve for the Glow. See you later!' With a cheery wave, she headed into the pumpkin patch.

I watched her go, desperately hoping her assessment of Genevieve's attitude toward cats was correct.

'She would have done us all a favor if she'd stayed in Portland,' Hattie grumbled.

'Linette?' I said with surprise. I'd met her only a few times, but she'd always seemed pleasant to me.

'Oh, goodness, no,' Hattie said quickly. 'I have no complaints about Linette. It's that friend of hers, Genevieve. She bought the house next door to mine and I haven't had a moment's peace since.'

'From my limited interactions with her,' I said, 'I can see that she's not easy to get along with.'

Hattie shook her head. 'That's an understatement. I've got four cats and Genevieve is out to get them, no matter what Linette says. It's one thing for someone not to be a cat person, but it's a whole other thing entirely to want to harm poor innocent animals.'

'What do you mean?' I asked with alarm. The thought of anyone wanting to hurt an animal in any way turned my stomach.

'My cats are usually in the house or in their catio – an outdoor enclosure I had built for them. But one day, I was going to take them indoors from the catio when Sylvester, my tuxedo cat, escaped and took off. He came home an hour later, but then Genevieve showed up at my door, claiming that Sylvester had destroyed her garden. At most, he might have done his business in one of her flower beds, but it couldn't have been anything worse than that. Sylvester isn't a destructive cat.' Hattie paused for a breath before continuing. 'Then she showed up two days later, claiming that my cats had been in her yard again. Which wasn't true, because none of them had escaped since the last incident. But that woman had the gall to threaten to poison my cats if I didn't keep them under control. Can you believe that?'

'That's horrible!' My already low opinion of Genevieve sank to far greater depths.

Callum, done chatting with his fans, joined our conversation.

'Do you really think she'd carry that threat out?' he asked with concern.

'I wouldn't put it past her,' Hattie said, tears welling in her brown eyes. 'And it's not just my cats at risk. She might blame every cat sighting on her property on my fur babies, but clearly there are other neighborhood kitties involved. If she starts lacing her yard with poison, all manner of animals could get killed.'

Anger and worry bubbled up inside of me like boiling water in a cauldron.

'One thing is for certain,' Hattie declared. 'Twilight Cove was far better off before Genevieve Newmont moved to town.'

On the way home from the pumpkin patch, Callum and I stopped at the grocery store to pick up a few items. By then, we both had growling stomachs, so we grabbed a bite to eat at the Moonstruck Diner. Despite my hunger and the tasty food, I couldn't eat much of my meal. Hattie's words kept replaying in my head like a broken record, causing my stomach to churn.

'Are you OK?' Callum asked from across the booth. He must have noticed the way I was picking at my food.

'I can't stand the thought of Genevieve poisoning someone's cats, or any animal,' I said, setting down my fork. 'She shouldn't be able to get away with something so awful.'

Callum reached across the table to give my hand a squeeze. 'Do you think there's anything that can be done?'

'I really don't know,' I said with a sigh. 'Maybe Auntie O will have an idea.'

Callum was still working on his salmon burger, so I tapped out a text message to my aunt, sharing what Hattie had said about Genevieve's threat. She replied right away, horrified and incensed.

I'll talk to Isaac, she wrote after venting her feelings about Genevieve. **Maybe he can at least warn her off.**

Isaac Stratton was the chief of the Twilight Cove Police Department and a friend of Olivia's. Her plan to bring him into the picture eased some of my worries. That allowed my appetite to make a comeback, so I turned my attention back to my food while chatting with Callum.

By the time we left the restaurant, darkness had fallen and the air had taken on a frosty touch. Soon I'd be spending my evenings curled up in front of a crackling fire with Flossie, Fancy, Stardust, and Callum. As much as I enjoyed spending warm evenings out on the back porch of the farmhouse, I was looking forward to cozy winter nights with my favorite animals and my favorite cowboy.

Twilight Cove had given me so much, had filled in the holes I hadn't realized were in my life before. While living in Los Angeles, I'd focused solely on my screenwriting career. When I visited Twilight Cove to help out Auntie O while she recovered from a broken ankle, I'd realized how much was missing from my life – like family, close friends, deep connections, and the unconditional love of animals. It hadn't taken me long to decide to move to the farm permanently. I'd never once regretted the decision and I knew there would be plenty to enjoy with every season.

When we reached Callum's truck, he cranked up the heat and we set off for home, me with my hands tucked up inside the sleeves of my jacket.

'Are you planning on an early night or do you want to hang out at the house with me and the animals?' I asked as we drove along the dark road.

'Quality time with all my favorite girls?' He reached out for my hand and gave it a squeeze once I slipped it out of my sleeve. 'I'm not going to turn down that offer.'

His words warmed me more than the truck's heater did.

He turned on to Larkspur Lane and flicked on his high beams. Unlike the streets in the middle of town, the country roads didn't have any streetlamps. As we followed a curve in the road, Callum turned down the headlights in case another driver was coming from the opposite direction. I caught sight of yellow beams of light up ahead when we rounded the bend, but something seemed off. I realized the next second that the lights weren't on the road.

Callum slowed the truck before I had a chance to say anything. 'Looks like there's been an accident,' he said, worry evident in his voice.

He pulled over and stopped at the side of the road. His truck's headlights lit up the accident scene. There was just one vehicle involved and I recognized it as soon as we came to a halt.

Genevieve's gold SUV sat with its rear wheels in the shallow ditch and its front bumper crushed up against a sturdy tree.

SIX

'I can't believe this!' Genevieve screamed as Callum opened the driver's door of her SUV.

'Are you OK?' he asked with concern.

I peered around him at Genevieve. At first glance, she appeared unharmed. I couldn't see any blood, at least. The airbag had deployed and an acrid smell wafted out of the vehicle.

'Of course I'm not OK!' Genevieve fumed as she unclipped her seatbelt and slid out of the car.

I noticed Callum's eyebrows hitch up slightly at her tone, but he still offered her his hand and helped her out of the SUV. Once she was steady on her feet, Callum slowly released her and took a step back to be at my side.

'Should we call an ambulance, Genevieve?' I asked. 'Where are you hurt?'

She turned her furious gaze on me. 'I'm not *hurt*. I'm *angry*! Look at my car!' She gestured at the front bumper and threw her hands in the air.

I took a step closer to the front of the vehicle. The bumper definitely needed to be replaced, but it looked as though the rest of the SUV had survived unscathed. Aside from some lost bark, the tree didn't appear too worse for wear either.

Callum put his phone to his ear. 'I'm calling it in.'

'Make sure they get the police here,' Genevieve demanded. 'I want a full investigation!'

Anyone who didn't know Callum well wouldn't have noticed the subtle look of disbelief he sent in her direction before he turned away. Even though I'd told him about Genevieve, that wasn't the same as actually experiencing her personality firsthand. I knew he was taken aback by her attitude, but he was doing a good job of keeping it to himself.

He walked a few paces along the grassy, dry ditch as he spoke on the phone. Genevieve joined me by the front of her SUV, letting out a hiss of anger when she got a good view of the front bumper hugging the tree trunk.

'This is sabotage!'

'Sabotage?' I echoed with surprise.

It looked as though she'd simply driven off the road and into the tree. I couldn't smell any alcohol on her breath, but that didn't mean she wasn't under the influence of something. Of course, it was possible someone else had caused the accident.

'Did someone run you off the road?' I asked.

'They *startled* me off the road. I came around the bend and there was Bigfoot standing right in the middle of the lane.'

'Bigfoot?'

She gave me a scathing look. 'You know – Bigfoot, Sasquatch. A big, ape-like man.'

Irritation rushed through me, but I tried to keep it in check. 'I know what it is, but are you sure that's what you saw?'

'Of course, I'm sure!'

The fire in her eyes was so intense that I had to fight the urge to back up a step. I didn't want to give her that satisfaction.

'And I bet I've got proof.' She pushed past me and rounded the open driver's door. 'I've got a dashcam.' She reached across to the passenger seat and grabbed her handbag. She rifled through it until she produced her phone. 'I can bring the footage up on the app.' She tapped the screen of her phone as Callum ended his call and came over to join us.

'What's going on?' he asked me as he sent a wary glance in Genevieve's direction.

'Genevieve saw something on the road when she came around the bend,' I explained. 'She had to swerve to avoid it.'

'Not some*thing*,' Genevieve corrected with a heavy dose of disdain. 'Some*one*. Dressed up as Bigfoot.'

Callum's eyebrows hitched up again. 'Bigfoot?' he mouthed at me while Genevieve was focused on the screen of her phone.

I shrugged.

'There!' Genevieve thrust her phone at us. 'Look.'

She played a video recorded by her dashcam. At first, it showed nothing but the car's headlights shining on the dark road. Then, as the vehicle rounded a bend, a creature came into sight, standing on the road.

Just as Genevieve had described, it resembled a hairy, ape-like man. A split second after it came into view, the creature raised its arms as if ready to attack the vehicle.

The footage went jumpy as the SUV swerved and left the road.

'As soon as I got over the shock of the crash, I looked out at the road and the thing was gone. First someone steals my pumpkins and now they scare me off the road. I could have been killed!'

The pumpkins hadn't exactly belonged to her, but I let that slide. That detail wasn't important and the rest of what she'd said was true. A Sasquatch had stood in the middle of the road and tried to scare her. Or, at least, someone dressed as a Sasquatch.

Although I normally wouldn't have been eager to side with Genevieve on anything, I had to admit that she was right. Someone likely had played a trick on her. Whether it had been specifically directed at her or at whatever motorist happened along the road, I didn't know.

'Did anyone know that you'd be driving this way at this time?' I asked.

'I was just at a book club meeting,' she replied. She'd calmed down a bit but still sounded huffy. 'Anyone else who was there knew when I left.'

'Did anyone leave ahead of you?'

Genevieve scowled. 'No. I was the first to go. But that doesn't mean someone couldn't have been lying in wait for me.'

Maybe that was the case, or maybe Callum and I could have been the victims of the prank just as easily.

'Whether you were targeted or not,' Callum said to Genevieve, 'it was a dangerous prank for someone to play. The police should be here soon.'

Just as he said those words, we caught the sound of an approaching siren on the cool night air. Seconds later, a police cruiser rounded the bend and slowed as it came upon the accident scene.

Officer Brody Williams climbed out of the cruiser. He was a tall man with an athletic build and short, dark hair. I'd met Brody soon after arriving in Twilight Cove in June and I now considered him a friend. He and Tessa had known each other for years and he'd joined us several times during the summer and early fall when a group of us got together to play baseball. I knew he enjoyed playing other sports as well, and he occasionally sold his beautiful Native American artwork at the local farmers' market.

We greeted Brody, who was all business, and an ambulance arrived less than a minute later. Callum and I backed off and let Genevieve tell her story to Brody, sharing the same footage she'd shown us. When the paramedics tried to check her over, she ungraciously warded them off with sharp words and flapping hands.

Another officer arrived on the scene and Callum and I provided her with our brief statements and our contact information. After that, Brody assured us that we could head home.

That night I dreamed of a banshee – who looked an awful lot like Genevieve – wailing and screaming as she chased a terrified Sasquatch through the forest. I would have laughed about the dream when I woke up, except for the real danger involved in the situation that had triggered it. Genevieve really could have been hurt – or even killed. Judging by the dashcam footage, there wasn't any doubt that the so-called Bigfoot had meant to scare Genevieve – or whichever driver happened to come along the road at that point. I hoped the police would catch the prankster before anything worse happened. Until the culprit had been identified, I knew I'd drive more carefully along the local roads at night.

After completing my morning farm chores, I piled into my car with Flossie and Fancy and headed for the local farmers' market, held in Twilight Park, an oceanside green space close to where Main Street met up with the beach. This was one of the last markets of the year. At the end of the month, it would shut down until the following spring. I wanted to make sure I had a chance to peruse the local wares before that happened.

When I reached the parking lot at the beach, I pulled into a free spot next to a flashy black sports car with California plates. The dogs and I crossed the lot to the grassy park, where two long rows of booths had been set up with a wide pathway in between. I zipped up my fleece jacket as a chilly breeze tickled the skin of my exposed hands, neck, and face. Unlike the day before, the sun was hiding behind a thick blanket of gray clouds.

As I drew closer to the vendors, I bit back a groan of annoyance. Genevieve was up ahead, standing near a booth selling handmade jewelry. I really didn't want to run into her again, but unless I detoured all the way around the back of the booths to the far end of the row, I'd have to walk right past her in order to shop.

I decided to keep walking straight and hope that Genevieve was too engrossed in her current conversation to notice me. She stood a couple of feet away from the nearest booth, talking with a preppily dressed man who appeared to be in his early twenties. He had fair skin and brown hair that was swooped back from his forehead and held firmly in place with gel.

'I just need a few hundred to tide me over,' the man said in a wheedling voice. 'Come on, Aunt Genevieve.'

'Barclay,' his aunt said with exasperation, 'the money you get each month from your trust fund should be more than enough to support you. If you can't learn to live within your ample means, that's not my problem.'

'It's just this month,' Barclay cajoled. 'I won't ask again.'

'That's what you said the last time.'

I made it safely past Genevieve without her spotting me. When I glanced back a few seconds later, her nephew slouched off with a scowl on his face. He pulled a key fob from the pocket of his jeans and the lights of the black sports car flashed with a beep. He climbed into the vehicle, slamming the door behind him. As he squealed his way out of the parking lot, I turned to face the nearest booth, determined to focus on my shopping and not think about Genevieve Newmont for the rest of the day.

SEVEN

As I wandered past various booths at the farmers' market, I stopped now and then to look more closely at the items for sale. Auntie O had a small vegetable garden on the farm, but I liked to pick up things from the market that she didn't grow. I bought a bag of potatoes from one local farmer and a butternut squash from another. As I made my way down the line of booths, I spotted Praise Adebayo sitting behind a table displaying a variety of jams and other preserves. I'd seen her at the market before and my aunt had mentioned once that Praise was known for her delicious jams.

I stopped at the booth and greeted Praise. While she conducted a sale with another customer, I checked out the various goods she had on offer. There was everything from mango chutney to green tomato relish, from apricot jam to blackberry jalapeño jam. Auntie O made a large batch of strawberry jam every summer and I ate it on my toast almost every morning. I didn't plan to change my breakfast habits much, but when I saw Concord grape jelly at Praise's booth, I decided to buy a jar. I loved grape jelly, but I hadn't had any for years.

I shared a few words with Praise after I paid and then I went on my way. I checked the time on my phone and decided I'd better leave the market. Although I glanced around on my way back to the parking lot, I didn't see Genevieve anywhere. Hopefully I wouldn't run into her again anytime soon, but I knew my chances of that were slim, especially since I'd agreed to do another shift of volunteering for the Pumpkin Glow that afternoon.

After stashing my purchases in the back seat of my car, I swung by the home of the animal sanctuary's teenage volunteer, Roxy Russo. I'd arranged to pick her up and take her to the farm so she could be there to greet our newest additions. We had two donkeys moving to the sanctuary and Roxy didn't want to miss their arrival. I pulled up in front of her house, an aging bungalow, and the front door opened before I'd even come to a full stop. She must have been watching for me through the window.

Three boys who looked to be about eleven or twelve years old were out front of the neighboring house, trying on different Halloween masks and making what I guessed were supposed to be monster sounds. As Roxy jogged across her front yard, one of the boys charged toward her, roaring and holding a Frankenstein's monster mask to his face.

'Cut it out, Robbie,' Roxy grumbled at him.

She yanked open the passenger door and dropped into the seat. She pulled the door shut and fastened her seatbelt as Robbie stuck his head in the open window and roared again before running away to a chorus of hoots and laughter from his friends.

Roxy rolled her eyes.

'Friends of yours?' I asked with a grin, already knowing the answer.

She huffed out a sigh. 'As if.'

She brightened when I turned the conversation to the donkeys and I was happy to see an excited light in her eyes. Roxy didn't always have an easy time at home or at school. Her mom struggled with alcoholism and I knew from Tessa – who taught at the local high school – that Roxy didn't have many friends. She'd been in a few fights, though not so far this school year. She'd recently reconnected with her father and that seemed to be going well so far. I hoped that would continue to be the case. Roxy was a good kid and truly loved the animals at the sanctuary.

We got to the farm early enough that we had time for a brief spell of playtime with Stardust before we heard Callum's truck pull into the driveway. We hurried outside with the dogs, leaving Stardust to watch from the kitchen window.

Callum waved through the open driver's side window as he slowly drove along the driveway, towing a horse trailer behind the truck. Auntie O emerged from the carriage house and walked with Roxy and me to the pasture where the donkeys would stay. The animals had been surrendered by an elderly man who could no longer take care of his farm or livestock. A small herd of cows had been taken in by another farmer and a local family had adopted the chickens.

The donkeys would stay with us, either permanently or until we found a suitable home for them elsewhere. They wouldn't be going anywhere for a while, though. We needed to make sure that they were completely healthy before adoption even became a possibility, and Auntie O had mentioned that they'd suffered from unintentional neglect over the past few months. For the next while we would keep the new donkeys separate from the ones already living on the farm, in case they had any contagious illnesses or medical conditions.

'How was the trip?' Auntie O asked as Callum climbed out of his truck.

'Uneventful. The girls were both great passengers.' He moved around to the back of the horse trailer.

Roxy opened the pasture gate as Callum backed the first donkey off the trailer.

'This is Tootsie,' he said as he led her into the pasture.

I joined Roxy by the gate. She eagerly took the lead rope from Callum and led Tootsie farther into the pasture, talking to her quietly the whole way. When she brought the donkey to a stop, I approached and let the animal sniff my hand.

'Aren't you a beauty,' I said as I stroked Tootsie's nose.

The smile had faded from Roxy's face. 'She's beautiful but . . .'

'I know.' My heart ached as I rested a hand on Roxy's shoulder.

Tootsie's coat was caked with mud and she had a few bald spots and sores on her skin. Her soulful brown eyes held unmistakable sadness.

'We'll get her all fixed up so she'll be healthy and comfortable,' I assured Roxy.

She nodded and stroked Tootsie's scraggly neck.

Callum led the next donkey into the pasture. 'And this is Twiggy.'

While Tootsie was a spotted donkey with a coat of light gray and white, Twiggy's coat was a reddish color called rose dun, as Callum had once told me. They both had brown eyes and one of Twiggy's looked like it might be infected. Her coat needed a good grooming, but she didn't have sores on her skin like Tootsie did.

I hoped it wouldn't take long for the animals to settle in and shed their sadness. I knew we all found it hard to see them suffering from neglect, but now that they were here at the sanctuary, Twiggy and Tootsie would have a good future ahead of them.

With the gate closed, we unhooked their lead ropes. Tootsie nibbled at some grass, but Twiggy simply stood there with a posture that reminded me of Eeyore. I stroked her neck as a fresh rush of sadness welled up inside of me. I blinked back tears as Callum came over to my side. He must have seen the emotion on my face. He rubbed my back while resting his other hand on the donkey's neck.

'We're going to give them a good life,' he assured me.

I nodded, swallowing back the lump in my throat.

'The vet will be here tomorrow to give them each a full checkup,' Callum added. 'Whatever treatment they need, they'll get.'

We let the donkeys have some time to take in their new surroundings, although Twiggy seemed far less interested in exploring than Tootsie. In the meantime, Callum filled their water trough and Roxy, Olivia, and I stayed by the fence, chatting quietly and watching the sanctuary's newest residents. Once Callum had finished filling the trough, he and I made a quick trip to the barn and returned to the pasture armed with grooming tools.

Callum and Roxy worked on Tootsie, while my aunt and I groomed Twiggy. Both donkeys behaved like angels, letting us brush their coats and pick out their hooves. The hooves would need to be trimmed, but the farrier was scheduled to come two days from now to take care of that. With the help of the vet, the farrier and all of us here at the sanctuary, I hoped that Tootsie and Twiggy would soon be happy donkeys, with their neglect a distant and fading memory.

Once we had Twiggy and Tootsie cleaned up as best we could for the time being, Auntie O got started on some garden work while Callum and I set off for Griffin Park with the dogs. We offered to give Roxy a ride home, but she wanted to stay at the farm to keep the donkeys company for a while longer. I would have liked to stay with her, but Callum and I had promised to help out with more preparations for the Pumpkin Glow that afternoon.

'I guess there's no point in hoping that Genevieve won't be there,' I said as Callum drove us through town.

'She definitely has a strong personality.'

I laughed. 'That's a diplomatic way of describing her. She seems determined to make everything as unpleasant as possible. But,' I added, 'I'm just as determined to enjoy the Pumpkin Glow, no matter how many hissy fits Genevieve throws in the lead-up to the event. Twilight Cove didn't have a Pumpkin Glow when I lived here in my teens so I've never been to one.'

'I've heard of similar events around the country,' Callum said, 'but I've never attended one either. No matter what Genevieve does, I'm sure the sculptures will still be amazing. I bet my parents would like to see them.'

'Then we'll take them if they get here before Halloween,' I

decided, doing my best to ignore the butterflies that always fluttered nervously in my stomach when I thought about meeting his parents.

After leaving the truck in a free spot down the street, we cut across the park to the pavilion. A small group had gathered there and hung around talking, looking at loose ends. I spotted Tessa in the group and made my way over to her.

'What's going on?' I lowered my voice. 'I thought Genevieve would be barking out orders at everyone by now.'

'Right?' Tessa whispered. 'But she hasn't shown up.'

That took me by surprise. Callum and I had arrived a few minutes later than we'd meant to. I was worried that Genevieve would yell at us when we got there, but it seemed she was even later than us. I wondered if she'd suffered injuries in the car accident, ones that didn't make themselves known until a while after the crash. That might explain her absence.

'It would be nice if she didn't show up at all,' Tessa said quietly. 'We'd have a lot more fun.'

'That, and I wouldn't be at risk of ending up in jail for wringing her neck.' She lowered her voice even further. 'We had another bust-up. I wasn't even sure if I should come here this afternoon.'

'Oh no.'

'I'll tell you about it later,' she promised as Catherine Adams clapped her hands together to get everyone's attention.

'Since Genevieve's not here yet and she's not answering my text messages, I think we should get to work,' Catherine said. 'We all know what we're here to do, right?'

Everyone answered in the affirmative.

Callum and I had volunteered to help put together a long, arched pergola that would be set up over the pathway, near the entrance to the park. It would have wooden spikes attached to it so that dozens of jack-o'-lanterns – lit with battery-operated LED candles for safety's sake – could be affixed to the structure, on the lattice work along the sides and overhead. When complete, the pergola would look like a tunnel of glowing jack-o'-lanterns.

The pergola had been used for the previous Pumpkin Glows and had been stored in several parts. It just needed to be put back together and anchored in place so it wouldn't blow over in a strong wind or if someone pushed at the structure, whether accidentally or on purpose. I wasn't great at building things, but Callum and Jamieson, the other volunteer helping us, were in their element. I let them do their thing and simply held things in place and passed them whatever tools they needed. Flossie and Fancy lay in the grass and alternated between snoozing and supervising our work.

When we finally had the pergola set up and safely anchored to the ground, I dusted off my hands and glanced around the park. Tessa and Catherine had nearly finished decorating the pavilion with orange lights and pumpkins. Another group of volunteers was busy using rakes and leaf blowers to clear away the leaves that had fallen from the deciduous trees along the pathway. They weren't going to clear the entire park of leaves; just the areas where the competitors would be building their sculptures.

As for Genevieve, she still hadn't appeared.

Despite her accident the night before, I was surprised that she'd pass up an opportunity to boss us around and criticize our work.

'Ready to head home?' Callum asked as he removed his work gloves.

'Definitely.' I stuffed my hands in the pockets of my jeans. The sun was sinking and the air was growing colder. I could see my breath puffing out in front of me in small clouds and I suspected we'd get a frost that night.

The dogs jumped up, tails wagging, and we set off across the grass, heading for Callum's truck. A dark shape swooped down from the sky and landed in a tree to my left. I looked up and smiled at the great horned owl perched on a branch. Although there were lots of other great horned owls living in the area, I knew this one was my friend Euclid.

He let out a 'hoo-hoo' that caught Callum's attention.

'Whoa,' he said, looking up. 'I don't usually see owls this close. Except for that one that likes to hang out at the sanctuary.' He studied Euclid for another second or two. 'Come to think of it, this one looks just like the one at the farm. It couldn't be the same one, could it?'

'I'm pretty sure it is,' I replied.

Euclid swiveled his head, looked down at us, and then flew to a branch in another tree, a little farther from where Callum and I stood. Flossie barked and the two spaniels dashed off into the copse.

'Flossie! Fancy!' I released Callum's hand and jogged after the dogs.

Callum followed a pace or two behind me, dry leaves crunching beneath our feet.

Above us, Euclid flew deeper into the small stand of trees and landed on another branch. He looked at the ground below him and let out another 'hoo-hoo'. Then he swooped off the branch, nearly skimming the ground before beating his wings and flying up into the sky.

A flash of emerald-green caught my eye. I looked to my right in time to catch a brief glimpse of someone running through the trees, heading away from us. Still moving, I turned my attention back to the dogs.

The spaniels sat down, facing away from us. As we drew closer, Fancy threw back her head and let out a long howl. The eerie, mournful sound chilled my blood and raised goosebumps on my arms.

I knew then that Euclid and the dogs had found something terrible.

Callum and I kept running, pulling up short when we reached the dogs.

I let out a gasp and Callum swore.

Genevieve lay sprawled on the ground, unmoving.

EIGHT

I dropped to my knees beside the dogs while Callum knelt on the other side of Genevieve. Her chest didn't seem to be rising and falling and her face was red. Callum checked her wrist for a pulse as I leaned in and placed my cheek just above her mouth and nose, hoping to feel her exhaled breath brushing against my skin. I felt nothing, but I did detect a faint scent.

I raised my head and looked to Callum. He shook his head, his face grim. Then he checked for a pulse at her neck. I could tell by the look on his face that he found no sign of life there either.

'She's still warm,' he said. 'Call 911.'

I already had my phone out.

Callum started chest compressions while I spoke to the emergency operator.

With the phone to my ear, I jogged out of the trees and yelled for help. The other volunteers came running. Jamieson had first-aid training and took turns with Callum doing CPR. It felt like it took hours for the first fire truck to arrive, though it was only about five minutes. An ambulance arrived less than a minute later.

The dogs and I had retreated with Tessa and the other volunteers to the park's main pathway, giving the first responders plenty of space to work. Callum and Jamieson joined us a minute or so after the paramedics arrived. Callum, his face ashen, came over to my side. I wrapped my arms around him and held on tight.

I tipped my head back so I could look up at him. 'Are you OK?'

He nodded, his expression bleak. 'I don't think she's going to make it.' He said the words quietly so only I could hear them.

I had a terrible feeling that he was right. I tightened my grip on him.

Fancy let out a quiet whine as she and Flossie sat at our feet.

With lights flashing, a police cruiser arrived at the park, cutting its siren before stopping in the middle of the road.

'Why don't we all go sit down in the pavilion?' Catherine

suggested. 'We should wait around until the police tell us it's OK to go home.'

She led the way and we all followed, a few people casting glances over their shoulders at the trees that hid Genevieve and the first responders from view.

'What do you think happened?' Tessa asked, falling into step with me, Callum, and the dogs.

I kept a tight hold on Callum's hand. It couldn't have been easy, trying to resuscitate Genevieve without success. Hopefully the paramedics would get her heart beating again, but with every minute that passed, that seemed less and less likely.

'I'm not sure,' I said, although I had a suspicion, one triggered by the scent of almonds I'd detected near Genevieve's mouth.

'I couldn't see any outward signs of injury,' Callum said. 'She's young for a heart attack, but it can still happen at her age.'

It didn't take long for more police cruisers to arrive and soon the area was awash in flashing red and blue lights. The paramedics loaded a gurney into the back of the ambulance and drove away. I couldn't see from my vantage point whether they'd taken Genevieve with them or if they'd left her behind for the medical examiner. As much as I hoped they'd be able to resuscitate her, a weight settled in my chest, heavy with the certainty that she was dead.

Brody Williams and another police officer walked over to the pavilion with serious expressions on their faces. They wanted to speak to us individually, starting with Callum and me, since we'd found Genevieve.

Brody pulled me aside and we stood just beyond the pavilion, Flossie staying at my side while Fancy followed Callum and the other officer. Streaks of orange painted the darkening sky, the beautiful sight a jarring contrast to the scene I knew lay within the stand of trees.

'Is Genevieve . . .' I had to take a breath before I could finish my question. 'Is she dead?'

'An official declaration hasn't been made yet, but resuscitation attempts have so far been unsuccessful.'

I pulled my hands up inside my sleeves as my stomach churned. Flossie whined and pressed her nose to my leg. I gave her a brief, grateful smile and stroked her head. She sat right next to me and leaned her comforting weight against my leg.

At Brody's request, I outlined how Callum and I had found Genevieve, leaving out the part about Euclid. Instead, I simply mentioned that the dogs had gone running into the trees and we'd followed.

I rubbed my arms as I spoke. The late afternoon chill had worked its way into my bones.

'When I checked to see if she was breathing, I noticed a faint scent of almonds,' I told Brody. 'And her face was red. Do you think she could have been poisoned with cyanide?'

'We don't know much at all at this point,' Brody said.

'Last night at the accident scene, she told Callum and me that she thought someone was out to get her.'

'She mentioned that to me too,' Brody said. 'Something about an incident with pumpkins?'

I nodded toward the pavilion. 'Those pumpkins were left here so the volunteers could use them to decorate the pavilion. The morning after they were delivered, a few of them were missing.'

'Why did Ms Newmont think the theft was directed at her?'

I shrugged. 'She's in charge – *was* in charge – of the Pumpkin Glow. They didn't belong to her, but maybe she thought someone was trying to sabotage her efforts to organize a good event. What about the Sasquatch incident?' I asked. 'Do you think that was directed at her or was she simply in the wrong place at the wrong time?'

'We haven't been able to track down the prankster yet so, at this point, we're really not sure.'

'If she was poisoned, it makes it seem like maybe the other two incidents really were directed at her,' I mused.

'We'll know more once we're further into the investigation,' Brody said without commenting on my remark.

'There's something else.' I told him about the person I'd seen fleeing from the copse when Callum and I had found Genevieve.

A subtle shift in Brody's demeanor suggested that the information had caught his interest. 'Was it a man or a woman?'

'I'm really not sure,' I admitted, wishing I could provide a better answer. 'All I really saw was a flash of green. Emerald green, I think. It might have been a coat.'

'Which way did they go?'

I pointed. 'Out toward the street on the other side of the trees.'

I wondered if the green-clad person had harmed Genevieve or had simply panicked when they stumbled upon her body. Although the latter scenario was a possibility, the person's behavior struck me as suspicious. Had they somehow given Genevieve the poison right there in the park, running away when they heard Flossie and Fancy approaching?

Brody already had my contact information, but he wrote it in his notebook anyway. By that point, the other officer had finished speaking with Callum.

'You two can head on home,' Brody said.

Callum reached my side just in time to hear those words. He and I thanked Brody and then crossed the grass, heading for the street, the dogs at our side. I took hold of Callum's hand and gave it a squeeze.

'Your hands are like ice,' he said, returning the pressure. 'We'll get the truck warmed up soon.'

By the time I got in the vehicle, I was shivering. Callum cranked up the heat and I held my hands in front of the vent, waiting for the blowing air to get warmer.

'Did you notice the smell of almonds on Genevieve?' I asked as Callum fastened his seatbelt.

His forehead creased. 'No.' He sent a quick glance my way. 'You're not talking about perfume, are you?' It was more of a statement than a question.

'Her face was red. I'm no medical examiner, but I've written plenty of fictional murders and I can't help but think she was poisoned with cyanide.'

Callum started the engine, his forehead still furrowed. 'Does Brody think she was poisoned?'

'Brody didn't tell me anything.'

'The police probably don't know much yet. If she was poisoned, it should show up in her bloodwork.'

I nodded as we pulled away from the curb. 'As long as they check soon. I think cyanide degrades quickly, but I could be wrong.'

'But you told him about your suspicions?'

'I did, and I probably wasn't the only one to notice the smell of almonds or the color of Genevieve's face. They'll probably test for cyanide right away.' I tucked my hands up into my sleeves. Even with the heat blasting, I could barely keep myself from shivering. 'Genevieve wasn't a nice woman, but to see her like that . . .'

Callum reached over and gave my arm a quick squeeze before returning his hand to the steering wheel.

'As unpleasant as she was, she didn't deserve to die,' I said. 'Or to be murdered.'

'Maybe there's still a chance she wasn't poisoned, that she died of natural causes.'

'Maybe,' I said, but I couldn't shake the ominous feeling that someone had purposely killed Genevieve.

When we arrived home, Callum walked me to the back door of the farmhouse. I gave him a quick kiss and then wrapped my arms around him, not letting go. He did the same with me.

After standing there, listening to the comforting beat of his heart, I tipped my head up. 'Are you OK?'

I was still worried about him. It was bad enough just seeing Genevieve like that. Trying and failing to resuscitate her . . . I suspected that was even worse.

'I'm all right,' he said quietly into my ear, still holding me close. 'It's a lot, but I'm OK. What about you?'

'Same,' I replied.

With a sigh that seemed to carry a lot of regret, he stepped back and took hold of my hands. 'We've got a busy day tomorrow, so we'd better try to get some rest.'

I put a hand to his face and stroked my thumb along his cheek. I had so many things I wanted to say to him. They were bubbling up inside me, but I couldn't find the right words. It probably wasn't the best time for them anyway. I gave him another quick kiss and we said goodnight.

Although Flossie and Fancy had taken to sleeping on their big dog bed with Stardust, that night all three animals hopped up on to my bed and curled up with me. Even though that left me with a sliver of space to squeeze into, I didn't complain. Having them close made me feel better, though sleep nevertheless eluded me. Stardust and the dogs didn't have the same problem; they fell asleep within minutes.

I was still awake, staring at the ceiling, when Flossie stirred just after midnight. She jumped down from the bed and put her front paws on the windowsill, letting out a whine.

'What's the matter, Flossie?' I carefully slipped out from beneath the covers and got up. Although Fancy raised her head, Stardust was still stretched out on her side, fast asleep.

I joined Flossie by the window and parted the curtains. Out beyond the barn, a bright light shone. I knew right away what it was.

After slipping back into the clothes I'd discarded earlier, I hurried downstairs with the dogs on my heels. Stardust had cracked her eyes open as I got dressed, but she didn't bother to get up. I tied my sneakers and pulled on a coat before opening the back door.

Once outside, the spaniels and I hurried across the lawn, past the barn, and out into the open field beyond Callum's cabin. My breath formed white clouds in front of my face and I tucked my hands in the pockets of my jacket. Overhead, vaporous clouds swirled as they drifted across the moon.

With Auntie O's blessing, Callum had set up a batting cage in the field so he could hit balls without them flying all over the farm. He had a pitching machine and a spotlight set up so he could see. He stood in the cage, wearing jeans and a raglan baseball tee, hitting each ball that the machine pitched at him.

He must have heard us approaching, because he took a step back and turned our way. A ball sailed past him to hit the netting, but then he pressed a button on the remote that controlled the pitching machine and it stopped spitting out balls.

'I see I'm not the only one still awake,' he said as he held aside the flap of netting that served as a door.

I joined him in the batting cage while Flossie and Fancy busied themselves with sniffing smells in the field.

'Is this what you do when you can't sleep?' I asked.

'Anytime I need to center myself.'

'Think it'll work for me?'

He grinned and handed me the bat. 'One way to find out.' He set a helmet on my head and tucked himself in behind me so my back was against his chest, just like when he'd first taught me how to hit a ball.

'I'm pretty good at hitting them on my own now,' I reminded him. 'The easy pitches, anyway.'

'You are,' he said with obvious pride that lit a warm glow in my chest. 'But I still like hitting them together.'

'Me too,' I admitted with a smile as he wrapped his arms around me and placed his hands next to mine on the bat.

With every crack of the ball against the bat, my thoughts slowed and tension seeped out of me. I could understand why this was Callum's go-to activity for relaxing and regaining his equilibrium. Although I was a newbie when it came to baseball, the sport had been his life, his primary focus, for decades. Swinging a bat, sending balls sailing through the air – this was his happy place. I was grateful to be part of it this time, grateful to have this man in my life.

With Callum at my back and in my heart, all my worries flew off into the night.

NINE

I yawned over my breakfast of toast and grape jelly the next day. By the time Callum had walked me back to the farmhouse and we'd said goodnight for the second time, it was one o'clock in the morning. Although I'd fallen asleep easily when I'd climbed back into bed, I wasn't used to staying up so late. I eyed my laptop where it sat at the far end of the rectangular kitchen table. My brain was fuzzy and I didn't feel the least bit creative. Not exactly good for a screenwriter. I had a few things I needed to do before I would have a chance to sit down and write, though. Hopefully by the time I returned to the house, my brain would be far more alert and the creative juices would be flowing.

After eating, I set off across the back lawn with Flossie and Fancy trotting ahead of me and Stardust between them, scampering along. Now and then she paused to pounce on a bug, and then she'd race furiously to catch up with the spaniels. Her antics made me laugh and helped to shake off some of my sleepiness.

Auntie O's late neighbor, Dorothy Shale, had rescued Flossie and Fancy after finding the pups all alone in the wooded hills outside of town. I'd made a trip to that area back in the summer, hoping to find clues as to how the spaniels had come into their special powers. Although I still didn't have any concrete answers, I believed that Witch's Peak – the place where Dorothy found the dogs – had something to do with their special abilities. I'd detected an unusual energy in the air there, and a local woman, Fae Hawthorn, had told me that ley lines converged in that area, making it a magically powerful place. However, exactly how that had caused the dogs to have their unique abilities, I didn't know.

Although I was now mostly content with knowing that I'd never be entirely sure how Flossie and Fancy got their powers, I did wonder if Stardust was anything like the dogs. They'd found the kitten abandoned not far from Witch's Peak when we'd hiked up there. So far, Stardust hadn't exhibited any unusual abilities – and I'd been watching for any such signs – but she was still young.

I wasn't sure if I wanted her to have magical powers or not. The dogs' unique abilities had helped me out numerous times in the past, but I worried about the wrong people finding out what they could do. No matter what the case with Stardust, I loved her dearly. That would never change.

I completed my morning farm chores while the dogs explored the smells around the barnyard and Stardust rode around on Callum's shoulder while he tended to the other animals. Once my chores were complete, the dogs and I hopped in my car and drove into town, leaving Stardust at the carriage house with Auntie O. I needed to pick up some dog and cat food, and I knew Flossie and Fancy wouldn't want to miss out on making a trip to their favorite store, the Pet Palace.

I tried to push aside my worries as I drove, but that wasn't as easy as it had been the night before when I was out hitting baseballs with Callum. Now thoughts of a possible murder in town swirled around in my head along with worries about Twiggy. Callum had told me that morning that the donkey wasn't eating. He suspected there was a problem with her teeth, one that made it too painful for her to eat.

The vet would be coming that afternoon to take a look at Twiggy and Tootsie, and I hoped she'd be able to make them both feel better and wouldn't find anything seriously wrong. Until the doctor had examined the donkeys, I would simply have to stay positive and hope for the best.

As soon as we got out of the car on Main Street, the spaniels tugged on their leashes, their tails wagging, eager to get to Cindy's store.

'No pulling,' I admonished, trying to slow them down.

They complied, but their tails drooped and they exchanged a glance with each other, one that suggested they weren't thrilled by my unhurried pace. Their tails started wagging again when we reached the shop door. Cindy came out from behind the counter to greet the dogs, crouching down to their level while Flossie and Fancy covered her with kisses.

When Cindy had to stop the cuddle fest to ring up another customer, I set off down the food aisle. Before I could pick anything off the shelves, Fancy nudged my leg.

'Hi, sweetie,' I said, somewhat absently, as I gave her a pat and then reached for a can of dog food.

Fancy gave me a more insistent nudge. This time she got my full attention.

'What is it?'

When she nudged me again, I moved in the direction she was trying to push me.

Satisfied that I was finally getting the message, she trotted off ahead of me, turning at the end of the aisle and going down the next one. When I peered into that aisle, I saw Fancy sitting in the middle of it, looking back at me expectantly. A little farther along, Miles Schmidt stood perusing a display of food and other supplies for pet fish.

'Morning, Miles,' I said.

He sent a distracted glance my way before looking back at the products on the shelf. 'Morning,' he mumbled.

I'd first met Miles when he volunteered to help out with the Trail of Terror. He was a member of the local theater group and would be playing the part of a zombie dentist. He would wander through the woods, revving his drill and hopefully giving the event attendees a good scare.

I almost asked him how he was doing, but then I remembered something Praise had mentioned.

'I'm so sorry for your loss,' I said instead.

His hand resting on a container of fish food, he looked at me, puzzled.

My stomach sank and I wished I could take my words back. 'You haven't heard?'

'Are you talking about Genevieve?' he asked, lowering his hand, the fish food forgotten. 'I know she died last night, but she and I weren't close.'

'Oh.' Now I was the one confused. 'I thought I'd heard that you were dating her.'

Maybe Praise hadn't actually said that, but she'd talked about Genevieve whispering sweet nothings in his ear and I'd taken that to mean they had a romantic relationship of some sort.

Anger flashed in his gray eyes. 'No,' he said, his voice flat. 'I wasn't.'

He grabbed a container of fish food off the shelf and strode off to the sales counter.

I remained rooted in place, feeling bad that I'd clearly said the wrong thing. I must have misunderstood Praise.

Doing my best to shake off the encounter, I got back to my shopping. Luckily, by the time I approached the sales counter, Miles had already left the store.

Soon after, we left too, with me carrying cloth bags filled with dog food, cat food, and a few treats. As I stashed the purchases in the trunk of my car, my gaze strayed across the street to Déjà Brew, the local coffee shop. A matcha latte would hit the spot, I decided, and it would hopefully clear some of the cobwebs from my brain. I couldn't take the dogs into the coffee shop with me, but Dolores Sánchez, one of Auntie O's friends, sat at an outdoor table with Hattie, the woman I'd met at the pumpkin patch.

After crossing the street, the dogs and I approached Déjà Brew, pausing outside the shop.

'Morning, ladies,' I greeted Dolores and Hattie.

Hattie returned my greeting as Flossie and Fancy trotted straight to Dolores to say hello.

'Morning, Georgie,' Dolores said before adding to the dogs, 'and to you too, you gorgeous girls.'

That got happy tail wags out of the spaniels.

'Georgie, do you know Hattie Beechwood?' Dolores asked.

'We met at the pumpkin patch the other day,' I replied.

'Her handsome young man helped me load my pumpkins into my car,' Hattie said with a smile.

Dolores smiled too. 'He certainly is handsome. How is he doing, Georgie?'

'Great,' I said before changing the subject, hoping to avoid any probing questions about my relationship with Callum. 'Dolores, would it be all right if I left the dogs with you while I pop inside to get a drink?'

'Of course,' Dolores said with delight, taking the leashes from me. 'I'd love to keep them company for a while. You take your time, Georgie.'

I left both women fussing over the dogs and entered the coffee shop. I paid for my matcha latte and then moved down the counter to wait while the barista prepared it. As I stood there, the conversations from the other patrons blurred together until someone at the nearest table mentioned a familiar name.

'Where's Barclay?' a young man grumbled. 'He was supposed to meet us here half an hour ago.'

My ears perked up as I recalled that Barclay was Genevieve's nephew, the one I'd seen with her at the farmers' market. I glanced over at the group of two men and two women, all of whom appeared to be in their early twenties and dressed in expensive clothing.

'Is there a casino in this town?' the other guy at the table asked. 'Because if there is, I bet that's where we'd find Barclay.' He sniggered before taking a drink of his coffee.

'This town is too sleepy to have a casino,' the first man said, still sounding disgruntled.

'Oh my gosh!' One of the women – a blonde with long, straight hair – typed furiously on her phone. 'He just texted me. His aunt died last night.'

'Seriously?' the other woman said.

'So does this mean he's not coming sailing with us?' the grumpy guy asked.

The blonde glared at him. 'You're so insensitive, Jeremy.'

Jeremy rolled his eyes and went back to drinking his coffee.

The barista set my drink in front of me, so I thanked her, picked up my latte, and headed out of the coffee shop with only a brief final glance at Barclay's friends. Barclay had wanted money from Genevieve. Could he have decided to poison her after she refused his request? That wouldn't help his situation any unless he was her heir.

I made a mental note to find out who would inherit Genevieve's estate. Then I told myself that I didn't need to worry about such things. Sure, I'd tried to solve murders in the past, but there was no need for me to do that this time. The police would take care of it. I had enough to worry about with the donkeys, all the other animals, the upcoming Trail of Terror fundraiser, and my screenwriting career all needing my attention. Not to mention the fact that I'd soon be meeting Callum's parents.

That last thought sent butterflies into a mild panic in my stomach. I was grateful for the distraction when Dolores invited me to join her and Hattie at their table once I was back outside.

Although it was October, I understood why the ladies had chosen to sit outside. Despite a chilly undercurrent to the air, the sun was pleasantly warm and it likely wouldn't be long before wet and cold weather put an end to sitting outdoors until spring.

'Did you hear that Genevieve Newmont died?' Dolores asked me once I'd taken a seat at their table.

'Callum and I found her in the park,' I said by way of response.

Shocked, Dolores and Hattie showered me with sympathy before asking if I knew what had happened.

'Nobody seemed to know last night,' I said, wanting to answer truthfully while keeping my suspicions to myself.

While Hattie and Dolores talked about how shocking it was that Genevieve – who'd appeared so healthy – had died so suddenly, I glanced up the street to see a man exiting the Moonstruck Diner. The same man I'd seen lurking at Griffin Park, watching Genevieve.

I stood up so quickly that I startled Dolores and Hattie.

'Sorry,' I apologized. 'I'll be right back.'

Leaving the dogs with Dolores and my drink on the table, I hurried up the street. The man, who had dark hair and light brown skin, climbed into a dusty black sedan and drove off. I watched him go and then turned into the Moonstruck Diner. Jackie, the owner, was carrying two plates of eggs Benedict to one of the retro diner's booths. After she'd delivered the meals, she smiled at me on her way back behind the counter.

'Morning, Georgie,' she greeted. 'Here for a bite to eat?'

'Just a quick question, actually. That man who just left the diner . . . he looked really familiar. Did you catch his name?'

'Enrique Ramos? You know him? He said he's from Portland.'

'The name doesn't ring a bell,' I said. 'Is he here on vacation?'

'Sounds like it.'

Jackie's gaze strayed to a young couple who'd just walked into the diner. She smiled and called out a greeting to them, and I knew I should leave her to get back to work.

'Thanks, Jackie.' I gave her a quick wave as I left the diner.

Enrique Ramos was from Portland. Genevieve had moved here from Portland a few months ago. Had Enrique been spying on Genevieve when he was lurking at the park? Or was he there for another reason?

If I saw him doing anything suspicious again, I'd report him to the police, I decided. Meanwhile, I needed to focus on my career, the sanctuary, and my relationship with Callum. I didn't need to be seeing murder suspects where there might not even be any.

As I made my way back to the coffee shop, my phone rang. Recognizing Brody's number, I answered as I walked. I hung up a moment later, any remaining hope that Genevieve had died a natural death now obliterated. Brody had asked me to come to the station to provide a more fulsome statement. He'd also done what he couldn't do the night before – he confirmed that the police viewed Genevieve's death as suspicious.

TEN

Since I'd arranged with Brody to meet him at the police station in half an hour, I had time to enjoy my latte first. When I returned to the coffee shop's outdoor table, Flossie and Fancy welcomed me back with wagging tails.

'Were you trying to catch up with that man who came out of the diner?' Dolores asked as I sat down.

I hesitated before responding, not wanting the women to think I was nosy, even though I couldn't really deny that trait. I preferred the word 'curious' to 'nosy' but sometimes those were the same thing.

'I wanted to find out who he was,' I replied after taking a sip of my drink to buy myself time to choose my words. 'I saw him at Griffin Park the other night.'

'I've never seen him before myself,' Hattie said. 'At least I don't think so. I didn't get a particularly good look at him.'

'He's from Portland, apparently.' I took another drink, my mind still whirring from my conversation with Brody. Although I'd strongly suspected that someone had murdered Genevieve, thanks to the signs of cyanide poisoning, having confirmation that the police suspected foul play had triggered whatever it was in my brain that always made me want to puzzle out mysteries until I had everything figured out. I wanted to quiet down that part of my brain so I could focus on other things.

Dolores' next words made that impossible.

'Whoever he is, I saw him arguing with Genevieve the other day,' she said between sips of her coffee.

That caught my attention. 'What were they arguing about?'

Dolores thought for a moment. 'He claimed that she owed him money. Or owed him something, anyway. Genevieve denied it. Vehemently.'

'That sounds like Genevieve,' Hattie said with a shake of her head. 'Even if the man was telling the truth, she thought she could get away with anything.'

'I guess it's a relief that there's no chance of her harming your cats now,' I said, suddenly seeing the other woman in a new – and suspicious – light.

'I'm not glad she's dead, but I am glad she'll no longer be living next door to me and my fur babies,' Hattie admitted.

I wondered if I should put Hattie on my suspect list. Then I silently chastised myself. I didn't have a suspect list. This time, I was staying out of the murder investigation.

'Did you hear that crazy story about Bigfoot chasing Genevieve off the road?' Dolores asked. 'That's the nuttiest thing I've heard in a while.'

'I'm sure that was a lie.' Hattie tsked before taking a sip of coffee. 'She probably made up the story just to get attention.'

'I heard she had dashcam footage,' Dolores said.

'Of someone in a Sasquatch costume,' I chimed in. 'I saw the footage. It looked like a cheap costume. Not very convincing at all.'

Dolores frowned. 'That was a dangerous prank for someone to play.'

Hattie agreed, and the conversation turned to the various Halloween pranks that had been played around town in years past. I only half listened, my mind wandering back to Genevieve. Maybe the person in the Sasquatch costume had meant the prank to be dangerous, even deadly. Had that been the killer's first attempt on Genevieve's life? Then, when she survived the accident, had the murderer decided to change tactics?

Apparently, it was impossible to keep my mind from trying to figure out the mystery. Hopefully the police would solve the case soon so I could put a stop to all the suspicions and theories bouncing around in my head.

Once I'd finished my latte, I excused myself and set off for the police station with Flossie and Fancy. When I'd mentioned that the dogs were in town with me, Brody had assured me that I could bring them along when I provided my statement. The brick building that housed the Twilight Cove Police Department sat just off Main Street, well up the hill from the beach. I found a parking spot a short way down the road and soon Brody was leading the dogs and me into an interview room.

Once we were settled, Brody had me once again go over how Callum and I had found Genevieve at Griffin Park. While I talked, he wrote down everything I was saying. After I'd shared all that I could remember, including the glimpse I'd caught of someone running from the scene, he asked me some further questions.

'Who was at the park when you arrived for your volunteer shift?'

It made sense that he'd want to know such things now that Genevieve's death was considered suspicious. I gave him all the names I could think of, including Tessa's, Catherine's, and Jamieson's.

'And did any of them disappear from sight at any time while you were working in the park?'

'I don't think so,' I replied, wishing I could be more certain. 'I didn't notice anyone coming or going, but I was focused on setting up the pergola with Callum and Jamieson. They definitely didn't leave at any time before Callum and I found Genevieve, but I can't be completely sure about any of the others.' I couldn't hold back my next questions. 'Genevieve was poisoned, right? Do you think the poison was administered right there at the park?'

'I can't answer that,' Brody said.

'Right.' That didn't surprise me in the least. 'Ongoing investigation and all that.'

He nodded. 'You know the drill.'

A nugget of worry formed in my stomach. I hated that I couldn't say for certain that Tessa and Catherine had stayed with the group the entire time. Then again, the two women could probably vouch for each other. Besides, it might not matter, depending on when Genevieve ingested the poison.

Something occurred to me. 'Genevieve was still warm when we found her, so I'm guessing she wasn't poisoned too long before that. Cyanide works quickly, right?' When I saw that Brody wasn't about to answer my questions, I continued, 'But we were all surprised when Genevieve wasn't there waiting for us when we first showed up at the park, which was ages before we found her in among the trees.'

I looked at Brody and he looked back at me.

'OK, sorry,' I said with a sigh. 'I know you can't give me any details. I was just thinking out loud. The fact that she didn't show up on time makes me wonder if she was delayed by the killer somehow, but if cyanide is fast-acting and she collapsed at the park . . .' My thoughts jumped slightly. 'Did she drive herself there after she was poisoned or before?' I shook my head. 'Sorry. Thinking out loud again.' Before Brody could say anything, I added, 'I know I'm not supposed to be trying to figure this out.'

'We definitely don't want a repeat of what happened at the

lighthouse at the end of summer,' he said. 'Or what happened back in June.'

On both of those occasions I'd tangled with killers.

'Believe me, I more than anyone want to avoid that,' I assured him.

'Good.' Brody met my gaze head-on. 'Let me and my colleagues take care of this investigation.'

'I fully intend to do that.'

I thought I might have detected the tiniest hint of disbelief in Brody's eyes, but I couldn't be sure. He was too good at schooling his expressions.

Realizing that I might know some important information, I relayed what Dolores had told me about Genevieve's argument with Enrique Ramos. Then I filled Brody in on Barclay's request for money from his aunt, and his reaction when she'd refused to comply. Brody included that in the statement, and then he had me go over everything he'd written.

It all looked right, so I signed it and the dogs and I left the interview room. On our way out of the station, I checked my phone and saw that I'd missed several text messages from Tessa, asking me to call her as soon as possible. That took me by surprise. She should have been at the high school, teaching. She didn't typically send texts or make personal phone calls during working hours.

Concerned, I put a call through to her number.

She picked up right away. 'Georgie,' she said, sounding distraught. 'I don't know what to do. The police think I killed Genevieve!'

ELEVEN

I drove to Tessa's apartment as fast as I legally could and arrived there in under five minutes. She lived on the top floor of a large Victorian house that had been converted into half a dozen separate units. She buzzed me in through the front door and the dogs and I clattered up the interior staircase. When we reached the third floor, Tessa stood in her open doorway, arms wrapped around herself and tear tracks on her cheeks. The spaniels and I hurried into her apartment. As soon as she had the door shut behind her, I gave her a fierce hug.

'I can't believe this,' I said as I held her. 'Are you sure you aren't mistaken? How could the police believe that you would kill anyone?'

I forced myself to stop talking, realizing that I needed to quit bombarding her with questions.

Tessa sniffled as I released her. Flossie and Fancy whined, pressing their noses to Tessa's legs. She crouched down and received kisses from them while she stroked their fur. When she stood up again, a single tear meandered its way down her face. She wiped it away with the back of her hand.

'I'm not mistaken,' she said, leading us farther into the apartment. She sank down on to her couch and tucked one leg beneath her.

I sat down in the armchair across from her while the dogs planted themselves by her feet and rested their chins on her knees. That got a hint of a tremulous smile out of Tessa as she stroked their silky heads.

'The police came by this morning, wanting to ask me a whole bunch of questions,' she said. 'Not Brody, thank goodness. I don't think I could bear it if I looked in his eyes and saw that he suspected me.'

Tessa and Brody had both grown up in Twilight Cove. Although Brody was a year younger than us, they'd known each other their whole lives. It was only in recent months that Tessa had confessed to me that she had a crush on the good-looking police officer.

'I don't think Brody would suspect you for a moment,' I said.

I replayed my recent conversation with him in my head, wondering if there had been any indication that he knew about Tessa's status as a suspect. He probably did, but he hadn't given anything away. He'd seemed serious throughout our meeting, but that was par for the course when investigating a murder.

My stomach clenched as I remembered how he'd asked me if anyone – including Tessa – had left the park while I was there volunteering. Now more than ever I wished I could have vouched for Tessa's every movement.

'His colleagues do,' Tessa said, interrupting my rapid thoughts. 'Chief Stratton was here with a detective from the state police force. The chief was trying to be kind, but the detective was all business. They didn't take me down to the station, but I was still terrified.'

I moved over to sit next to her on the couch so I could hug her again. 'I'm so sorry, Tessa. If they want to talk to you again, you should have someone with you.'

'You mean a lawyer?' She wiped away another tear and let out a watery laugh that was devoid of humor. 'I never thought I'd need a lawyer. Not a criminal one, anyway.'

She burst into tears.

'Oh, Tessa.' I gave her another squeeze, wishing I could magically make everything better for her.

'And here I thought I had enough trouble with the missing fog machine,' she said through her tears. 'That seems so unimportant now.'

'What missing fog machine?' That was the first I'd heard of any such thing.

'My senior drama class is putting on a short Halloween play for the other students,' she explained. 'We were going to use the department's fog machine, but when I went to get it out of storage to make sure it was working properly, it was gone. I might have to replace it out of my own pocket.'

'That doesn't seem right.'

She shrugged. 'I'm the head of the drama department. It was under my charge and there's no room in the budget to get a new one.' She cried harder again. 'That's the least of my problems now.'

I rubbed her back. 'I'm so sorry you're going through this, Tess. Can you tell me why the police suspect you?'

She nodded, drawing in a shaky breath as she wiped her tears away. I jumped up and grabbed a box of tissues from across the room and brought it back to her. She pulled one out of the box and cleaned away the tear tracks on her cheeks.

'Somebody told the police about the argument I had with Genevieve at Griffin Park,' she said eventually. 'You know, when she accused me of leaving her measurements out for everyone to see.'

'That wasn't much of an argument,' I said. 'Not really. Certainly not enough to make you seem like a solid murder suspect.'

'But then there was that other argument. I never got around to telling you about it. I ran into Genevieve on Main Street the next day and she demanded to know when I'd have her costume ready.'

'You'd already told her you weren't making her a costume.'

'She didn't care about that. She always assumed she'd get whatever she wanted, no matter what.' Tessa dabbed at her eyes. 'When I told her, again, that she'd have to get a costume from another source, she flew into a rage. She called me all sorts of terrible names and threatened to ruin my career as a teacher.'

'How could she do that?'

Tessa shrugged. 'Spread lies about me, maybe? Who knows? She was an awful, *awful* woman. But I didn't kill her.'

'I know you didn't,' I said without a shred of doubt.

Fancy gave a quiet 'woo' of agreement.

A ghost of a smile appeared on Tessa's face for a brief moment. She patted Fancy's head and then Flossie's. 'I'm so lucky to have friends like the three of you.'

'We're lucky too,' I said.

This time it was Flossie who voiced her agreement with a woof.

That got another fleeting smile out of Tessa. 'I guess someone told the police about that second argument too,' she continued. 'There were probably several witnesses. I don't remember who was around. I walked away from Genevieve while she was still screaming at me and I was so angry that I could hardly see straight. To make matters worse, I was alone for a while at the park, not long before you found Genevieve. I took a walk along the path to see if any leaves had blown into the cleared areas. Some had, so I raked them up. Nobody can vouch for my whereabouts while I was doing that.'

That wasn't good news, but I tried not to let on that her lack of an alibi worried me.

'Tessa,' I said, 'I'm absolutely certain that you can't be the only suspect. Genevieve was horrible to so many people.'

'But did she argue with any of them publicly in the days before her death?' Tessa asked, sounding doubtful.

I thought about the question before answering. 'She did. I can think of at least two people she argued with. I witnessed one myself. She argued with her nephew at the farmers' market. It wasn't a major blow-up, but he wanted money from her and she wouldn't give it to him.'

'Do the police know about that?'

'I mentioned it to Brody earlier. There was another argument too, one I heard about secondhand. A man told Genevieve she owed him something, which she denied. I saw that same man hanging around Griffin Park the day before Genevieve died.'

'Is he anyone I know?' Tessa asked with a flicker of interest.

'He's from Portland, apparently. Enrique Ramos.'

She shook her head. 'Never heard of him.'

'I told Brody about him as well. He'll make sure every angle gets considered.'

Tessa didn't look too convinced. 'The state police take charge of murder investigations. Brody can only do so much.'

'He'll do everything he can. I'm sure of it.'

'But what if that's not enough?' Tears welled in her beseeching brown eyes as she looked at me. 'Georgie, I know I shouldn't ask this, but will you help me clear my name?'

'Of course,' I said without hesitation. 'You can count on it.'

TWELVE

Before leaving Tessa's apartment, I tried to convince her to come back to the farm with me. After her early morning visit from the police, she'd called in sick, not feeling up to going to work. She didn't want to risk being seen around town when she was taking a sick day, and she said that all she wanted to do was take a nap in an attempt to rid herself of the headache she had brewing.

I left her reluctantly, even though she seemed far calmer now that I'd agreed to help her clear her name. I had asked her to get in touch with her cousin Valentina, who worked at the police station in a civilian capacity. Valentina had loose lips and loved nothing more than to gossip. In the past, she'd provided us with valuable inside information and I was hoping that she could do the same again. The more we knew about the investigation into Genevieve's murder, the more I'd have to work with when helping Tessa.

When I pulled into the farm's driveway, Dr Mahika Sharma, one of Twilight Cove's veterinarians, was just leaving in her truck. I waved as we passed each other and, as soon as I'd parked by the farmhouse, the dogs and I set off toward Tootsie and Twiggy's pasture. Callum and Auntie O were over there, inside the fence with the donkeys.

'I'm sorry I wasn't here for Dr Sharma's visit,' I said as I reached the fence. 'Something came up while I was in town.'

'Anything serious?' Callum asked as he stroked Twiggy's nose.

'I'll fill you in later,' I said without really answering his question. 'How did things go with Twiggy and Tootsie?'

Auntie O ran a hand along Tootsie's neck. 'Dr Sharma vaccinated them, dewormed them, and floated their teeth.'

'Floated?' I opened the gate to let myself into the pasture.

'Filed,' Callum clarified. 'Twiggy's teeth were particularly bad. They were so sharp they were cutting into the inside of her mouth.'

I cringed. 'Poor donkey.' I gave Twiggy a sympathetic pat.

'That's probably why she hasn't been eating,' Auntie O said. 'It's been too painful.'

My heart ached and tears prickled at my eyes, but I managed to keep them at bay. Even so, Callum didn't miss the emotions bubbling up inside of me.

'Hey.' He kissed my forehead. 'I know it's hard to see them suffering, but their teeth are all fixed up now. As Twiggy's mouth heals, she'll be back to eating without any problem.'

I nodded as I stroked Twiggy's nose. Her eyes were only half open, as if she were falling asleep.

'Dr Sharma sedated them,' Callum explained. 'They're both a little out of it still.'

I gave Twiggy's nose another pat and then moved over to greet Tootsie, who looked just as sleepy as her companion. 'What about Tootsie's sores and Twiggy's eye?'

'The eye is infected, just like we thought,' Auntie O said. 'Dr Sharma put some medication into it and I'm going to pick up more meds from the clinic later today so we can continue treating it every day for the next while.'

'And Tootsie's got sweet itch,' Callum added.

'What's that?' I'd never heard of it before.

'A hypersensitivity to midges,' he replied. 'The raw spots on her back are from scratching herself against fence posts or trees to the point of breaking her skin.'

'I'm picking up medication for that later today too,' Auntie O said. 'And we can help her out in the future with a special coat, antihistamines, and by stabling her at dusk and dawn during midge season.'

One of the several knots of tension residing in my chest unraveled slightly. I stroked Tootsie's nose and looked into her half-open eyes. 'So, hopefully, in a few weeks – or even sooner – you'll both be as good as new, huh, Toots?'

'That's the plan,' Auntie O agreed with a smile, giving Tootsie an affectionate pat on the neck.

'They'll probably feel a bit better as soon as tomorrow,' Callum said, 'thanks to having their teeth filed today and getting their hooves trimmed in the morning.'

At least things were looking up in that respect. If only I could say the same about Tessa's situation. Hopefully I *would* be saying that in a matter of days.

As we spent more time comforting the donkeys and keeping them company, I told Aunt Olivia and Callum about Tessa's predicament.

Neither one of them believed for a second that Tessa had anything to do with the murder.

'But the police are certain Genevieve was murdered?' Auntie O asked.

'They're treating her death as suspicious,' I said. 'That's the wording Brody used. It's possible to accidentally get poisoned by cyanide, but I don't know if they've been able to eliminate that possibility or not.'

'How does one even get hold of cyanide these days?' my aunt asked.

I considered the question. 'Straight cyanide? I'm not sure. But—'

'Certain fruit seeds and pits release cyanide when ingested,' Callum finished for me.

I looked at him, impressed.

'Hey,' he said with a grin, 'I may not write thrillers or mysteries, but I do read them.'

A thought struck me. 'Maybe that's what happened to Genevieve. A cyanide capsule will kill you pretty much instantly. But if you ingest, say, cherry pits, it will take longer to feel the effects of the poison.'

'So it's possible that Genevieve unknowingly ingested something like cherry pits and then collapsed a while later,' my aunt mused. 'Then it really could have been an accident.'

'I hope that's what happened,' I said. 'And I hope the police can find proof to support that theory. Then there won't be any suspects and Tessa won't have to worry.'

'But they clearly haven't proved it was an accident yet,' Auntie O said.

'No.'

'And they might have evidence to the contrary,' Callum added.

'That could be,' I agreed.

It really would help to know what information the police had about Genevieve's movements before she died and how she'd ended up with cyanide in her system.

Fortunately, I had a possible way of getting that intel. By the time I'd returned to the farmhouse after spending more time with the drowsy donkeys, I had a text message from Tessa, letting me know that her cousin Valentina had agreed to meet with us the very next day.

* * *

I tried to spend the rest of the day writing. Between worrying about Tessa, wondering what had really happened to Genevieve, and getting distracted by a certain gray kitten who was running and jumping – with the dogs giving chase – all over the house, I didn't have much success. Fortunately, I didn't have any looming deadlines. One of my projects was currently in postproduction and I was waiting for notes from a network on another script. I had a couple of other screenplays out on submission to various producers and production companies, but that was mostly a waiting game. It could be days, weeks, or even months before I heard back from any of them. Some might never get back to me at all.

Although I had another screenplay that I wanted to get started on, it wasn't under contract, so the fact that I hadn't been writing much over the past few days wasn't a big deal. Still, I tended to feel twitchy and restless when I had a story brewing and didn't get it down on the page. The thriller that I wanted to write was set in the mountains of the Pacific Northwest and involved a terrifying game of cat and mouse, with the protagonist up against the antagonist, inclement weather, and the dangers of the wilderness. I could picture the opening scenes clearly in my head, but I only managed to get the first one written before I gave up.

I took the dogs and Stardust outside, where they cavorted about in the grass, playing together. I spent time watching them and I also visited Tootsie and Twiggy again. The following twenty-four hours seemed to pass in slow motion, but at least the farrier's visit the next morning helped to distract me. By the time he left, the donkeys had nicely trimmed hooves and already seemed more comfortable as they moseyed around the pasture.

In the afternoon, shortly after school let out for the day, I drove into town on my own to meet Tessa and Valentina at a teahouse located in an old Victorian house near Main Street. I knew from an earlier text exchange that Tessa had gone to work that day and I hoped it had been a good distraction for her. When I met her outside the teahouse, I gave her a fierce hug, my heart hurting for her. She had dark rings under her eyes and lacked her usual bubbly energy.

Once inside the teahouse, the hostess led us to a table near a beautiful, tiled fireplace. Rather than an actual fire, it held an elaborate candelabra with a dozen flickering tealights. Although diners occupied several other tables, no one was too close to us. That came as a relief, since we didn't want anyone overhearing our upcoming conversation.

We ordered for the three of us and Valentina joined us within minutes, wearing an all-black outfit and oversized sunglasses. Her glossy, dark hair was styled into perfect waves and she brought with her a hint of flowery perfume.

'What's with the glasses?' Tessa asked as her cousin got settled in her chair.

'It's probably not the best idea for me to be seen with you right now,' Valentina whispered. 'After all, I work for the police and you're a murder suspect.'

'Like I need to be reminded.' Tessa reached over and pulled the glasses off Valentina's face. 'Wearing these indoors will only draw *more* attention to us. Besides, everyone in this town knows who you are and knows that the two of us are cousins.'

'I was just trying to be cautious,' Valentina said with a huff before studying her sparkly purple nails. Now that she wasn't wearing the sunglasses, I could see that the paint on her nails matched her eyeshadow.

'We're hoping you can help us out,' I said to Valentina, trying to placate her so she'd be willing to share information with us. 'Last time there was a murder investigation in this town, you had valuable intel.'

That seemed to appease her. 'I am in the thick of things,' she said, perking up. 'Of course, I can't share *everything*. I have a responsibility to keep some things confidential.'

Tessa and I exchanged a brief glance. We knew that keeping secrets was far from Valentina's forte.

'We understand that,' I said, despite my thoughts. 'But we're trying to clear Tessa's name, so we'd be grateful for any tidbits you can give us.'

We paused our conversation as a waitress brought our individual pots of tea. She returned a moment later with tiered serving plates, one for each of us. They held a variety of finger sandwiches, scones, and delicate desserts. My stomach grumbled at the sight. I'd eaten a light lunch, hours earlier, knowing that I'd be dining at the teahouse.

'Can you confirm that Genevieve was poisoned with cyanide?' I asked in a low voice once the waitress had left us alone again.

'She was,' Valentina said as she spread a generous amount of apricot jam on a scone. 'But not from a cyanide capsule or anything crazy like that.'

'Cherry pits?' I asked.

'Nope.' Valentina smiled, apparently pleased that I hadn't guessed correctly. She leaned forward and whispered, 'Apricot kernels. Ground up and mixed into baked goods.'

THIRTEEN

I held back a wince as Valentina took a big bite of her scone, slathered as it was in apricot jam. Although I felt confident that the teahouse's offerings weren't laced with cyanide or any other poison, I couldn't help but wonder if Genevieve had bitten into the tainted baked goods that had killed her just as blithely as Valentina had done with her scone.

'Was there any sign of baked goods with her in the park?' Tessa asked me.

I selected a smoked salmon and herb tea sandwich. Despite thoughts about poisoned food, my appetite hadn't disappeared. 'I didn't see any. All she had with her was her handbag. It was certainly big enough to have food in it, but that doesn't seem too likely.' I thought for a moment as I took a bite of the delicious sandwich. 'Besides, I think when you ingest cyanide in that form, it can take a while to affect you.'

Valentina nodded as she polished off the last of her scone. 'According to the medical examiner, it could take anywhere from about twenty minutes to three hours to start showing symptoms. When the police searched the victim's home, they found anti-nausea medication sitting out on the kitchen island. And they found evidence in the park that she vomited on the way from her courtesy car – apparently, her own vehicle was being repaired – to the place where she was found.'

'So she was feeling the effects before she left her house,' Tessa surmised.

'Which means she ingested the poisoned food before leaving for the park.' I took a sip of my blackcurrant tea before directing the question at Valentina. 'Did the police find the baked goods at Genevieve's house?'

Valentina shook her head as she savored a finger sandwich. 'Not a trace of tainted food or of any apricot kernels.'

'So they don't know where the food came from?' I asked.

'Not yet,' Valentina confirmed.

Tessa looked to me. 'I didn't even know that apricot kernels were poisonous, but there's no way I can prove that to the police.'

'No,' I agreed. 'So we'll just have to figure out who *did* give Genevieve the poison.'

'Please tell me that I'm not the only suspect,' Tessa said to her cousin.

'Definitely not.' Some of the tension eased out of Tessa's shoulders with Valentina's response. 'But things wouldn't be so bad for you if you hadn't argued with the woman in public. Twice.'

'If I knew she was going to be murdered, I would have held my tongue.' The tension had returned to Tessa's shoulders and irritation crept into her voice. 'But if you'd had to deal with her, you would have argued with her too.'

'Tessa just stood up for herself,' I said in defense of my friend. 'Genevieve really was awful to her.'

'Hey, I know you didn't do the deed, prima,' Valentina said as she finished off another sandwich, 'but it doesn't look good for you.'

Tessa selected a sandwich but set it on her plate instead of eating it. 'The police must have stronger suspects.'

Valentina shrugged. 'I don't know how he ranks compared to you, but they're definitely interested in the victim's nephew.'

'Barclay,' I said with a nod. 'He wanted money from Genevieve and she refused to give him any.'

'He gets money every month from a trust fund,' Valentina added, 'but, apparently, he goes through it in a flash.'

'But will he inherit anything from his aunt?' I asked.

'I don't have that info yet,' Valentina said, sounding disappointed. 'But I know that one of the detectives from the state police was going to speak with Genevieve's lawyer in Portland today. So I might be able to fill you in tomorrow.'

'Do you know why the police think it's unlikely her death was accidental?' I asked. 'Maybe someone didn't know the kernels were poisonous or used them by mistake?'

'There were notes at her house,' Valentina said between bites of a mini eclair.

'What kind of notes?' Tessa prodded.

'Threatening ones. And, apparently, the victim thought someone was out to get her.'

I nodded at that. 'She mentioned that after her car accident.'

Valentina didn't know what the threatening notes had said and she didn't have any further intel to share, so we spent the rest of our time at the teahouse chatting about the delicious food and the town's upcoming Halloween events, including the Trail of Terror. Tessa joined in the conversation now and then, but she was distracted and glum.

I hated seeing her like that and I knew I wouldn't be able to stop looking for answers until her name was cleared and she was back to the happy, effervescent Tessa that I knew.

After leaving the teahouse, I gave Tessa another hug and assured her that we'd succeed in proving her innocence. Despite my confident façade, worry swirled in my stomach as I watched her drive away. I hoped her reputation and career wouldn't suffer any damage before we – or the police – had a chance to crack the case and identify the real killer.

As I turned to walk to my own car, I saw Praise unloading a box from the trunk of her vehicle, which was parked behind mine at the edge of the street. When I drew closer, I saw that the lid-less box held a variety of jars filled with jam and jelly.

'Do you sell your preserves to the tea house?' I asked after exchanging greetings with her.

'I'm not their only supplier, but they do like to use local products whenever possible.'

'I love the grape jelly I bought from you at the market the other day.'

She smiled. 'Thank you. I'm glad you like it.' She adjusted her grip on the box. 'I'd better get these inside.' She took a step away from me and then paused. 'Oh, Georgie, I wanted to thank you for the volunteering you've done for the Pumpkin Glow.'

'It's my pleasure. Is it still on now that Genevieve is gone?' I hadn't heard any news in that regard.

'The organizing committee voted last night to put me back in charge. The event is going ahead as scheduled. And,' she added as she smiled again, 'now it will be the event that it was meant to be.'

Calling out a goodbye, Praise set off along a paved pathway that would take her around to the back of the teahouse.

As I was about to get into my car, I decided to leave it there for the time being and walk over to Scissor Me Timbers, the local hair salon. I wanted to make an appointment to get my hair trimmed and tidied up before Callum's parents arrived in Twilight Cove. My wavy brown hair had grown out to almost chin length and was looking a little shaggy. I liked having it a bit shorter, but still long enough to tuck behind my ears.

I'd almost reached the salon when I saw Linette walking along the sidewalk in my direction. She seemed like she was off in her own world and would have walked on by without noticing me if I hadn't spoken.

'Linette, how are you doing?' I asked.

She stopped and looked at me as though startled to find someone next to her. 'Oh, Georgie, I didn't see you there. Did you say something?'

'I just asked how you're doing,' I said. 'I'm so sorry that you lost your best friend.'

Although I didn't understand how anyone could be close friends with Genevieve, it was entirely possible that Linette knew a side of her that I'd never glimpsed, and I couldn't bear the thought of anything bad ever happening to Tessa, my own closest friend. So, no matter my feelings about Genevieve's personality, my heart went out to Linette.

'Thank you. I appreciate that, Georgie.' Tears glimmered in her eyes. 'I'm sorry I can't stay and chat. I've got an appointment here at the salon.'

'That's no problem,' I assured her. 'And that's where I'm headed too.'

I followed her into Scissor Me Timbers. A middle-aged woman with spiky, black-and-purple hair welcomed Linette with a hug before leading her to a hair washing station near the back of the salon.

I approached the reception desk, surprised to see Hattie Beechwood seated behind it.

'I didn't realize you worked here,' I said.

It was the first time I'd entered the salon. I'd had my last haircut in LA when I'd gone back there to pack up my belongings so I could move to Twilight Cove permanently. That was way back in the early summer, which was why my hair was starting to look a little unkempt. I'd dropped Auntie O off at the salon and picked her up on a couple of occasions, but I'd never set foot inside.

'On a part-time basis,' Hattie said with a smile. 'Do you have an appointment?'

'No,' I replied. 'I was hoping to make one. I've never been here before.'

'Hmm. Aleah always does your aunt's hair, but with those waves of yours . . . Amy-Lee would be a good match.' Hattie consulted the computer. 'She has an opening right now. Does that work for you?'

'Sure,' I said.

Hattie got up from her seat. 'I'll just double-check with Amy-Lee to make sure she can take you now.'

She hurried off to the back of the salon, returning a moment later with a slender, fair-skinned woman who appeared to be just a little older than me, in her mid-thirties. The dark brown hair on the sides of her head was cut super short, but on top she had glossy curls. She had a silver ring through one eyebrow and a stud in her nose, along with several piercings in each ear.

Amy-Lee introduced herself and then accompanied me to one of the hair washing stations. A few minutes later, when she led me to her styling chair, I realized that luck had smiled upon me.

Seated in the chair next to me was Linette Mears, and she and her stylist were talking about Genevieve's death.

FOURTEEN

'I'm so sorry about your friend,' the stylist said as she combed out Linette's hair. 'I remember how happy you were that she'd moved to Twilight Cove.'

Linette reached up and patted the stylist's hand that rested on her shoulder. 'Thank you, Demi.' I could see in the mirror that Linette's eyes had misted up. 'It's all so hard to take in. And I received another blow this morning.'

'How so?' Demi asked with concern as she picked up her scissors.

Fortunately, Amy-Lee had left me briefly to grab a clean cape, so I could listen in on the conversation unfolding next to me.

'I just spoke with Genevieve's nephew, Barclay,' Linette explained. 'The police told him that Genevieve was poisoned. Poisoned! I think it must have been a terrible accident, but the police seem to think that foul play is a strong possibility.'

Demi expressed her shock and their conversation turned to crime rates in general and the fact that nowhere was truly safe anymore.

Amy-Lee returned and spent a few minutes studying my hair and asking what I wanted done. As my stylist began cutting, Hattie came by, bearing a plate of chocolate-chip cookies.

'I made them fresh this morning,' Hattie said as she offered me the plate.

Although the cookies looked delicious, I politely declined, explaining that I'd just come from the teahouse. I didn't think I could fit another bite in my stomach.

Hattie assured me that she understood and offered the plate to Linette next.

'I really shouldn't,' Linette said as she eyed the cookies with obvious longing.

'You deserve some comfort food,' Demi encouraged her.

'Maybe you're right.' Linette wiggled her hand free from beneath her cape and accepted a cookie. 'Delicious,' she proclaimed after taking a bite.

Hattie beamed at the compliment and moved on to offer cookies to the other clients in the salon.

'Hattie's always spoiling us with her goodies,' Amy-Lee said as she continued snipping away at my hair. 'I can never resist what she brings. I've already eaten three of those cookies today. It's a good thing that I can barely make toast because if I could bake, I'd be eating cookies and cupcakes every day.'

'If only we could do that without any health consequences,' I said with a smile.

'I'm with you there. I have such a sweet tooth.'

'Oh, me too,' Demi said, her scissors flashing as she worked. 'Are you a baker, Linette?'

'Have been since I was a little girl,' Linette replied. 'I've always enjoyed baking for friends and family.'

'I'm sure Genevieve must have enjoyed that,' I said.

'Goodness, no. She was always watching her figure. She wouldn't so much as touch any sort of dessert or baked good.' Linette hesitated. 'Although . . .'

'Although?' I prodded. I wanted to know what she'd left unsaid. Considering what Valentina had shared about how Genevieve got poisoned, what Linette had just revealed didn't seem to fit.

'Genevieve certainly didn't like anyone to know that she ever indulged, but sometimes she would. In private.' Linette produced a tissue from somewhere beneath her cape and dabbed at her eyes. 'She had a particular weakness for dark chocolate.'

'But she didn't eat your baking?' I checked, wondering if Linette belonged on my suspect list, despite the fact that she seemed to be truly saddened by her friend's death.

'She'd never touch anything I baked,' Linette replied. 'Even when she indulged, she stayed gluten-free. She had an intolerance, you see, and I always use my grandmother's recipes. She's the one who taught me to bake. Back in her day, gluten-free really wasn't a thing.'

From there, the conversation turned to health fads and then to the weather. I tuned out Linette and Demi, holding my own conversation with Amy-Lee. We talked about where we were from – Amy-Lee had moved to Twilight Cove eight years ago from Wyoming – and other standard getting-to-know-you topics.

When she finished styling my hair, I admired her work in the mirror. My waves had a healthy gleam and I looked much more put together thanks to my new, tidier haircut.

After leaving Amy-Lee a generous tip and assuring her that I'd be back in a few weeks, I made my way out of Scissor Me Timbers, running into Linette again in the reception area. Although her appointment had ended before mine was over, Linette had lingered to purchase a bottle of shampoo from the shop area at the front of the salon.

'Georgie,' she said as I held the front door open for her, 'I heard there was some . . . unpleasantness for the Pumpkin Glow volunteers, that perhaps Genevieve was a bit . . . difficult.'

That was an understatement, but I held back that comment. It wasn't the sort of thing Linette needed to hear when grieving the loss of her friend.

'Anyway,' she continued, 'I know Genevieve wasn't always the easiest person to work with – I attribute that to her upbringing – but I hope you won't think too poorly of her now.'

I was saved from having to respond by a woman waving from across the street and calling out a greeting to Linette.

'That's my neighbor, Suzanne,' Linette explained. 'I'm meeting her for dinner. I hope to see you around, Georgie.'

I said a quick farewell as she crossed the street.

A hint of guilt accompanied my relief. If not for the interruption by Suzanne, I would have had to lie to save Linette's feelings. As much as I didn't like to think or speak ill of the dead, I just couldn't manage to view Genevieve in a positive light.

My next stop was the local grocery store. Auntie O had texted me while I was at the salon, asking me to pick up some nachos that she could add to the spread of food she was preparing for her Gins and Needles meeting. She and the other members of the group took turns hosting, and that night the ladies would gather at the carriage house.

Inside the store, I turned down the snack aisle. Two women stood chatting near the potato chips. I gave them a brief smile as I scooted past them to reach the nachos. As I perused the selection on the shelves, I couldn't help but hear the women's conversation.

'My husband and I were out walking the dog last night before bed and we saw lights at the cemetery,' one of the women said. She was tall, with light brown skin and glossy, black hair that reached nearly to her waist.

'What kind of lights?' the other woman asked. She had a mass of curly blonde hair and stood several inches shorter than her friend.

'I don't know. Spooky lights. One was really bright and the others were dimmer. The bright one stayed in place but the dimmer ones were bobbing and moving about. Then the bright one went out. Chad wanted to go and check them out, but I wouldn't let him.'

'Good call,' the blonde woman said with a dramatic shiver. 'They might have been ghost lights.'

'I was thinking more along the lines that there's a murderer among us, so it's not good to take any chances.'

The blonde's face paled. 'Running into a killer would be almost as bad as running into ghosts.'

'*Almost*?' her friend echoed, incredulous. 'I'd rather meet a ghost than a very-much-alive murderer any day.'

'Maybe it was the victim's ghost,' the blonde suggested with a gleam of excitement in her eyes.

'Hmmm,' her friend said noncommittally.

Their conversation turned to their kids' soccer team and I gave myself a mental kick, reminding myself why I was at the store. I grabbed a bag of nachos and then a second one just to be safe. If Auntie O didn't need both bags, I'd serve the leftover nachos to my friends the next night. Tessa and Roxy had agreed to meet me and Callum at the farmhouse to carve the pumpkins that would decorate the pathways for the Pumpkin Glow.

As I headed toward the checkout counters, I wondered what I should feed Callum's parents when they arrived. Burgers, or something more sophisticated? I almost made a detour to the bread aisle to get an idea of what was available, but then had second thoughts. Even if I served hamburger buns or dinner rolls, shouldn't they be homemade? After all, I wanted to make a good impression.

Nerves swirled in my stomach. Maybe it was best not to think about that yet.

I got into line behind the curly-haired blonde who'd been chatting with her friend in the snack aisle. There was a man ahead of her, putting some items on the conveyor belt. It took me a second to realize that it was Genevieve's nephew, Barclay. I couldn't help but notice that his collection of groceries consisted of corn nuts, soda, cheese sticks, and a six-pack of beer.

'Would you like a paper bag?' the cashier – a young woman barely out of her teens – asked Barclay. 'They cost extra.'

'Nah. Forget it,' he replied.

I looked at the rack of magazines next to the checkout counter for something to do as I waited. In front of me, the blonde woman put a divider on the belt and started unloading her groceries.

'I'm sorry, sir, but your card has been declined,' the cashier said to Barclay.

That drew my attention away from the magazines.

'What?' Barclay's face reddened. 'That can't be right. Try again.'

The cashier, her cheeks now pink, did as requested. Barclay inserted his card into the machine and his frown deepened.

'I'm sorry, sir,' the young woman said, looking like she wished she could disappear.

Muttering under his breath, Barclay shoved the card into his wallet and pulled out some cash. He counted the bills. It seemed he had just enough.

He practically tossed the bills at the cashier. She fumbled and nearly dropped one, but then she managed to count them and handed over the twenty-five cents in change that he was owed.

Mumbling what sounded suspiciously like swear words, Barclay loaded the groceries into his arms and stormed out of the store. He left a cloud of awkwardness hanging in the air in his wake, but by the time it was my turn to pay, the young cashier had apparently recovered. She smiled at me and happily made small talk as she scanned my nachos. I responded at all the right moments, but my mind remained on the incident with Barclay.

It seemed his money problems were more than just trifling.

That made me wonder once again if Barclay stood to gain financially from his aunt's death.

FIFTEEN

When I got back to the farm, I dropped off the nachos at the carriage house. Flossie, Fancy, and Stardust had spent the last couple of hours with my aunt and I found them romping around in the grass beyond the back patio. The dogs greeted me with excited barks and wagging tails while Stardust mewed and wound figure eights around my ankles until I picked her up for a cuddle. I asked Olivia if she needed any help, but she assured me that she had everything under control. She wanted me to stop by later so I could enjoy some of the food she'd prepared for her friends and I readily agreed, despite the fact that I was still full from my time at the teahouse. Her kitchen smelled amazing and I didn't mind in the least that I wouldn't have to cook any dinner that night.

I left Stardust at the carriage house for a while longer so I could take the dogs for a walk through the woods. When we returned, we picked up Stardust and she sat on my shoulder as I crossed the lawn to the farmhouse. I considered spending an hour or two writing, but then decided I should learn how to make my own bread. I wanted to have at least one practice run before Callum's parents arrived. Two or three practices would probably be better. Unless I turned out to be completely hopeless at the process. Then I'd have to go with bread from the bakery, or bread made by Auntie O or Callum.

I flipped through one of the many cookbooks Auntie O still kept on a shelf in the farmhouse kitchen. Since I was a beginner bread maker – and only a moderately skilled baker in general – I decided to start with a basic loaf of white bread. Hopefully that would be simple enough for me.

While I worked, the dogs snoozed on the kitchen floor with Stardust curled up between them like the cutest and fluffiest dust bunny ever. Although she had white paws and a white patch on her chest roughly in the shape of a star, she was mostly gray, with hazel eyes that almost matched my own.

By the time I left the dough to rise for the first time, the animals had woken from their nap. Stardust batted a ball around the kitchen, chasing after it and skittering and sliding across the floor. I laughed at her silliness while Fancy cheered her on with an enthusiastic 'woo-woo' and Flossie bounced around with excited barks.

I tossed the ball across the room a few times, much to Stardust's delight. The dogs grew even more animated, so I opened the back door and let the animals charge out on to the lawn, where they proceeded to chase each other around. I didn't worry about letting Stardust outside anymore. Not during the day, anyway. Flossie and Fancy had become her dedicated guardians and always kept a close eye on her. She tended to stick close to the house or the barn, but if she ever showed signs of wandering, the dogs quickly herded her closer to home.

After sitting on the porch for a while, watching the animals play, I returned to the kitchen to tackle the next stage of breadmaking. I was up to my elbows in flower, kneading the dough, when the back door opened. Stardust and the dogs skittered into the kitchen ahead of Callum, who wore jeans and a plaid shirt – with the sleeves rolled up – over a T-shirt. His wavy blond hair was a little windswept, but the look suited him. I smiled at him over my shoulder as I continued to knead the dough.

'Perfect timing,' I said to him. 'I could use a master baker's advice on when to stop kneading this bread dough.'

'I'm not sure I'm a master,' he said as he washed his hands at the kitchen sink, 'but I'm always happy to lend you my expertise, no matter its level.'

I knew he was being modest. He'd learned to bake from his grandmother when he was a kid and still whipped up tasty creations on a regular basis. His chocolate brownies were heavenly and his sourdough bread tasted even better than the delicious loaves the local bakery sold. That was one of the reasons I'd never tried making my own bread before. With Callum and my aunt around, and with a great bakery in town, I always had a delicious supply on hand. Nevertheless, I wanted to hone my own skills.

Callum dried his hands and then came up behind me and wrapped his arms around my waist, watching over my shoulder as I kneaded the dough. It took extra concentration to keep my hands moving. Callum's proximity had a decidedly distracting effect on me.

'Did you get your hair cut?' he asked as he gave me a gentle squeeze.

'I got a walk-in appointment earlier today.'

'You look beautiful.'

I almost laughed. 'Covered in flour?'

'You always look beautiful, covered in flour or not, new haircut or not.'

His sincerity made me smile, but I kept on kneading the dough. 'Thank you, but as much as I like the compliments, I really do need your expertise. I have to get good at this before the end of the month.'

Callum kissed my neck and it took all my strength to keep focused on the task at hand instead of turning in his arms to kiss him back.

'Why's that?' he asked, trailing kisses up toward my ear.

'Why's what?' I asked, thoroughly distracted now.

'Why do you need to get good at making bread so quickly?'

Right. I tried to refocus on our conversation.

'I want to be able to serve homemade bread to your parents. Made by me. Not that I know what else to feed them. But there's a good chance that any meal we decide on will include bread.'

Callum stopped his kisses but kept his arms around my waist. 'I can always make bread for the dinner if you don't want to use store-bought.'

I kneaded the bread harder, channeling my nervous energy into the task. 'I want to make a good impression.'

'Hey.' Callum put his hands over mine and held them still. 'First of all, you're going to pummel that thing to death.' He took half a step back and turned me around, resting his hands on my hips. 'Second of all, you don't need to make bread to make a good impression on my parents.'

'I just want . . .' I sighed, rethinking everything. 'I'm being ridiculous, aren't I?'

'It's not ridiculous that you want my parents to like you.' A slow grin took shape on his face. 'In fact, I take that as a very good sign.'

'It is a good sign.' I fought down the nervous flutters in my stomach, determined to put my feelings – some of them, at least – into words. 'This thing we've got, it's important to me. I want to fit in with your family. I want them to believe that we're a good match.'

'Georgie,' Callum said, staring into my eyes in a way that stole the breath out of my lungs, 'they already believe that.'

My forehead scrunched. 'They haven't even met me yet.'

'Maybe not, but they know that I can't stop talking about you every time I'm on the phone with them. They know how happy you make me. They already love you because of that. As soon as they actually get to meet you, they're going to adore you.'

I buried my face in his chest and he wrapped his arms around me. 'If we decide to serve bread, maybe it's best if you make it,' I said. 'I don't want to end up serving them hockey pucks.'

Callum gave me a squeeze and spoke into my hair. 'Georgie, they really won't care if you make hockey pucks, bread baseballs, or hardtack. We could serve them take-out fast food and they'd be fine with that, as long as they get to spend time with us. I get that you're nervous, because I'd be a little nervous meeting your dad, but you really have nothing to worry about.'

I pulled back just enough so I could look him in the eye. 'OK. I'll try to stop being so silly.'

He kissed my forehead. 'Not silly. Just worrying unnecessarily.'

'That's something I'm very good at.'

A humorous glint lit up his green eyes. 'I happen to know something else you're very good at.'

'What's that?' I asked.

'This.' He kissed me then, so sweetly and deeply that I lost track of time, the world around us, my worries – everything except us.

When our lips finally parted, I felt like I was floating in the air and I was pretty sure my eyes were glazed over.

Callum grinned at me in a way that made my stomach do a giddy somersault. 'As much as I'd like to stay longer, I need to give Twiggy and Tootsie their meds.'

I glanced at the ball of dough I'd forgotten on the counter. 'I'll set this in a bowl to prove and then I'll come help.'

He waited for me to do that and we set off for the barn hand in hand.

By the time I returned to the farmhouse after helping Callum with the donkeys, several cars were parked over by the carriage house. I put my bread in the oven to bake, crossing my fingers that it would turn out well. Then I fed Flossie, Fancy, and Stardust and quickly washed up before leaving the animals to their dinners and heading over to Auntie O's place. During the warmer months of the year, she and her fellow Gins and Needles ladies typically gathered on the back patio, but the autumn chill in the air was keeping them indoors this time.

I let myself in through the unlocked front door and paused for a moment to breathe in the delicious smells. Auntie O had spent much of the day cooking and baking, and I knew she'd be serving a soup full of autumn vegetables and wild rice, spinach dip with sourdough bread, and homemade cheesecake.

Auntie O spotted me and waved me into the kitchen, where she pressed an empty plate into my hands. 'Help yourself, dear. There's plenty of food for us to get through.'

A chorus of greetings came from the women gathered in the kitchen and living room.

'Come and join us,' Dolores called, patting the spot next to her on the couch. As always, she wore a muumuu, this one made from black-and-purple fabric.

I balanced a cup of soup on my plate before I added some finger foods around it.

'We hear you're the one who found Genevieve Newmont when she died,' Leona Powell said. In her sixties, with cropped gray hair, Leona still led an active life and had a fiery personality.

'Callum and I did,' I confirmed.

The ladies offered me their sympathies and expressed their shock and dismay at the fact that the police now considered Genevieve's death as suspicious.

'How are the preparations for the Pumpkin Glow going, Praise?' Clara Olmstead asked after a while. She was the oldest and most petite member of the group, with bright blue eyes and fluffy white hair. 'I hope Genevieve didn't leave things in too much of a shambles.'

'I'm getting everything on track,' Praise replied from where she sat in one of the armchairs, a plate resting on her lap. 'But we did have a few more pumpkins go missing from the pavilion at Griffin Park.'

'What's going on in this town?' Esther Yoon – Cindy's mother – asked no one in particular. 'Murder, thefts, and now ghost sightings.'

'Ghost sightings?' Dolores echoed with interest.

'Well, maybe not ghosts, exactly,' Esther amended, 'but I heard that multiple people saw mysterious lights in the cemetery the other night.'

From there, the conversation turned to the upcoming Trail of Terror fundraiser. Those members of the Gins and Needles group who wouldn't be participating in the production promised that they would purchase tickets for the haunted walk.

I'd just finished off my delicious food and was taking my dishes into the kitchen when the French doors that led out to the patio rattled.

'Oh, look at that!' Esther exclaimed happily. 'We've got visitors!'

I set down my plate as I spotted Flossie and Fancy on the other side of the doors, their noses pressed up against the glass and their tails wagging.

'I must not have latched the farmhouse door properly,' I said, although I knew perfectly well that I'd not only closed it but locked it. That, however, wouldn't stop Flossie.

Auntie O opened the French doors. 'Come on in, girls.'

Tails still wagging and tongues lolling out of their mouths, the spaniels made the rounds, greeting each member of the group in turn. Fortunately, they didn't try to help themselves to any food within their reach, although they did give an appreciative sniff now and then when they greeted someone with food on their plate. I thought I saw Esther slip them each a morsel of the cookie she was eating, but I pretended I hadn't noticed. I didn't want the dogs to develop a habit of begging for food, but I'd been guilty of giving them bites of my own meals on occasion and so far they were still polite.

I loaded my dishes into the dishwasher while the dogs enjoyed the attention the ladies bestowed on them.

'I think I'll head out now,' I said to Auntie O as she mixed cocktails in the kitchen.

Once everyone had finished eating – for the time being, at least – cocktails would be served and the ladies would bring out their knitting and needlework projects.

'Take a slice of cheesecake for yourself and one for Callum,' Auntie O said, abandoning the cocktails while she grabbed a clean plate.

I wasn't about to refuse the offer, so I waited until she'd slid two slices of chocolate cheesecake on to the plate and handed it to me. Then I gave her a kiss on the cheek and waved goodbye to the other ladies.

On our way to the front door of the carriage house, Fancy veered off and disappeared into the ground floor bedroom. I set the plate of cheesecake on the entryway table and followed her. Flossie pushed past me so she could catch up with her sister.

'Fancy, what are you doing?' I whispered when I found her nosing through the guests' coats piled on Auntie O's bed. 'Leave those alone.'

Fancy ignored me and Flossie moved in to help her.

'Hey!' I protested as Flossie grabbed a black coat with her teeth and yanked it off the top of the pile.

I was about to scold the dogs further when Fancy snatched the coat that Flossie had just uncovered. She pulled it off the bed with her teeth and dropped it at my feet.

I stared at it for a moment before picking it up and holding it out in front of me.

The long, wool coat was the exact shade of green I'd seen at Griffin Park on the night Genevieve died.

SIXTEEN

'Everything all right?' Auntie O asked, poking her head into the bedroom.

My heart thudded a little harder than normal as I turned to show her the green coat. 'Who does this belong to?'

My aunt came farther into the room. 'That's Praise's coat. Why?'

'Fancy must have picked up an interesting scent. She was nosing around and I was worried she might have slobbered on it.'

'We can get it cleaned for Praise if it's a problem.' Olivia took the coat from me and inspected it. 'I don't see any marks.'

'I couldn't find any either,' I said, trying to stay focused on our conversation as my mind raced.

'No harm done, then.' Auntie O returned the coat to the bed and gave Flossie and Fancy each a pat on the head.

I picked up the black coat Flossie had grabbed and added it to the top of the pile. 'All right, girls, let's get out of here.'

This time both spaniels followed me to the door and out into the night. As soon as I had the carriage house door shut behind me, I shivered, and only partly from the frosty air.

Praise probably wasn't the only person in Twilight Cove who owned a garment in that shade of green. However, I couldn't ignore the fact that she had a motive for killing Genevieve. She'd fought with the woman two nights before the murder and she'd clearly been upset that Genevieve had taken over her position as organizer of the Pumpkin Glow. Now that Genevieve was dead, Praise had that coveted role back.

But was that really worth killing for?

I knew that people killed for less all the time.

Maybe having another suspect to add to my list should have encouraged me, because it meant that Tessa was far from the only person with an apparent motive to kill Genevieve, but I didn't want one of Auntie O's friends to be a murderer.

I thought back to how angry Praise had been when she confronted Genevieve here at the farm. I had to add her name to the suspect list, no matter how much I didn't want her to be guilty.

I decided that I needed to write down a physical list. My mind was whirring so much that I couldn't keep track of all the information I'd gathered so far. I wanted to have an encouraging report to share with Tessa when she came over the next evening, so that meant I needed to get to work.

First, however, I had bread to take out of the oven and cheesecake to share with Callum. I hoped the kick of sugar would give my brain the boost it would need to unravel the mystery of Genevieve Newmont's death.

The next afternoon, after spending the morning writing in the farmhouse kitchen, I sat on the fence of Tootsie and Twiggy's pasture and watched the donkeys as they grazed. The sight warmed my heart. Both donkeys were clearly more comfortable since having their hooves trimmed and Tootsie had even shown a spark of energy when I'd tossed a ball into the pasture earlier. She'd trotted after it and pushed it around with her nose for a while before losing interest.

Now that her teeth had been filed and the cuts in her mouth were healing, Twiggy had started eating, much to my relief. Her eyes were already looking better and the same was true of Tootsie's coat. The sores on her back no longer looked as painful and I hoped that her coat would grow back soon. Both donkeys had lost some of the desolate air that had hung over them when they first arrived at the sanctuary, and that filled me with happiness.

As I sat there watching Twiggy and Tootsie, the sun disappeared, blocked out by gray clouds as they moved swiftly across the sky. The breeze swirled around me, cutting through my coat and making me shiver.

I was about to go inside and have a hot drink when Euclid swooped down from the sky and landed on the fence next to me.

I smiled at the owl. 'Hello, Euclid. It's good to see you.'

I hadn't seen him since the night Genevieve had died. That wasn't unusual. He visited me and the dogs fairly frequently, but he also occasionally disappeared for a few days. I figured he probably spent those times hunting farther afield or doing whatever else owls did.

Euclid looked at me with his big yellow eyes and I couldn't help but feel that he was trying to tell me something.

I spoke to him in a low voice. 'ESP would be helpful. I feel like you have so much you could tell me, so much wisdom you could share.'

Euclid swiveled his head and then took off from the fence, flying over to the carriage house, where he landed on the roof. He was too far away for me to tell for sure, but I had a feeling he was looking back at me.

I hopped down from the fence and headed in that direction. He'd trained me well enough that I knew if he ever gave any indication that he might want me to follow him, I should do just that.

Hattie Beechwood's burgundy sedan sat parked by the carriage house. I hadn't seen her arrive, but Auntie O had mentioned that she was stopping by to pick up donations for the charity shop where she volunteered. Clothing and other donated items were sold at the shop and the profits went to the local animal shelter, a cause near and dear to Auntie O's heart and my own as well. My aunt had asked if I had anything I wanted to donate, but I'd cleared out all the clothes I no longer wore when I moved to Twilight Cove from Los Angeles.

The dogs had been off watching the goats in their pasture, but they ran over to me and then slowed to trot along at my side. When I got close to the carriage house, Euclid gazed down at me. Maybe it was my imagination, but I thought he gave me a look of approval before he lifted off and circled above us once before soaring off toward the woods.

'What do you think he was trying to tell me?' I asked the spaniels.

Fancy let out an 'a-woo' while Flossie bounded over to the carriage house's front door. It opened just as she reached it. Auntie O emerged, carrying a cardboard box, and Hattie followed her outside.

'I'll get the trunk open for you,' Hattie said, hurrying over to her car. 'Oh, hello, Georgie,' she added when she noticed me.

Hattie opened the trunk of her car and Auntie O placed the box inside.

'Thank you so much for the donations,' Hattie said as she shut the trunk.

'It's always my pleasure to help animals in need,' Auntie O said. 'And it's nice to have a bit more room in my closet.'

Hattie smiled. 'A good excuse to go shopping, if you ask me.' She opened the driver's door of her car but then paused. 'Did you hear about the lights people have been seeing at the graveyard?'

'A couple of nights ago, right?' I asked.

'And again last night,' Hattie said.

Auntie O considered the news. 'Has anyone checked them out?'

'I heard that Matthew Mayfield tried to chase them down, but then all the lights blinked out,' Hattie replied. 'If it was humans responsible, they were gone by the time Matthew got across the graveyard.'

'I'm sure it was humans responsible,' Auntie O said.

'You're probably right,' Hattie agreed. 'And that's my preferred explanation. I don't like to think of ghosts haunting the area.' She paused, as if letting that thought sink in. She gave a slight shudder, so subtle that I almost missed it, and then changed the subject. 'I've also heard that more pumpkins were stolen from the Pumpkin Glow.'

'We heard that too,' I said. 'Hopefully there's still enough to keep the pavilion looking festive.'

'I hope someone catches the thief or thieves.' Hattie shook her head. 'They struck at Miles's house last night too. He was absolutely furious.'

'They stole pumpkins from his house?' I asked.

'Not pumpkins, but other decorations.'

'I can see why Miles would be upset,' Auntie O said. 'He loves decorating for Halloween and always spends hours putting out all those decorations.'

'And some of them cost a pretty penny too,' Hattie added. 'It's a bit silly of the thieves, don't you think? Miles would recognize his decorations if they showed up on someone else's lawn, but what's the point of stealing decorations if not to use them?' She didn't seem to expect an answer. 'Anyway,' she continued as she climbed into her car, 'I've got a few more stops to make, so I'd better get moving. See you again soon!'

With a cheery wave, she turned her car around and then drove off down Larkspur Lane.

'I wouldn't want to be the thief who stole from Miles Schmidt,' Auntie O remarked.

'Why's that?' I asked.

'He's a nice enough man, but he does have a temper. I remember once when he was in school, one of his classmates played a prank on him. Miles bided his time, but nearly a year later he sought revenge.'

'A year?' I echoed with surprise.

'Yes,' my aunt confirmed with a shake of her head. 'He messed with the other kid's costume for the school play so his pants fell down on stage. One thing's for certain – Miles knows how to hold a grudge.'

SEVENTEEN

I recalled the brief conversation I'd had with Miles at the Pet Palace. He seemed angry when denying that he and Genevieve were dating at the time of her death. Now I wondered about the reason for his strong emotions. Maybe Auntie O could enlighten me.

'From the way Praise talked about Genevieve having sway over Miles, I thought the two of them were an item,' I said to my aunt. 'But when I offered my condolences to Miles the other day, he seemed angered by the suggestion that he'd had any romantic link to her.'

'Ah, small-town drama,' Auntie O said as we walked toward Tootsie and Twiggy's pasture. 'They did date, but not for long. My take on the matter was that Miles was quite smitten with her and Genevieve buttered him up before dropping him like a hot potato.'

I shook my head. 'I don't understand people like Genevieve.'

'Nor do I,' Auntie O said. 'She had a major sense of entitlement, that's for sure. Romantic relationships end all the time, of course, but it seemed like she was using Miles. Once she was in charge of the Pumpkin Glow, thanks in part to Miles voting in her favor, she acted like he no longer existed.'

'You don't suppose . . .' I trailed off.

Auntie O glanced my way as we reached the pasture. 'You think Miles might have killed Genevieve?'

'I have no idea,' I said, speaking the truth, 'but he seems to resent her, and his history suggests that he can strike out when harboring a grudge.'

Olivia rested her arms on the top rail of the fence and considered what I'd said. 'I hate to say it, but it does seem like a possibility. They say that poison is a woman's murder weapon – though I don't know how true that is – but I feel like it's a method Miles would gravitate toward. Like with that prank he played on his classmate. Hands-off revenge is his style.'

Tootsie wandered over to greet us, bringing smiles to our faces. It was the first time she'd come to us for attention of her own accord.

After a few minutes of watching from a distance, Twiggy came over to receive pats on the nose too.

'They're doing so much better,' I said, brimming with happiness.

'Improving more and more each day,' Auntie O agreed. She looked my way. 'How did the bread-making go?'

I groaned and lowered my forehead to the top of the fence for half a second. 'Not well.' I'd mentioned my experiment to my aunt the day before, but now I was glad that she and Callum were the only ones who knew about it. 'It turned out tough and chewy and just completely wrong.'

Auntie O gave my arm a sympathetic pat. 'It takes practice, dear. You'll get there.'

Not before Callum's parents arrived.

The sound of a car pulling into the driveway made us both turn.

'Is that Linette?' I asked, recognizing the vehicle. We started walking in that direction. 'Were you expecting her?'

'Not today,' Auntie O replied.

As soon as Linette climbed out of her car, we could see that she'd been crying. Her face was splotchy and her eyes were red.

'Linette, dear,' my aunt said, putting an arm around her shoulders. 'What's going on?'

'I'm so sorry to do this, Olivia,' Linette said, fighting tears. 'I have to pull out of the Trail of Terror. I know it's last minute, but I'm hoping you can find someone to replace me.'

Auntie O frowned with concern. 'Why don't we go inside and sit down?'

She guided Linette into the carriage house and I followed. Once Linette was seated on the couch, with a box of tissues in front of her, Olivia perched next to her and I sat in a nearby armchair.

'Why do you want to pull out?' my aunt asked. 'Is it too much right now, having just lost your friend?'

'Actually, I thought it might be a good distraction for me.' Linette sniffled. 'But then I heard through the grapevine that Genevieve had wanted my role. I didn't know that. If I *had* known, I would have given her the part. But now it's too late.' She burst into tears.

Olivia patted her back. 'Was Genevieve ever involved in theater before she moved here?'

Linette shook her head as she struggled to get her tears under control. 'But I know she wanted to try new things when she got to Twilight Cove. I wish she'd told me that she wanted the role.'

I exchanged a glance with my aunt. Neither of us was about to mention that Genevieve had tried to bribe her way into the part.

'You earned the role fair and square,' Olivia reminded her. 'If Genevieve was a good friend, she'd want you to continue with the event. If you feel like it's too much to take on because of your grief, I can understand that and we'll find someone else to take the part, but I don't want you to give it up out of some misplaced sense of guilt.'

Linette wiped at her cheeks with the tissue as her tears subsided. She took a moment to consider Olivia's words.

'I suppose you're right. Genevieve would want me to be happy. I know a lot of people didn't see her the way I did, but she was a good friend. She just had . . . issues.' She thought for another moment. 'I really do think it would be a good distraction for me.'

'I think so too,' my aunt agreed.

'Your audition was amazing,' I reminded her. 'You're really going to be a crowd-pleaser.'

'Thank you, Georgie. And you too, Olivia. I'm sorry I had this breakdown in front of you.'

'Nonsense,' Auntie O said. 'It's perfectly understandable and we don't mind at all.'

I nodded my agreement and Linette gave us a watery smile.

When she left the farm a few minutes later, she seemed far calmer than when she'd arrived.

'I feel so bad for her,' I said as we watched her turn out of the driveway and on to the road, 'but I really don't understand how she was such good friends with Genevieve.'

'That's one of life's mysteries, but everyone has many sides to them,' Olivia pointed out. 'I suppose Linette saw a side to Genevieve that we never experienced.'

I nodded at that before parting ways with my aunt. I returned to the farmhouse, where I responded to some emails and added a few more pages to my latest script. After Tessa had finished work for the day, she came over to the farm and we covered the large kitchen table with newspaper in preparation for our pumpkin-carving session.

The pumpkins that Callum and I had picked up from the pumpkin patch currently sat out on the back porch. We carried some of them inside and I got out knives and special pumpkin scooping tools that I'd picked up in town a few days earlier. By the time we'd done all that, Callum and Roxy had joined us.

'Can we make the jack-o'-lanterns scary or do they have to be happy?' Roxy asked as she sized up the pumpkin sitting on the table before her.

'Scary, happy, goofy, whatever you want,' I said.

I'd received confirmation of that in a recent email from Praise. Genevieve had sent a previous email stating that she wanted only high-quality carving, preferably with no pumpkins that were too goofy or 'otherwise ridiculous', as she'd put it. In her email, Praise had stated that jack-o'-lanterns carved at any skill level and with pretty much any type of face would be welcome. As long as the jack-o'-lanterns weren't somehow offensive, they'd be used as decorations for the Pumpkin Glow.

While I didn't like that it was Genevieve's murder that allowed Praise to be in charge of the event, I was glad that she now held the reins. I believed the Pumpkin Glow would be much more of a success under her guidance.

'Is it true that you're a suspect in the murder investigation?' Roxy asked Tessa point-blank.

Tessa's face blanched. 'Does everyone know?'

'That's the rumor going around,' Roxy said. 'But I don't think any of the other kids at school believe it. I definitely don't. And if somebody says that you did do it, well . . .' She stabbed a big knife into the top of her pumpkin.

Tessa's face regained some of its color. 'I appreciate you wanting to stick up for me, Roxy, but please don't get into any arguments or altercations on my account. I didn't kill Genevieve and everyone will know that soon enough.'

Roxy's face lit up. 'Georgie, does that mean you're on the case?'

'What makes you ask that?' I hedged.

'Tessa knows the real killer is going to be identified soon. I figure that's because she's got you to clear her name.'

'It's not like I'm Nancy Drew or something,' I protested.

The other three laughed.

'Why is that so funny?' I demanded, pretending to be hurt.

Callum put an arm around my shoulders and gave me an affectionate squeeze. 'We know you can't resist a mystery. There's no point in denying it.'

'OK, fine,' I conceded. 'I am looking into the matter, for Tessa's sake.'

Still holding the knife, Roxy pumped her fist in the air, causing the blade to flash. 'I knew it!'

'Hey,' Callum cautioned, leaning away from her. 'Be careful with that thing.'

With a grin, Roxy stabbed the knife back into her pumpkin. 'I want to know everything, starting with your suspects.'

I glanced at Tessa and Callum. I didn't like the idea of drawing Roxy into the investigation. She was only fifteen, after all, and she'd put herself in a risky situation in the past in the name of trying to solve a murder. I could tell that Tessa and Callum had the same misgivings.

Roxy didn't miss our silent communication. She rolled her eyes. 'Come on. It's not like I'm going to go running off to confront the suspects, and what if I have something valuable to contribute?' She leveled a glare at us, as if challenging us to dispute that she could be of help.

I caved. 'All right.'

Her expression brightened again.

I set aside the pumpkin lid I'd just cut out and wiped my hands on a paper towel. 'I wrote out a list yesterday.' I grabbed the notebook from across the room. 'And I want to add two more names.'

Before returning to the table, I jotted down Hattie Beechwood and Miles Schmidt. Then I put the notebook in Roxy's waiting hand. Tessa and Callum gathered behind her so they could read over her shoulder.

'Who's Barclay?' Roxy asked as she read the first name. 'And who names their kid that?'

'Genevieve's nephew,' I said, not bothering to answer her second question. 'He needs money and asked Genevieve to give him some, but she refused.'

'Praise?' Tessa said in surprise as she looked at the list. 'She seems so nice.'

I explained how upset Praise had been that Genevieve had taken over the Pumpkin Glow. 'They argued right here at the farm. And that's not all.' I explained that Praise's coat could have been the flash of color I'd seen as the mystery person fled from the copse where Callum and I had found Genevieve.

'Who's Hattie?' Callum asked, reading the next name on the list.

'Remember that lady we met at the pumpkin patch? You helped load her pumpkins into her car.'

'Right,' he said.

For Tessa's and Roxy's benefit, I explained that Genevieve was

Hattie's neighbor and had threatened to poison Hattie's beloved cats.

'What a bi— witch,' Roxy said, rephrasing her sentence when she caught Tessa's warning look. 'Anyone who would even threaten to hurt an animal should be locked in jail forever.'

'I don't disagree with you,' I said.

'If Genevieve threatened to poison Hattie's cats, she might have seen it as some sort of poetic justice to then poison Genevieve,' Callum said.

I nodded. 'My thoughts exactly.'

'I've never heard of Enrique Ramos,' Roxy said, still studying the list.

'That's because he's not from here.' I grabbed one of the scoops I'd bought and got to work scraping out the inside of my pumpkin. 'But he knew Genevieve and argued with her before she died.'

'We need to find out more about him,' Roxy declared as she, too, began scooping seeds and guts out of her pumpkin.

Callum already had the inside of his pumpkin cleaned out. 'Maybe Linette knows him.'

'She might. Good point,' I said, giving him a smile. 'You'd better watch out. It seems the sleuthing bug is contagious.'

He grinned and picked up a knife. 'Puzzles aren't my forte, but I'm happy to help where I can.'

I dropped a scoop of pumpkin innards into one of the large bowls I'd set out for that purpose. 'Maybe I can find a way to ask Linette about Enrique without letting on why I want to know about him.'

'Is she a suspect too?' Roxy asked. 'Her name wasn't on the list.'

'She did know Genevieve the best,' Tessa pointed out.

'Linette crossed my mind when I was making the suspect list,' I said, 'but she's known Genevieve forever. Why wait until now to kill her if she had a problem with her?'

'Maybe Linette inherits under Genevieve's will and needs money?' Callum hypothesized.

'That's something we definitely need to find out.' I took a second to think before continuing. 'But if she doesn't inherit then I'm not sure what her motive would be. Besides, she seems genuinely cut up about Genevieve's death.'

'We can't discount her entirely yet,' Tessa cautioned. 'We need to talk to her. Then we can decide whether or not she belongs on the list.'

'Good idea,' I agreed.

I leaned to the side so I could see the face Callum was carving into his pumpkin. He'd made slender triangles, pointed inward, for the eyes, an isosceles triangle for the nose, and now he was adding a mouth with fangs.

'Is he supposed to be scary?' I asked. I guessed that was the intent, but all the features were a little uneven and off-kilter, which gave the jack-o'-lantern a goofy and endearing appearance.

'Supposed to be, yes.' Callum took a step back to study his work. 'But I was born with zero artistic talent so he looks like a goofball trying to be scary.'

'I love it,' I said, meaning it.

Tessa started carving her pumpkin. 'I have an idea. I've almost finished the alterations on Linette's costume for the Trail of Terror. I was going to swing by her house and drop the costume off when I was done, but . . .'

'That would give us the perfect excuse to drop in on her and have a chat,' I finished.

Tessa grinned. 'Exactly.'

'I bet I can find out more about Mr Schmidt.' Roxy gave a shudder. 'Talk about creepy – having a potential murderer for a teacher.'

'Wait – Miles is a teacher?' I asked. 'How did I not know that? Never mind,' I added before anyone else could speak. 'I only met him for the first time when he volunteered for the Trail of Terror so I guess it's not surprising that I don't know much about him.'

'He teaches math at the high school,' Tessa said.

'He's boring,' Roxy added with a roll of her eyes.

Callum cut a lid out of his second pumpkin. 'Math was my favorite subject in school. Well, maybe my second after PE.'

'I don't hate math,' Roxy said. 'But Mr Schmidt just stands there at the front of the room and drones on and on. Math may not be the most exciting thing in the world, but it really doesn't have to be *that* boring.'

'As much as I should probably stand up for my colleague, I've seen Miles in action and he's not the most . . . vibrant teacher,' Tessa said. 'Which is weird, because when he's on stage playing a character, he completely transforms. I'm not sure why he can't channel a bit of that energy into his work as a teacher.'

'I agree that we need to find out more about him. But,' I said, looking at Roxy, 'That's probably better for Tessa to look into.'

'You don't trust me?' Roxy challenged.

'I don't want you getting into any danger,' I said.

Roxy frowned but got back to carving without putting up any further argument.

I steered the focus of our conversation to another suspect. 'Tessa, when we get a chance to talk to Linette, we should also ask her about the nephew, Barclay. As Genevieve's best friend, there's a good chance she knows him. Maybe she has an opinion on whether he could be the killer.'

Tessa smiled, and the sight eased my concern for her, at least a little bit.

'With all of us on the case,' Tessa declared, 'the murderer doesn't stand a chance.'

EIGHTEEN

Despite Tessa's confidence in our ability to identify Genevieve's killer, I still hoped the police would crack the case before we had a chance to do much detective work. Nevertheless, I appreciated the fact that our investigation had reignited Tessa's spark. Actively working to clear her name had definitely raised her spirits.

After completing my morning farm chores and putting in a couple of hours of writing the next day, I loaded the jack-o'-lanterns we'd carved – all twelve of them – into the back of Auntie O's old farm truck, which I'd asked to borrow so I could transport the pumpkins into town. Praise had decided to store the donated jack-o'-lanterns at her place for a couple of nights before delivering them to Griffin Park. She hoped that would reduce the chance of another theft occurring before the Pumpkin Glow got underway.

I'd hoped for a chance to speak with Praise, and perhaps to ask her some subtle questions, but she didn't answer when I knocked on her front door. The email she'd sent out to the volunteers, detailing her plan to keep the jack-o'-lanterns at her house for the time being, had directed us to leave any such pumpkins in her backyard if she wasn't home. With nothing but my own two arms to carry the pumpkins, I had to make several trips between the truck and Praise's back porch, where I found about twenty other jack-o'-lanterns already waiting. Fortunately, Callum and I hadn't chosen any particularly large pumpkins, so I was able to carry two at a time on each trip.

Once I had all the pumpkins moved to the back porch, I paused outside the driver's door of Auntie O's truck. I hadn't bothered to rush while moving the pumpkins in the hope that Praise might return home while I was still there, but I had no such luck. There was no sign of her and I didn't feel like hanging around to wait. Besides, I didn't have a good excuse for doing that and I didn't want to let on to one of my suspects that I was trying to solve Genevieve's murder.

I was about to climb into the truck when Euclid swept down

from the sky and landed on the roof of the vehicle with a clacking of his talons. As always, his beauty took my breath away and brought a smile to my face. He was such a gorgeous bird, with a depth of intelligence in his yellow eyes. He fixed those eyes on me now, holding my gaze for a moment before taking off. He landed on a branch in a tree halfway down the street and looked back at me.

'All right, Euclid,' I said quietly. 'I'm coming.'

I got into the truck and drove slowly along the road. Euclid flew ahead of me, landing on a tree branch or lamppost whenever he needed to wait for me to catch up. He led me to a residential street lined with ornamental cherry trees. The road must have looked stunning in the spring when all the trees were in bloom.

As I drove slowly along the street, Euclid flew up into the sky and disappeared. I barely had a chance to wonder why he'd led me to that particular place when I spotted Linette standing in front of a white, two-story house with black trim. She was currently in conversation with none other than Genevieve's nephew.

I pulled into a free spot at the curb and parked the truck, lowering the windows and staying in the driver's seat. Fortunately, Linette and Barclay didn't notice me, even though I was close enough to overhear their conversation. Although, I probably could have heard Barclay from the very end of the street. He wasn't exactly trying to stay quiet.

'I can't believe she did this to me!' he ranted. 'She told me ages ago that I was her heir, but she left all her money to my mom instead!'

I had to listen a little more carefully to hear Linette.

'She changed her will a couple of years ago. She thought you didn't appreciate the money you already had and she was worried that you'd mishandle any she left to you.'

'Are you saying she thought I was a spoiled brat?' Barclay practically roared.

Linette held up a placating hand. 'Of course not.'

I suspected that was exactly what Genevieve had thought and that Linette knew that was the case.

'I think she was hoping that you'd have time to mature,' Linette said, remaining calm, 'and then she would have changed her will again.'

'Why aren't you mad?' Barclay demanded. 'You were her best friend for decades and all she left you was a lamp that can't be worth more than a hundred bucks.'

Linette's demeanor didn't change. 'I'm touched that she left me that memento. I wasn't expecting anything at all. Genevieve knew that I received a sizable inheritance from my parents. That's how I was able to retire early. I don't need more money.'

'Well, I do!' Barclay raged. 'I'm completely broke!' He kicked at the base of the house's front steps and then swore and hopped around, favoring his right foot.

I guessed from Linette's body language that she let out a heavy sigh. 'Barclay, it is what it is. There's nothing we can do about it now. And, frankly, you're only broke because you gamble too much.'

'I'm trying to become a professional poker player!' He swore again. 'Forget it. You don't understand.' He stormed away from Linette and climbed into his sports car, slamming the door. Seconds later, he swerved away from the curb with a squeal of tires and took off down the street.

Slowly, I climbed out of Auntie O's truck. When I shut the door, Linette looked my way. I raised a hand in greeting.

'Was that Genevieve's nephew?' I asked as I walked over to her, pretending I didn't know for sure.

This time I did hear Linette's sigh. 'Barclay, yes. He and Genevieve were quite close when he was younger. Once he hit his late teens, he got a bit wild and they drifted apart. Genevieve didn't approve of his frivolous and foolish spending habits.' She gave her head a shake. 'Anyway, I'm sure you don't want to hear about their family drama.'

As much as I actually did want to hear about any drama in Genevieve's family, I didn't contradict Linette. 'I was in the neighborhood,' I said instead, 'and wanted to stop by to let you know that the alterations on your costume are nearly finished.'

Linette's face brightened. 'I can't wait for the Trail of Terror. I really appreciate that you and Olivia talked me into keeping the role. It's given me something to look forward to, and knowing that I'll be helping out the sanctuary's animals while doing something I enjoy . . . that brings me a sense of happiness in an otherwise bleak time.'

'I'm glad it's providing you with something positive to focus on,' I said.

Linette pulled her phone from her pocket and checked the time. 'I would invite you in, but I've got an appointment that I need to get to.'

I took a step back. 'Don't worry about that. I really just stopped by for a moment. Either Tessa or I will drop off your costume once it's ready.'

'That sounds wonderful.' Linette managed a small smile. 'Thank you again, Georgie.'

'I'm just glad we were able to help you in some small way.'

I said goodbye and drove off as she hurried into her house.

Barclay might not have inherited any money under Genevieve's will, but he'd clearly expected to. His aunt wasn't willing to give him any money while she was alive, so maybe he'd thought the only way to get what he was after was for her to die.

He was definitely staying on my suspect list.

I didn't make it very far before I slowed Auntie O's truck to a near stop. One street away from Linette's house, I spotted Hattie Beechwood raking leaves in front of a cute bungalow. I lowered the passenger-side window and waved when she looked my way. She leaned her rake against the trunk of a maple tree and walked over as I pulled up to the curb and parked.

'I didn't realize this was your neighborhood,' I said. 'It's a beautiful area.'

Like Linette's street, this one was lined with ornamental cherry trees. Hattie also had a maple tree and several shrubs in her front yard.

Hattie looked around with a smile. 'I love it during all seasons, but in the spring it's a sight to behold.'

'I'm sure,' I said. 'I'll have to remember to drive this way during cherry blossom season.' I glanced at the houses on either side of Hattie's bungalow, my curiosity awakened. 'Which house was Genevieve's?'

Hattie pointed to the one to the right of her house. 'The gray one with black trim. I'm looking forward to getting new neighbors once the house is sold. Whoever they turn out to be, I figure they'll be better than Genevieve.'

I wasn't sure what to say to that, but she didn't wait for a reaction from me.

'Would you like to meet my cats?' she asked.

'Sure.' I climbed out of the truck.

Some people might have found Hattie's offer strange, but as a fellow animal lover, I was quite happy to meet her feline companions. She led me through a gate and into her backyard. It was only as we rounded the back of the bungalow that I realized I'd just followed one of my murder suspects into a somewhat secluded area. Thanks to mature trees and bushes, her yard wasn't overlooked by any of the neighbors, and I didn't know if there was anyone close enough to hear if I screamed for help.

I pushed those thoughts aside. I planned to remain vigilant around Hattie, but even if she had killed Genevieve, she had no reason to want me dead. I didn't think there was any way she could know that I was trying to crack the case so I could clear Tessa's name.

'Wow.' I drew to a stop when I saw the cats' enclosure.

It wasn't just an ordinary catio. The main structure – all enclosed with chicken wire – was about ten feet tall and at least fifteen feet long by ten feet wide, but that wasn't the end of it. Two wire-enclosed tunnels stretched away from the main structure. One ran along the grass to a smaller enclosure at the back of the yard, while another tunnel, held up by wooden supports, stretched along the side fence, near its top, providing a raised walkway. Two cats lounged on raised platforms in the main enclosure, another sat in the raised tunnel, watching birds in a nearby tree, and a fourth cat was in the ground-level tunnel, apparently hunting for bugs.

'This is amazing,' I said, impressed. 'What lucky cats.'

Hattie beamed. 'Thank you. But I think I'm the lucky one. They're such delightful companions. I figure this is the least they deserve.'

'I'm surprised they even think about trying to escape.'

'Sylvester does have a bit of a wild side.' She pointed to the black-and-white tuxedo cat in the raised tunnel. 'He's always looking for an adventure. At least now I don't have to worry about that witch next door trying to harm him if he gets out.'

The sound of crunching leaves came from somewhere nearby. Hattie turned to face the fence across the yard from the catio, the one that separated her property from Genevieve's. She held still, staying quiet, so I did the same.

The sound came again.

'It sounds like someone's in Genevieve's backyard,' Hattie whispered.

'Maybe a family member?' I suggested, also keeping my voice low.

Without responding, Hattie swiftly but quietly crossed the lawn to the fence. I followed, my curiosity awakened once again. Not that it ever truly slept.

Hattie found a knothole and put her eye to it. 'I can't see anything,' she said in a frustrated whisper.

She couldn't have been more than five and a half feet tall, so she had no chance of seeing over the six-foot fence. I had four inches of height on her so my prospects were more promising.

Dry leaves crunched again, followed by a creak of wood. I tested the sturdiness of one of the many decorative rocks that lined the edge of Hattie's yard. It wiggled only slightly, so I held on to a fence post as I stepped on to the rock. That got me just high enough to peek over into the next yard.

The grass needed cutting and an apple tree had dropped brown leaves all over the yard, but that wasn't what really caught my attention.

Standing on the back porch, peering through one of Genevieve's windows, was Enrique Ramos, another one of my suspects. He held a tool in his right hand, one with a slender metal blade.

I dropped down out of sight. 'Does Genevieve's yard have a back gate?'

The large apple tree had blocked my view of the back fence.

Hattie gestured to me to follow her. 'This way.'

Quietly, she led me through a gate and out into an unpaved alley. We crept along, making as little noise as possible so as not to alert Enrique to our presence. When we reached the gate in Genevieve's back fence, Hattie motioned for me to go first.

With my heart thundering in my chest, I unlatched the gate and eased it open, hoping it wouldn't creak or groan. Fortunately, it seemed that Genevieve had kept it well oiled.

As soon as I took a step into the yard, I could see that Enrique was now at the back door, perhaps trying to jimmy the lock

'Excuse me?' I called out. 'Can I help you?'

Enrique spun around, his eyes so wide that it was almost comical. Then he leaped off the porch and ran straight at me.

NINETEEN

I slammed the gate open wide as I pushed Hattie out into the alley.

'Look out!' I yelled at her as Enrique ran toward us, brandishing the metal tool.

I braced myself for his attack, but he tripped on an exposed tree root and fell flat on his face in the overgrown grass. He let out a cry of pain and rolled on to his back.

I stood frozen, not sure what to do. When Hattie peeked around me to see what had happened, I kicked myself into action and fished my phone out of my pocket. 'I'll call the police.'

As I made the call, Hattie warily crept closer to Enrique.

'Careful,' I cautioned her just as the emergency operator answered my call.

I quickly explained that we'd caught someone trying to break into a recently deceased person's house.

'Get me an ambulance!' Enrique groaned. 'I think I broke my leg.'

I passed that information on while Hattie stood over Enrique, her wariness now gone.

'It's your own fault,' she said, planting her hands on her hips.

He pointed my way. 'She scared me.'

'You deserved to be scared,' Hattie scolded. 'You were breaking into this house.'

'That's not true. I was just looking in the window.'

'Ha.' She nudged the discarded tool with the toe of her shoe. 'Then what was this for?'

Enrique clutched his left leg and groaned. 'I just want what's mine.'

I handed the phone over to Hattie, explaining that the operator wanted Genevieve's address. I had no idea what the house number was or even the name of the street.

'What do you mean you just wanted what's yours?' I asked, looking down at the man. Now that I was seeing him up close for the first time, I guessed his age to be about fifty-five or so. 'Did Genevieve owe you money?'

'She owed me restitution of some sort,' he grumbled. 'She told me she was opening a restaurant in Portland. She lured me away from my previous job and promised me I'd be the head chef at her new place. And then what did she do? She dropped the whole plan and moved out of town. She left me high and dry. I tried to get my old job back, but it had already been filled. It's hard enough competing with all the up-and-coming youngsters. Now I'm jobless and I deserve compensation. I just wanted her to do the right thing.'

'She can't do anything – right or wrong – anymore,' I said. 'She's dead.'

I watched him closely for any indication of surprise.

'But you already knew that,' I surmised when he displayed no such signs.

He didn't deny it. Instead, he just groaned again.

'So, what?' I prodded. 'You thought you'd break into her house and steal any valuables you could find?'

'No!' He huffed out a breath, his face etched with pain. 'She always boasted about the antique watch collection that she inherited from her father. She showed me one of the pocket watches. I'm betting the thing was worth a few thousand dollars all on its own and she had at least a dozen others.' He was about to say more but then clamped his mouth shut, perhaps realizing somewhat belatedly that he wasn't helping his case. 'I was just looking in the window, that's all. There's no crime in that.'

'We'll leave that for the police to decide,' I said.

A siren wailed, drawing closer. Within moments, Officer Brody Williams was on the scene with another uniformed officer. An ambulance arrived shortly thereafter.

Hattie and I provided brief witness statements and then we were allowed to leave the scene. I passed through Hattie's yard but didn't linger, instead going straight back to Auntie O's truck. I realized as I was driving away that I hadn't yet told Brody about the fact that Praise owned a green coat that matched what I'd seen at Griffin Park when Callum and I came upon Genevieve's body. I didn't know for sure that Praise was the one who'd fled from the park that night, but I figured I should probably let Brody know that she owned a coat in that color since she had a motive to want Genevieve dead.

I didn't turn back, however. Instead, I drove to the farm and texted the information to Brody. Then I started a group chat with

Callum, Tessa, and Roxy, and filled them in on everything I'd witnessed and discovered that day.

'You've been busy,' Callum remarked when he showed up at the farmhouse that evening to join me for dinner.

'Accidentally,' I said. 'I set out to talk to Praise, but never saw her. Everything else happened by chance.' And with a little help from Euclid, but I didn't mention that part.

Over dinner, I shared more details of what I'd learned and what Enrique had said while lying on the ground, waiting for the ambulance to arrive.

'He seems like a strong suspect,' I said as we cleaned up the kitchen after eating, 'but he's not the only one.' I gave my head a shake, feeling frustrated. 'I'm not sure I'm any closer to clearing Tessa's name.'

'Hey.' Callum shut the dishwasher and pulled me in close to him. 'How can I help?'

I rested my cheek against his chest. 'I'm not sure, but I appreciate that you want to. I don't even know what I should do next.'

'Maybe you need to think about something else for a while,' he suggested. 'Sometimes that makes things clearer.'

'True,' I agreed.

'I was hoping you might join me for an evening out tonight.'

I raised my head and smiled. 'What do you have in mind?'

He grinned. 'It's a secret, but the dogs can come and you should dress warmly.'

That sent my curiosity into high gear. 'I'm intrigued.'

'Does that mean you're in?'

'I'm definitely in.' I looked to Flossie and Fancy, where they lay curled up with Stardust in the corner. 'What about you, girls?'

The spaniels jumped to their feet, startling the sleepy kitten. Flossie barked and Fancy threw back her head and howled. They ran to the door and stood there, looking back at us, tails wagging.

I laughed. 'Then what are we waiting for?'

TWENTY

'So, where are we going?' I asked, once the dogs and I had joined Callum in his truck.

As instructed, I'd dressed in several layers, including a puffy down jacket and a winter hat to keep my ears warm. I noticed that Callum had a thermos sitting in one of the cupholders, but I didn't know if it was full or empty. I couldn't see any other potential clues as to our destination.

'It's still a secret,' Callum said as he turned out of the driveway and on to Larkspur Lane.

'Grrr.' My frustration was laced with good humor.

Fancy echoed my sentiment with an 'a-woo'.

Callum laughed, but didn't give in. The country road had no streetlamps and the moon was just a crescent in the clear sky, so he flicked on his high-beam headlights.

'You know I'm not good with suspense,' I complained.

'Unless you're dishing it out in your screenplays.'

'Exactly,' I said. 'But I'm definitely not in control of the narrative right now.'

'Nope.' Callum grinned. 'And you'll have to sit tight a little longer. You'll see where we're going when we get there.'

Flossie groaned in the back seat.

This time, I laughed. 'My thoughts exactly, Flossie.'

Callum drove north of town, along the coastal route. Minutes later, he pulled off the road, on to a dirt track I hadn't ever noticed before, probably because it was nearly overgrown with trees and bushes on both sides.

'Shortly after I moved to Twilight Cove, I was out exploring one day and found this place,' Callum said. 'I remembered it from when I was a kid, visiting my grandparents during the summer, but I almost didn't see the turnoff with all the overgrowth.'

All I could see by the light of the high beams was the dirt track and the surrounding trees. Soon, however, we rounded a bend and broke free of the woodland. I realized that we'd driven on to a point of land that reached out into the ocean.

Callum parked the truck with it facing south. 'This is it.'

Intrigued, I climbed out of the vehicle and let the dogs out of the back seat. I moved cautiously closer to the edge of what I worried was a cliff, but then I realized that we were probably only fifteen or twenty feet above sea level. A rocky slope led down to the ocean. It was probably easy to navigate by daylight, but I didn't want to try it at night. The tide was out, but not very far, and I could hear the waves lapping against the shore.

'It's a bit cold for a nighttime swim,' I said to Callum when he came to stand by my side. 'I hope that's not what you have in mind.'

'I didn't tell you to bring a swimsuit,' he pointed out.

'True. That's a good sign. As long as you aren't thinking of skinny dipping.'

'We'll save that for the warmer months.'

'Sure,' I said in the most non-committal way possible.

He chuckled as he took my hand and led me to the back of the truck. 'I hope you like stargazing.' He lowered the tailgate.

I smiled as I climbed into the bed of the truck. 'I love it.'

I craned my neck back to look up at the sky. Stars glittered like an endless spray of diamonds overhead. Here, outside of town, with no light pollution, the night sky was a sight to behold.

'Hang on,' Callum said before I could sit down.

He grabbed a blanket off the top of what I realized was a small stack of them. He spread it out on the bed of the truck and then produced two pillows.

'Stargazing in style,' I said. 'I like it.'

I sat on the blanket and Callum settled down next to me. He unfurled a second blanket to cover us and I shifted over so I could snuggle up to him.

Flossie and Fancy jumped up into the bed of the truck to join us. Flossie lay down at my side, pressing her body against mine, and Fancy did the same with Callum. I could already tell that the body heat from Callum and Flossie would keep me warmer than the blanket.

We lay there together, looking up at the stars. We could see the Milky Way stretching across the sky like a cosmic river. We pointed out familiar constellations and Callum named a few I'd never noticed before. After a while, we fell quiet, simply enjoying each other's company and the beauty of the night sky.

As I gazed upward, a faint band of light appeared overhead. I blinked, thinking it was just a finger of hazy cloud, but then another band appeared. They stretched and curved in a slow, sinuous dance.

I sat up. 'Is that . . .?' I let the question trail off, too awestruck to finish.

Callum sat up beside me and confirmed my suspicion. 'The aurora borealis.'

I glanced at him and saw the grin on his face. 'You knew this would happen!'

'I hoped it would,' he admitted. 'The forecast said there was a good chance we'd be able to see it this far south tonight.'

I stared up at the sky in wonder as more bands joined the others, bending and shifting. The light was mostly white, with just the faintest hint of green.

'This is amazing!' I exclaimed. 'I've never seen the Northern Lights before!'

'I was hoping you'd like it.'

'Like it?' I gave him a quick kiss before returning my gaze to the sky. 'I love it. It's incredible.'

Callum climbed down from the truck. 'It probably looks even more amazing through a camera.'

From beneath the spare blankets, he pulled out a tripod and a black camera case.

'You really thought this out,' I said, impressed.

He started setting up the tripod. 'I wanted it to be a date to remember.'

'Any time I spend with you is memorable,' I assured him, 'but this is . . . extraordinary.'

I climbed out of the truck and the dogs hopped down too. They sniffed at the base of the tripod and then flopped down in the grass, unaware of or uninterested in the celestial show taking place overhead.

Once Callum had the camera set up, he set it to take long exposures. We watched the screen when each new picture came up on the display.

'Amazing!' I kept exclaiming.

The photos captured far more color than we could see with our eyes. The camera picked up bright green, purple, and a hint of red. Callum set the timer and we got in a few pictures, with the spaniels joining us. In the photos, we were silhouettes, backlit by the magical colors of the Northern Lights.

Eventually, after an hour or so, the aurora faded away. By then I was shivering, although I hadn't noticed until that moment. Callum brought out the thermos – which turned out to be full – and poured me a cup of hot chocolate. I cradled the cup in my hands as I listened to the ocean and marveled at the beauty around me, even without the Northern Lights to dazzle me.

Callum put the camera and tripod away, stashing them in the bed of the truck. As he pulled his hand back there was a cascade of pinging sounds.

'Crap,' he muttered.

I hurried to his side. 'What happened? Did you hurt yourself?'

'No,' he replied, sounding disappointed. 'The bracelet you made me snagged on something and broke. The beads went everywhere. I'm sorry, Georgie.'

I set my empty cup down in the bed of the truck and took his hand. 'It's fine. I'm not upset.'

He stepped closer and put his arms around me. 'I am. I loved that bracelet and its coded message.'

I'd made the bracelet for him back in August, using black and white beads to spell out 'I really like you too,' in morse code. I'd meant it as a response to him telling me earlier that summer that he really liked me. Sometimes I struggled to voice my feelings, so the bracelet had helped me to say the words that I couldn't articulate.

I put a hand to his face. 'Don't worry. I'll make you a new one.'

He pulled me in close for a long kiss. When it ended, he kept his arms around me and looked into my eyes. 'I brought you here for a reason.'

'Other than to see the aurora?'

'Other than that,' he confirmed. 'I wanted the perfect moment to tell you something and I don't think it gets more perfect than this. Except for the broken bracelet.'

'I'll replace it,' I reminded him as nerves jangled inside me. 'What is it that you wanted to tell me?'

He brushed a stray lock of hair off my face and tucked it behind my ear. 'I love you, Georgie.'

'You do?' The words popped out of me in surprise.

He grinned. 'Yes, Georgie, I do. I love you.'

A warm glow of emotion burst into life inside of me. It was as if the aurora borealis had shot down from the sky and lit up inside my chest.

I couldn't speak in that moment, but I didn't need to. The way Callum kissed me was so magical that something inside of me transformed, grew stronger. When the kiss ended, I rested a hand on his chest, right over his heart.

'I'll make you that new bracelet,' I promised, 'but it's going to have a different coded message this time.'

'Yeah?' Even with just starlight to go by, I could see the hope in his eyes.

I met his gaze straight on. 'I love you too, Callum McQuade.'

Fancy let out a happy howl and somewhere in the distance an owl hooted.

Despite the heat of the kiss that followed, I couldn't help but shiver from the chill of the deepening night.

Callum wrapped me in a hug. 'Let's get you home so you don't freeze.'

On the ride back to the farm, I kept a hand on Callum's knee, not wanting to break contact with him. I felt so happy and full of love that I could hardly think straight, and I didn't mind at all.

After Callum parked at the farmhouse, he held my hand as he walked me up to the back porch to say goodnight.

We kept prolonging the parting with another kiss, until finally I rested my cheek against his shoulder with a sigh.

'I don't want this night to end,' I said.

'Neither do I,' Callum whispered in my ear.

I raised my head and met his gaze. 'Then it doesn't have to. Not yet.'

I took him by the hand and led him inside.

TWENTY-ONE

I woke up the next morning deliriously happy, snuggled up in Callum's arms. I was too comfy and too content to move, even though I could hear Herald the rooster crowing outside and I knew it must be nearly time to head out to the barn to take care of the morning chores.

'You awake?' Callum asked quietly. He spoke into my hair since I had my head tucked into the crook of his neck.

I tipped my chin up so I could meet his gaze. I thought my heart might explode when I saw the love and affection in his green eyes.

I snuggled even closer to him. 'I am, but I want to stay like this forever.'

'Same,' he said and I could hear the smile in his voice. 'Unfortunately, I don't think the farm is going to run itself.'

'Five more minutes.'

Low laughter rumbled in his chest. 'Let's make it seven.'

That sounded good to me, but not so much to Flossie and Fancy. They jumped up on the bed and climbed over us, licking our faces and pawing at the covers. Laughing, I tried to hide my face under the blankets, but Flossie grabbed them with her teeth and tugged until she had me uncovered. Then Stardust joined the fray, pouncing on our feet.

'OK, OK,' I said as I laughed.

Callum sat up and scooped Stardust into his arms. 'We surrender, so you can put those claws away.'

Stardust responded by swatting at his nose before slipping out of his arms and running wild around the room.

The animals weren't satisfied until we'd actually climbed out of bed. Then they clattered down the stairs to wait for breakfast in the kitchen. Once they were fed, I made toast for Callum and me, and we ate together at the kitchen table.

'I could get used to this,' I said as I rinsed our plates at the sink a little later. I liked sharing ordinary moments with him. And romantic ones too, of course.

Callum wrapped his arms around me from behind and kissed my neck. 'So could I.'

I turned around and kissed him. I easily could have lost myself in the kiss, but Fancy let out a loud 'a-woo' and Flossie pawed at the back door. I was afraid that Flossie might get impatient enough to unlock and open the door herself, so I broke away from Callum and did it for her. The dogs dashed outdoors, with Stardust scampering along behind them.

'Good thing we've got them to keep us on track,' I said.

Callum pulled me back to him. 'Sort of good,' he amended. He gave me a quick kiss and tucked my hair behind my ear. 'I'm going to head over to my cabin to change and then I'll meet you at the barn.'

'It's a date,' I said with a smile.

He ran his hands down my arms until my hands were in his. He gave them a squeeze before stepping back and letting my fingers slide out of his grasp. When he reached the door, he stopped and looked back. 'Georgie?'

'Yes?'

'I love you.'

My smile probably outshone the sun. 'I love you too.'

I didn't think I'd ever get tired of saying that.

After all the morning chores were taken care of and I'd spent some time keeping Twiggy and Tootsie company, I returned to the farmhouse. I spent the next few hours writing. I made a bit of progress, but not as much as I should have in that amount of time. My thoughts kept drifting to Callum, his parents' upcoming visit, and Genevieve's murder.

Eventually, I gave up and shut my laptop. I was about to take the dogs for a walk when I received a text message from Tessa. She must have been on her lunch break because she was at work and she never texted while she was teaching.

Guess what I heard in the staff room this morning? the message read.

Before I had a chance to type out a response, she sent another text.

Miles dressed up as Bigfoot for Halloween last year!

I let that message sink in. **Then he's probably the person who scared Genevieve off the road!** I typed out.

And the killer? Tessa's next message read.

Could be, I wrote in response.

Could he have wanted revenge on Genevieve for the way she'd treated him?

Did he own the Bigfoot costume or did he rent it? I asked.

Tessa had probably gone back to teaching because I didn't hear from her again until late in the day.

Not sure, she wrote back eventually.

I'll try to find out. I sent the message while I was in the middle of my evening farm chores.

Roxy had come over after school to help out. After mucking out the stalls in the barn, she'd gone to visit Twiggy and Tootsie, who seemed like different donkeys from the ones who'd arrived at the sanctuary a few days earlier. Their moods had brightened significantly and they interacted with us now, coming over to us for attention. Once in a while, they even played with the big ball that I brought out for them each day. Soon we would introduce them to the other donkeys and hopefully they'd all become fast friends.

With my tasks complete, I joined Roxy by Twiggy and Tootsie's pasture. She sat perched on the top of the fence, so I climbed up to sit next to her and filled her in on what Tessa had told me during our text exchange.

'Mr Schmidt is totally the killer,' Roxy declared when I'd finished. 'When the car accident didn't kill Genevieve, he had to try something else.'

'Let's not get carried away,' I cautioned. 'If he rented the costume years ago, he wouldn't still have it.'

'He could have rented it again,' she countered

'True enough,' I conceded. 'Is there a costume shop in town?' I didn't recall ever seeing one.

'No, but there's one in Britton Bay and that's only half an hour away. We should go and find out if they rented a Bigfoot costume to anyone recently.'

'I'm not sure they'd tell us that, but they'd probably tell the police.'

'We can figure this out faster than the police can,' Roxy said.

'We?' I echoed, giving her a sidelong glance.

'If you don't let me help, I might go rogue and do it on my own.'

'Roxy . . .'

'I can help,' she insisted.

'Fine,' I relented, 'but only in ways that involve zero danger, which means don't do things on your own.'

She rolled her eyes but didn't argue any further. 'So are we going on a road trip?'

'The store is probably closed for the day so there's no point in going until tomorrow. In the meantime, maybe someone around here knows if Miles rented or owned the costume.'

Roxy glanced over her shoulder and smiled. 'Like Olivia.'

I followed her line of sight and saw my aunt heading our way. When she reached us, Roxy didn't waste any time raising the question that was on our minds.

'Olivia, do you know if Mr Schmidt owned the Bigfoot costume he wore for Halloween last year?'

'Miles Schmidt?' Olivia asked.

Roxy nodded. 'The math teacher.'

My aunt considered the question. 'He's very involved in the local theater group. I suppose he could have borrowed it from there, but I'm afraid I don't know for sure. You'd be better off asking another member of the theater group.'

'Like Linette?' I had second thoughts as soon as I suggested her name. 'But she's new to town, so she might not know.'

'She's been here for more than a year,' Auntie O said. 'And she knows Miles better than I do. She dated him briefly, after all.'

'She did?' I said with surprise.

Roxy made a face. 'Ew. I don't need to know about my teacher's love life.'

My aunt gave me an astute look. 'Are you thinking Miles could be the one who caused Genevieve's car accident?'

'It's a possibility,' I said.

She frowned. 'If there's even a chance that Miles is dangerous, I don't want either of you near him.'

'He's volunteering for the Trail of Terror,' I reminded her.

'But there'll be plenty of other people around during the event,' she said. 'I know you're trying to clear Tessa's name, but promise me you'll be careful if you speak to Miles, or anyone else you might suspect.'

'We'll definitely be careful.' I nudged Roxy with my elbow. 'Won't we?'

'We're always careful.'

My aunt raised an eyebrow at that, but then she set off to look after the chickens.

'Come on,' I said to Roxy. 'I'll give you a ride home.'

'Not yet,' she said. 'Callum promised me a riding lesson.'

Callum had started teaching her how to ride Sundance back in September. Roxy had always wanted to learn how to ride a horse, but she'd never had any lessons before. I suspected that her mom couldn't afford to pay for activities like that. Fortunately, Callum was happy to teach Roxy for free. Even if he wasn't already rich from his lucrative major league baseball career, he still would have done it for nothing.

He'd even offered to fund the sanctuary so we wouldn't need to raise money through the Trail of Terror and similar events. Auntie O had turned him down, since he was already managing the farm in exchange for nothing more than a free place to live. I knew that he hadn't given up on the idea of financing the sanctuary, though.

I took the dogs for a walk and when we got back, we hung around the riding ring and watched the remainder of Roxy's lesson. Although Roxy didn't have to pay a cent for Callum's coaching, the deal was that she had to take care of Sundance before and after each lesson. Not that she minded. She loved spending time with the animals, and Sundance was one of her favorite sanctuary inhabitants.

By the time she'd finish grooming Sundance and cleaning the tack, darkness had fallen. Since her mom was working that evening and she'd be going home to an empty house, Roxy stayed for dinner. After that, we set off in my car while the dogs stayed with Callum.

'Did you see the Northern Lights last night?' Roxy asked as I drove along Larkspur Lane, heading for the center of town.

'I did,' I said with a smile. 'It was incredible. How about you?'

Roxy nodded. 'I sat on the roof of our house and got some pictures with my phone.'

'On the roof?' I echoed with concern. 'That doesn't sound very safe.'

She waved off my comment. 'I do it all the time. It's fine.' She changed the subject. 'We should talk to Linette tonight.'

'It's a little late for dropping in on someone,' I said.

'It's not that late.'

She was right, and if I were honest, I was as eager as she was to get on with our investigation.

'I'll tell you what,' I said, 'we'll drive past her house. If the lights are on, we'll stop and have a quick chat with her.'

As it turned out, we never made it to Linette's place. On our way there, we turned down Genevieve's street. I pointed out her house as we drove past at a crawl. As expected, the house was completely dark. Maybe I was imagining it, but it seemed to have an eerie and forlorn air about it.

'Creepy,' Roxy said as she stared out at the house. Then, 'What was that?'

I stopped the car.

I'd seen it too.

The beam of a flashlight bobbed up and down in Genevieve's backyard.

TWENTY-TWO

Roxy reached for the passenger door handle.

'Whoa,' I said to stop her. 'We're staying right here and calling the police.'

She slumped back in her seat. 'I guess I don't want to be *that girl* from a horror movie.'

I was glad she'd seen the wisdom in my decision. I put through the call, making sure to mention that the house in question had belonged to the recent murder victim.

'The prowler will probably be long gone by the time the cops get here,' Roxy grumbled when I hung up.

Fortunately, her prediction didn't turn out to be right. The light continued to flash and bob, sometimes disappearing but always showing up again shortly thereafter. We were watching it move about when a police cruiser turned on to the street with its lights flashing but its siren off.

Roxy and I got out of the car to greet the two officers. They introduced themselves as Perlman and Escobar.

'Please wait in your vehicle,' Escobar requested once we'd identified ourselves as the people who'd reported the prowler. 'We'll go check it out.'

We retreated to my car and watched as the officers disappeared into Genevieve's backyard, flicking on the powerful beams of their flashlights.

A minute passed, then another. No criminals fled through the front yard, but we had no way of knowing what was happening behind the house.

Roxy sat up straighter. 'Someone's coming.'

Two bright flashlight beams shone from the side yard, drawing closer. Soon we could see the shadowy outlines of Escobar and Perlman, herding four smaller silhouettes ahead of them.

'Kids?' I said with surprise.

Roxy and I climbed out of my car. We crossed the lawn to meet up with the officers and they didn't object to our presence.

'Robbie Howard?' Roxy blurted once we were close enough

to see the kids' faces by the light of the police officers' flashlights.

All four boys appeared to be about twelve years old.

Roxy turned to me. 'Remember the brat with the mask when you picked me up the other day?'

I remembered. 'That's him?'

Roxy crossed her arms over her chest and glared at Robbie and his friends. 'He lives next door to me. Were you trying to break into the murder victim's house?'

'No!' Robbie exclaimed. 'We weren't doing anything wrong!'

The other three boys stayed silent. They kept their gazes on the ground and looked decidedly worried.

Officer Perlman held up a camcorder. 'They were filming a horror movie.'

'Seriously?' Roxy said, like that was the most ridiculous thing she'd ever heard.

'It's going to be awesome,' Robbie said proudly.

Roxy rolled her eyes.

'And all those props you were using?' Escobar prodded.

Robbie stared at his feet.

'They've got pumpkins and an animated Grim Reaper,' Escobar explained to Roxy and me. 'A fog machine and other stuff too.'

'There's no way that's yours,' Roxy said, still glaring at Robbie.

'Pumpkins and Halloween decorations.' Dots connected in my mind as that thought sank in. 'Did you kids steal the pumpkins from Griffin Park? And the decorations from Miles Schmidt's house?'

'And the fog machine from the high school!' Roxy exclaimed just as I remembered Tessa's story about the missing machine. 'How did you know about it? You don't go to my school.'

'My cousin does,' Robbie said. 'He told me about all the cool stuff they have there. But we didn't steal anything,' he insisted. 'We just borrowed some stuff. We're going to put it back when we're done filming our movie.'

'You'll be returning everything first thing in the morning,' Perlman corrected him. 'As for right now, we're taking you kids home and having a chat with all of your parents.'

The boys looked as though they'd suddenly landed in a real-life nightmare.

Perlman herded the kids toward the cruiser.

'Thanks for calling it in,' Escobar said to me. 'It doesn't look like there's any harm done. We'll pick up the fog machine and everything else in the morning.'

I thanked him and his partner for responding to the call and Roxy and I got back in the car.

'I bet they're responsible for the lights seen at Griffin Park and the graveyard,' Roxy said.

'I think you're probably right about that,' I agreed. 'So that's a couple of mysteries solved – the recent thefts and the ghost light sightings.'

'Now we're just left with the murder to solve,' Roxy said.

And that was the toughest one of all.

Inspiration struck me within moments of opening my eyes the next morning. With my head once again tucked cozily in the crook of Callum's neck, I told him my plan. He didn't try to dissuade me from carrying it out, but he did ask to be part of it.

His offer came as a relief. I didn't want to venture into the lair of a possible murderer on my own, but I also didn't want the opportunity to gain some valuable information to slip through my fingers. Having Callum's company when I showed up at Miles's house that morning would make the plan far safer.

We had to take care of the most pressing farm chores before we could go anywhere, but that didn't matter. As eager as I was to put my plan in motion, I didn't think Miles would appreciate it if I showed up on his doorstep before dawn. At the same time, I wanted to catch him before he left for work. In the end, we set off in Callum's truck shortly after seven thirty, with the dogs riding in the back seat. Finding Miles's address had been easy. I'd simply looked him up in an online directory.

Although Miles had come to the farm for the Trail of Terror meetings, I couldn't remember the type of car he drove so I didn't know if it was parked out front of his house when we arrived. A light was on in the house, though, so I took that as a positive sign.

'What happens if he doesn't want to talk?' Callum asked as he parked his truck by the curb.

I shrugged. 'Then we leave and try to find another way to get the information we need.'

Miles lived in a gray stucco house on a quiet street lined with homes on generous lots. Although several of the neighboring houses had lights on, nobody was out and about at the moment. I didn't bother putting the dogs on their leashes and they stuck close to us as Callum and I headed for the front door.

Flossie and Fancy sat down as I knocked and waited for a response. At first, I thought maybe Miles wouldn't answer, but then I heard approaching footsteps.

When he opened the door, Miles seemed surprised to see us. I couldn't blame him, especially considering the early hour.

'Georgie,' he said, clearly puzzled by my presence, 'what can I do for you?'

I quickly introduced him to Callum and then said, 'I was hoping you might have a few minutes to chat about your missing Halloween decorations.'

Miles didn't seem any less puzzled, but he stepped back and held the door open. 'I don't have a lot of time. I need to leave for work soon, but come on in.'

'Is it OK if the dogs come too?' I asked.

Miles hesitated. 'Are they well-behaved?'

'Very,' I said, hoping Flossie and Fancy wouldn't prove me wrong. They *were* well-behaved dogs, but they were also smart and sometimes had their own agendas.

Miles shut the door behind us and led the way to the back of the house. 'I hope you don't mind me making my lunch while we talk.'

'Of course not,' I assured him.

I caught a glimpse of a fish tank in the living room as I followed Miles. I wondered if he had other pets, but I didn't see any signs that he did. We ended up in the kitchen, where Miles had bread, mayonnaise, butter, deli meats, lettuce, sliced tomato, and cheese set out on the island.

'Have the police contacted you about your missing decorations?' I asked as he started buttering the bread.

'No. I reported the theft, but they didn't seem terribly interested, even though I lost over a thousand dollars' worth of props.'

Callum raised his eyebrows when he heard that figure.

'My friend and I noticed some prowlers at Genevieve's house last night,' I explained. 'It turned out to be some kids filming a horror movie. They had a bunch of pumpkins and props that they admitted didn't belong to them.'

Miles looked up from his sandwich-making. 'Did they have my stuff?'

'I don't know for sure,' I replied, 'but I think at least some of what they had might belong to you. You'll probably be hearing from the police soon.'

'Hopefully they didn't break anything,' Miles grumbled as he layered tomato, lettuce, cheese, and deli meats on the bread. 'Especially the animatronics.'

I remembered what the police had said. 'A Grim Reaper?'

'Did you see it?' Miles asked eagerly. 'Is it OK?'

'I didn't see it, but the police mentioned that was one of the props the kids had.'

Miles scowled as he slapped the second piece of bread on top of the sandwich and plunked the whole thing into a plastic container. 'If they broke anything, they'd better pay for it.'

I shared a glance with Callum, not entirely sure how to broach the next subject. He gave the slightest shrug of one shoulder, which I took to mean, 'go for it'.

'I guess you heard about the car accident Genevieve had before she died,' I said.

Miles gave a snort. 'Didn't she claim a monster scared her off the road?'

'Bigfoot,' Callum said with a nod.

Miles frowned at that but said nothing as he put the sandwich container in an insulated lunch bag.

I pushed onward. 'I heard that you were Bigfoot for Halloween last year. Did you rent the costume?' I quickly added, 'I'm wondering if maybe the culprit rented it from the same place as you did.'

Really, I was wondering if Miles owned the costume, but I didn't want him getting defensive and refusing to answer my questions.

He fetched an apple from the fridge and added it to his bag. 'I didn't rent the costume. I own it.'

'Nobody borrowed it from you recently?' I checked.

'Of course not.'

'Not even without you knowing?' Callum asked.

Miles let out an exasperated sigh. 'It's in the basement. I'll show you.'

Callum and I followed as he opened the door to a stairwell and jogged down to the basement. Flossie and Fancy stayed behind on the main floor so I was glad to have Callum at my back. Venturing alone into the basement of one of my murder suspects would have made me worry that I was going to be *that girl* from a horror movie that Roxy hadn't wanted to be the night before.

I expected a dank, dark, creepy basement, but the room at the bottom of the stairs was fully finished and brightly lit by overhead lights and some weak daylight coming in through two high windows. There was a pool table at one end of the long room and two racks of costumes closer to us.

'That's quite the collection you've got,' Callum remarked.

'I've been in theater for years,' Miles said. 'And I enjoy dressing up at Halloween.'

He frowned as he moved the costumes around on the racks. After searching the first rack, he turned to the second, his frown deepening.

'That's odd,' he said, going back to search the first rack again.

'What is?' I asked, although I thought I already knew.

'The Bigfoot costume,' Miles said, confused. 'It's gone.'

TWENTY-THREE

'Are you sure this is where you left it?' Callum asked as Miles looked through the outfits again.

'This is where I keep all my costumes.' Miles rubbed his forehead. 'I'll have to figure this out later. I need to get to work.'

'Do you remember the last time you saw the costume?' I asked as we followed him up the stairs.

'Not really,' he replied. 'I haven't used any of those costumes recently. For the last play I was in, I used an outfit belonging to the theater.'

When I reached the main floor, my heart gave a worried flip-flop in my chest. Flossie sat waiting for us in the hallway, but Fancy was nowhere to be seen. Thankfully, Miles didn't seem to notice her absence. He headed straight for the kitchen and started rustling through the refrigerator.

'Where's Fancy?' Callum mouthed the question behind Miles's back.

I shrugged as I glanced around.

A flicker of movement caught my attention from down the hall. A piece of paper seemed to be suspended in the air, a foot or so off the ground. My eyes widened and I whipped my head around. Callum had his back to me as he talked to Miles about the pool table in the basement, and Miles was far enough into the kitchen that he wouldn't have a view of the hall.

My pulse racing, I darted quietly in the direction of the levitating paper.

'Fancy!' I hissed. 'What are you doing?'

The air shimmered and Fancy took shape before my eyes. As soon as I'd seen the levitating paper, I'd known that she'd camouflaged herself so she could sneak around Miles's house undetected. The paper, however, gave her away.

She dropped it at my feet. Fully visible now, she looked at me and wagged her tail. Flossie came down the hall to join us and gave Fancy's find an interested sniff.

I could hear the men's voices coming closer, so I snatched up the paper and stuffed it in my back pocket, just in time. The men emerged from the kitchen, Miles with his lunch bag in hand.

'I'm afraid I need to leave now,' Miles informed us.

'Of course,' I said, trying my best to look casual as I headed for the foyer, the dogs at my heels. 'We don't want to make you late.'

I opened the front door and made sure that Flossie and Fancy scooted out ahead of me. I didn't want to give them a chance to get into any further mischief. Miles grabbed a messenger bag from the hall table and followed us out, locking the door behind him.

'I hope you get all your Halloween decorations back,' I said as Callum and I descended the steps after the dogs.

Miles mumbled his thanks and then headed for a red hatchback parked in front of his house.

'So,' Callum said once we were seated in his truck, 'do you think the costume's really missing or was that all an act?'

'I've been wondering the exact same thing. After all, Miles said himself that he's been involved in theater for years. He could be acting. Maybe he used the costume to scare Genevieve, not realizing that someone would remember that he'd dressed up as Bigfoot for Halloween last year. Maybe he decided to pretend that the costume was stolen from his house so he'd appear less guilty.'

'Although he didn't have a chance to go and hide it once we started asking our questions,' Callum pointed out.

'True, but maybe he realized before we ever showed up that someone might link him to the costume. If that's the case, he could have hidden it or thrown it out days ago.'

'But we don't have any way of knowing whether he told us the truth or not.'

'No,' I said vaguely, my thoughts on the paper that felt like it was burning a hole in my back pocket.

I hesitated before speaking again. I didn't know how to tell Callum about the dogs' special abilities. I knew he'd never say or do anything that would expose the dogs or put them in danger in any way, but I didn't know for sure if Flossie and Fancy would let him witness what they could do. If I told him about their powers and he couldn't see with his own eyes that I was telling the truth, would he think I was crazy? Even if he did witness firsthand what the spaniels could do, would he find it all too strange to deal with? Would he worry that he and I were both losing our minds? I didn't know, but I hated keeping secrets from him, especially with our relationship growing stronger all the time.

Deciding on a compromise, I shifted in my seat so I could tug the paper out of my back pocket.

'Fancy found this in Miles's house,' I said as I unfolded the crumpled paper.

Callum glanced into the back seat. 'Do you have sticky fingers, Fancy?' he asked. 'Or should I say sticky paws?'

Fancy answered with a 'woo' that could have been an affirmative response or encouragement for me to hurry up and look at what she'd found.

'Oh,' I said when I saw what was on the paper.

It was a pencil sketch of Genevieve. It wasn't the most skilled drawing and it didn't have a whole lot of detail, but I could still tell who it was meant to be.

I handed it to Callum.

'Is that Genevieve?' he asked.

I responded with a question of my own. 'Why would Miles have a sketch of Genevieve in his house?'

'Didn't you say they dated for a while?' Callum handed the paper back to me and started the truck's engine.

'They did.' I studied the rough drawing, wishing it could magically give me some answers to the questions rattling around in my head. 'But does this look like a sketch someone would make of their sweetheart?'

The proportions were slightly off, making it look as though one eye was larger than the other and the nose was a little off-kilter.

'Maybe that's just the best Miles could do,' Callum suggested as he drove down the street and then turned in the direction of home. 'If I tried drawing your portrait, you probably wouldn't even recognize yourself in it.'

'So I shouldn't expect a gift of a hand-drawn portrait anytime soon?' I teased.

'Not unless you like stick-figures.'

I smiled and folded the creased paper.

Callum's expression grew more serious. 'Do you think . . .' He trailed off and glanced at the dogs in the rear-view mirror.

'What?' I prodded.

He seemed to measure his words before speaking. 'Fancy grabbed a random piece of paper from Miles's house, but it doesn't seem so random.'

My heart beat faster. 'I don't think it was random.'

This time, he glanced my way.

'They're smart dogs,' I said. 'Uncannily so, sometimes.'

Callum kept his eyes on the road now. 'Yes, I've noticed.'

'You have?' I said with surprise. Just what else had he noticed?

'Sometimes I swear they can understand every word I'm saying.' He glanced at Flossie and Fancy in the rear-view mirror again. 'Right, girls?'

Flossie gave an enthusiastic woof of agreement.

I relaxed into my seat. Maybe that was all he'd noticed?

I looked over my shoulder at the spaniels, who were happily watching out the windows. As nervous as the prospect made me, I wished they would put on a full display of their abilities in front of Callum. Then again, if that happened, he'd probably wonder why I didn't trust him enough to tell him what they could do before he witnessed it with his own eyes. So maybe it would be better if I told him and risked having him think I was crazy?

I wrestled with that question for the rest of the trip home. Twice, I almost blurted out the truth to Callum, but each time I chickened out. Then, when I was about to try for a third time, we arrived back at the farm. The next thing I knew, Callum had given me a kiss and set off for the barn and my chance was gone. Although, really, I could have chased after him and told him right then and there, but I still couldn't decide if that was the right move or not.

My internal dilemma had left my stomach in knots, so I set off on a long walk with the dogs, hoping for some clarity. The exercise helped to calm me down, but it didn't clear my mind.

That evening, Tessa and Roxy came over to the farmhouse, where we gathered at the kitchen table, the dogs at our feet and Stardust curled up on Roxy's lap. I'd let them know in the group chat that I'd found something of interest at Miles's house, but I hadn't provided any specifics. When I showed them the sketch of Genevieve, they both believed it was significant.

'Mr Schmidt was obsessed with Genevieve,' Roxy said, her eyes wide and lit with a spark of excitement. 'She dumped him and then he started stalking her. He decided if he couldn't have her, no one could, so he killed her.'

'That's definitely a possibility.' I filled them in on the supposedly missing Sasquatch costume.

'He's the killer,' Tessa declared once I'd finished.

'He's totally lying about the costume going missing,' Roxy said in agreement. 'He probably tossed it in a dumpster somewhere after scaring Genevieve off the road.'

'And there's more evidence against him,' Tessa said.

Roxy narrowed her eyes. 'Have you been holding out on us?'

'It's something I just found out an hour ago,' Tessa told her. 'I figured since I'd be seeing the two of you this evening I'd tell you in person instead of by text.'

'Tell us what?' I pressed, not wanting to wait in suspense any longer.

'There's been some talk among the staff at the school about having a holiday bake-off, with the teachers competing and the kids watching.'

Roxy smiled at the idea. 'That would be funny.'

'But what's that got to do with the murder?' I asked.

'Some of the teachers were joking that they didn't want to enter if Miles was taking part, because he was sure to win,' Tessa explained.

'Mr Schmidt is a baker?' Roxy asked at the same time as I said, 'Miles bakes?'

'Apparently he's amazing at it,' Tessa said. 'He used to bring in treats to the staff room until a health nut took over as principal. That would have been right around the time I started teaching, so he's never brought treats in my era. But one of my colleagues who's been teaching for decades said he could even make gluten-free treats taste like the real deal.'

I let those words sink in. 'So even Genevieve could have eaten his baking.'

'And they dated, so he probably knew that she didn't eat gluten.' Roxy stroked Stardust's fur as she declared, 'I knew it! Mr Schmidt is a math-loving murderer.'

TWENTY-FOUR

Roxy wanted to drive straight to Miles's house that night to search for more evidence against him, evidence solid enough to take to the police, but Tessa and I vetoed that idea. Not that I wasn't tempted to investigate Miles further, but I thought the smart thing to do would be to take what we already knew to the police and let them decide what to do with it. Tessa agreed, but Roxy wasn't so enthused by the idea. She would have preferred to continue investigating until we had some truly damning evidence against Miles so we could practically deliver him to the police on a platter. Fortunately, we managed to convince her to hold off on any further sleuthing. At least, I thought we had.

After completing my morning farm chores the next day, I drove to the police station with Flossie and Fancy accompanying me. I'd volunteered to take on the task of sharing what we knew since Tessa would be working at the high school all day and Roxy would be attending classes. I didn't relish the thought of telling the authorities what we'd learned about Miles. There was a definite possibility that the state police would be less than impressed that my friends and I had been sticking our noses into the investigation. It therefore came as a great relief when I asked for Brody at the reception desk and was told that he was available to see me. Speaking with him would be far less intimidating than dealing with a detective I didn't know.

When Brody appeared, he led me and the dogs into the bullpen, a large open area filled with numerous desks. Another officer called to Brody, so he turned to me and said, 'I'll be right back,' before crossing the room to join his colleague.

I was left standing next to a desk that was currently unoccupied, like most of the desks in the bullpen. Brody disappeared down a hallway with the colleague who'd called him away. That left two other officers in the room, both of whom were busy working on their computers.

I stood there awkwardly, hoping Brody wouldn't take too long. I pulled out my phone and started scrolling through my social media feeds without really paying attention to what was on the screen.

Having my phone to focus on always helped me feel less awkward in situations where I had nothing to do but stand around and wait.

Fancy gave a sudden jerk on her leash, catching me unaware and pulling the lead out of my hand. When I looked up from my phone, she'd disappeared. Except, I could see her leash trailing along on the floor.

Panic gripped my chest, squeezing my heart and lungs. I glanced at the police officers, but both remained engrossed in what they were doing.

A few desks away, a paper slipped to the floor. I wanted to call to Fancy, but if I did so even under my breath, one or both of the police officers in the bullpen would likely hear me. The last thing I wanted to do was draw attention over this way, especially now that the piece of paper seemed to be floating toward me, a few inches above the ground.

It dropped at my feet and the air shimmered as Fancy reappeared. She wagged her tail and sat down. She and Flossie looked up at me, waiting expectantly.

As surreptitiously as possible, I snatched the paper up from the floor. It appeared to be some sort of official report, but it was hard for me to take in the details. My heart was pounding so hard that blood roared in my ears and I kept glancing from the paper to the police officers, not wanting to be caught looking at the document that I was most definitely not meant to be reading.

Nevertheless, I noticed Genevieve's name on the paper. As I managed to absorb more information, my pulse upped its tempo even further. I heard male voices and realized that Brody and his colleague were about to reappear. I let the paper fall to the floor. It fluttered down and away from me, landing in the kneehole of the nearest desk. Someone would no doubt find it soon and think a draft of air had sent it drifting over this way. At least, I hoped that was what they would assume.

'Sorry about that,' Brody apologized as he rejoined me.

'No worries,' I said, trying my best to appear innocent and at ease, even though my pulse was racing fast enough to make me lightheaded.

He looked at me closely. 'Are you OK, Georgie? You're looking a bit pale.'

I rested my hand on the edge of the nearest desk to steady myself. 'I'm just feeling a bit woozy.'

Brody took my elbow and led me to an interview room, not releasing me until I was safely seated in a chair. Flossie and Fancy sat on either side of me, and Flossie touched a paw to my leg. I stroked her head to reassure her, knowing that she and her sister were worried about me.

'Put your head between your knees if you think you're going to pass out,' he instructed.

'It's not that bad,' I said. 'I'm feeling better already.'

I didn't have him convinced.

'I'll get you some juice.' He left the room before I could object and he returned a minute later with a paper cup filled with orange juice.

Now that I was well away from the document that could have landed me in hot water if someone had caught me with it, my heart had slowed to its normal pace and I no longer felt woozy. I drank down the juice anyway, and only partly to placate Brody. My bout of panic had left my mouth as dry as a desert.

When I finished the juice, I thanked Brody. 'I feel fine now.'

'I'm glad to hear it.' He took the seat across from me as the spaniels lay down at my feet. 'Now, what was it you wanted to talk to me about?'

'I don't want you to get mad,' I said to begin.

Brody's eyes narrowed with suspicion. 'Now I know I won't like what you're going to tell me.'

'It's nothing bad,' I rushed to say. 'I just have some information that I thought I should share with you.'

His suspicion hadn't faded, but he seemed ready to listen. 'Go on.'

I told him about the fact that Miles and Genevieve had dated briefly. It turned out he already knew about that. The fact that Miles owned a Bigfoot costume was definitely news to him, though. While he didn't say so out loud, I could tell that he grew more interested when I mentioned that Miles claimed his costume had gone missing.

Although I wanted to tell Brody about the sketch of Genevieve, I decided not to bring that up. He wouldn't be impressed that I'd surreptitiously removed something from Miles's house. Besides, the sketch didn't really prove anything. If he'd had dozens of photos and drawings of Genevieve in his house, like a creepy stalker, then it would be more relevant, but so far I knew of only the one sketch.

'Do I even want to know why you were at Miles's house?' Brody asked.

'I was just letting him know that the police might have recovered some of his stolen Halloween decorations.'

Brody nodded. 'The kids and their horror movie. I heard about that. By this evening, everything will have been returned to its rightful owners.'

'That's good to hear,' I said before changing topics slightly. 'What happened to the guy who was trying to break into Genevieve's house the other day?' I didn't think I should reveal that I knew Enrique Ramos's name, since that would alert Brody to the fact that I'd been snooping.

'He's got a broken leg and he's been charged with possession of a burglary tool.'

'Is he in the hospital?' I asked.

Brody shook his head. 'It wasn't a bad break. He was released once he had a cast put on.'

I drummed my fingers against my leg. 'Do you think he could have killed Genevieve? He clearly harbored a lot of anger toward her.' As guilty as Miles seemed, I couldn't forget that I had other viable suspects as well.

'We're looking into the possibility.' Giving me a stern look, he added, 'Which means you don't have to.'

I held up my hands in surrender. 'I was just curious about what had happened to him.'

'Uh huh.'

I clearly didn't have him fooled.

'Thanks for hearing me out,' I said as I got to my feet.

The dogs jumped up from where they'd been lying by my chair. Brody stood up too. 'Please be careful, Georgie. Even if you went to Mr Schmidt's house for an innocent purpose' – he clearly wasn't convinced that was truly the case – 'you still walked into the home of a possible killer.'

'I didn't go alone,' I said in my defense. 'I had Callum and the dogs with me. But,' I added quickly when I saw his unimpressed expression, 'I hear you.'

'Do you?' He remained skeptical, but I knew he was genuinely concerned for my safety.

'I do. Really. I'll be careful.'

'I hope that goes for Tessa too.'

'We look out for each other,' I assured him.

'I know you want to help her . . .'

'She didn't kill Genevieve.' When he said nothing, I added, 'You should know that.'

'I do know that. She wouldn't hurt anyone.'

'Have you told her that you know she's innocent?'

A pained expression passed over his face before he could hide it. 'I thought it would be best if I kept my distance. She might not want to see me right now. I am, in a way, the enemy.'

I didn't want to break Tessa's confidence by telling Brody about her feelings for him, but there was still something I *could* tell him. 'She would never see you as her enemy.'

He took a second to let that sink in and then nodded. I hoped that meant he would let Tessa know that he believed in her. It might not ease her worries completely, but it would mean a heck of a lot to her.

Brody let me leave the station without any further warnings, and soon the dogs and I had climbed back into my car. I didn't drive off right away. This was the first chance I'd had to think about what I'd seen on the report Fancy had stolen. Genevieve had died from cyanide poisoning that resulted from ingesting apricot kernels. I'd already known that, thanks to Valentina, but now I also knew that the baked goods containing the apricot kernels had been made of almond flour and apricot jam as well. Plus, the report had revealed that Genevieve had ingested the food less than an hour before her death.

Did that information help my investigation at all? I wasn't sure.

I shifted in my seat so I could look back at Fancy where she sat next to her sister. 'You nearly made me pass out. I thought for sure you were going to give yourself away.'

Fancy stood up on the seat, her tail wagging, and gave me a big kiss on the cheek.

My heart melted. I smiled and kissed her snout. 'I can't stay mad at you, but please be more careful in the future.'

She responded with a 'woo-woo' that may or may not have been a promise to do as I'd requested.

I released a breath, getting rid of some of my tension along with it. The dogs' secret was still safe. That knowledge helped to calm me down and I finally started up the car and drove away from the police station.

When Tessa had come over to the farmhouse the evening before, she'd brought Linette's finished costume for the Trail of Terror. I'd meant to bring it with me, but I'd forgotten it back at the farm. Maybe that wasn't such a bad thing, I decided. Now that I had to return home, I could ask Auntie O if she wanted to accompany me to Linette's house to drop off the costume. I hoped to get some valuable information out of Linette during the visit and I thought it might help to have my aunt there, since Linette knew her better than she knew me.

Luckily, my aunt wasn't busy and agreed to come with me to visit Linette. She wanted to check in and see how Linette was coping with the death of her friend. I felt a pang of guilt, since my motives weren't as noble, but then I reminded myself that I was searching for a killer and trying to clear my best friend's name.

Those goals were honorable enough for me.

TWENTY-FIVE

When Linette opened her door to find my aunt and me on the front porch with Flossie and Fancy, she happily welcomed us into her home. I handed over the costume Tessa had altered for her and Auntie O presented a jar of her homemade strawberry jam. Linette accepted both with gratitude. She invited us to sit down for a cup of tea, so we followed her to the sunny kitchen at the back of the house.

Flossie and Fancy paced around the room, not wanting to settle, so I ended up letting them out on to the back porch. Linette provided them with a bowl of water and I left them lapping away at it. As Linette brewed a pot of orange pekoe tea, my aunt and I sat at the kitchen table. I didn't think I should dive right into my probing questions about Genevieve, so I stayed quiet while Olivia asked about the funeral arrangements.

'Genevieve's sister is taking care of that,' Linette said as she poured hot water into a stout blue teapot. 'She lives in Portland, so that's where the service will be once the police release Genevieve's body.'

Linette turned away as she said those last words, but not before I caught her blinking rapidly. When she faced us again a few seconds later, she'd recovered her composure.

'Is that Barclay's mother?' I asked, hoping to steer the conversation in the direction of Genevieve's nephew.

Linette carried the teapot over to the table. 'That's her. Laura.' She fetched cream, sugar, and small spoons next.

'Were Genevieve and Barclay close?' my aunt asked.

'They were once.' Linette sat down at the table and poured the tea into pretty cups, each one decorated with a different flower. 'Laura and her husband are quite wealthy. They really spoiled Barclay as he was growing up. He was a fun kid, but once he hit his teens he became a bit wild and the selfish streak he'd always had seemed to take over.'

That matched with what Linette had already told me about their relationship.

'I saw him with Genevieve at the farmers' market one day,' I said after thanking Genevieve for the cup of tea she'd passed me. 'He was asking her for money and she didn't seem impressed.'

Linette frowned. 'That wasn't the first time he'd asked her for money. He gets plenty every month from his trust fund, but he likes to hit the casinos and he's always overspending. Genevieve was hoping he'd become more sensible as he matured, but that has yet to happen. She cut him out of her will a while back. That was probably for the best. Any money that falls into Barclay's lap seems to disappear in a flash.'

I didn't need to ask if Barclay was upset when he found out about being cut out of the will, because I'd witnessed his reaction for myself. There were, however, other things I wanted to find out.

'Did I hear someone mention that Barclay is an avid baker?' I asked, knowing full well that I'd never heard any such thing.

Linette appeared puzzled by the question and Auntie O sent a questioning glance my way.

'You must be mistaken,' Linette said. 'I doubt Barclay even knows how to cook an egg, let alone do anything fancier. I'm sorry to say that he's a lazy young man. He doesn't do anything for himself if he can help it.'

While Auntie O asked if Linette would travel to Portland for the service – she did plan to do so – I only half listened as I considered what I'd learned. It was highly unlikely that Barclay had made any poisoned baked goods to give to Genevieve, but that didn't mean he couldn't have purchased some professionally made treats and somehow added ground-up apricot kernels before presenting them to his aunt. That was true for any of my suspects, although Barclay might have known about Genevieve's habit of turning down desserts in public but indulging in secret. Still, I didn't think that helped me much.

I tried not to let myself get discouraged, but I didn't know what else to ask about Barclay. If I came right out and asked about his whereabouts on the day of the murder, Linette would know I suspected him. That might not bother her, but then again it might upset her enough to ask Auntie O and me to leave. I decided the direct approach should be my last resort and instead tried a different strategy.

'It's so hard to believe that somebody might have intentionally poisoned Genevieve,' I said after drinking half of my tea. 'Do you know if the police are getting any closer to finding who's responsible?'

Linette shook her head sadly. 'The police haven't told me anything and I don't know who would harm Genevieve. I know she rubbed people the wrong way, but murder? That's extreme.'

Auntie O and I murmured our agreement.

'What about Barclay?' I asked. 'Does he have any insights?'

Linette laughed, although the sound didn't hold much humor. 'I don't think Barclay has much insight into anything. He's too focused on himself to be aware of anyone else.' She got up from the table. 'I have some delicious chocolate-covered blueberries you should try.' She fetched a package of the treats from a cupboard. 'If only so I don't eat the whole bag myself,' she added with a smile.

She took a bowl down from another cupboard and poured the chocolate-covered berries into it. When she set the package down, I got a look at it and recognized the brand name.

'You got those at the Urban Moon?' I asked. 'In Los Angeles?'

The Urban Moon was a trendy health-food store. I'd been there only once, with a friend of mine, while I was still living in LA, but I knew a few people who liked to shop there for healthy and organic snacks. I personally found the Urban Moon's products to be overpriced and overhyped, but the business had thrived in LA since it opened eight years ago.

'I drove down to LA to visit a cousin last month,' Linette said as she set the bowl on the table. 'She took me to the shop. Everything was so expensive, but I have a weak spot for chocolate and blueberries, so I couldn't resist buying these.'

'They're certainly tasty,' Auntie O said after sampling one of the berries.

'Delicious,' I agreed after taking one for myself.

My aunt and Linette began talking about the local theater group, the Twilight Players, while I got up to check on the dogs. They were lying in a patch of sun on the back porch. They raised their heads to look at me when I peeked out the door, but they went back to snoozing when I told them we'd be staying a while longer.

As I returned to the table, I searched my brain for a way to find out more about Barclay or anyone who might have wanted to hurt Genevieve. Linette was telling my aunt about a play she'd written, one she hoped would be performed by the Twilight Players next year. Normally, hearing that someone was a writer would have piqued my interest, but this time I was too busy thinking to join the conversation. By the time Olivia and I fetched the dogs and headed out the front door, I still didn't have as much information as I'd hoped to gather during the visit.

Linette walked us out of the house and down to the front yard. I knew I was running out of time, so I decided to go with my last resort and try a direct approach.

I stopped on the pathway that led from the front porch to the sidewalk, as if a thought had just struck me. 'You don't think Barclay could have wanted Genevieve out of the way, do you?' I asked Linette.

She paled. 'No. No, of course not.'

She answered a little too quickly, her wide-eyed gaze darting over my shoulder.

I turned to see Barclay striding along the sidewalk toward us. His black sports car sat parked at the curb two houses down.

'Right,' I said as I watched him approach. 'Of course not.'

My aunt and I thanked Linette for the tea and got into Auntie O's truck with the dogs. Since I had the keys, I got into the driver's seat again, once the dogs were safely in the back of the cab. I lowered the windows, hoping to overhear Barclay's conversation with Linette.

'Who are they?' he asked, sending a hard stare in our direction.

'Just some friends who stopped by for a visit,' Linette replied.

'Can I crash at your place tonight?' Barclay asked as he and Linette started toward her house. 'I'm probably leaving town tomorrow, but I'm strapped for cash . . .'

I couldn't hear the rest of their conversation.

'Anything wrong, Georgie?' my aunt asked when I didn't make a move to leave.

'No,' I said quickly. 'Sorry.' I started the engine and pulled away from the curb.

As we drove down the street, I glanced back at Linette's house one last time.

Barclay stood on the front porch, watching us go.

That afternoon, I shared my investigative woes with Twiggy and Tootsie as I groomed them. They listened patiently, but – unsurprisingly – they didn't offer any insights. Voicing my thoughts out loud made me all the more determined to find further information about my suspects. Spinning my wheels wouldn't help Tessa, and every day that went by with a cloud of suspicion hanging over her head was one too many.

She'd texted me at noon, upset that students and other staff members were whispering about her behind her back. At least, she thought that's what they were doing. I hoped it was just her imagination, but with the way gossip always spread through Twilight Cove, she was most likely right.

Once Twiggy and Tootsie were cleaned up – and looking much better, not just thanks to their recent grooming – I brushed out the coats of the other donkeys as well. With that done, I returned to the farmhouse, with Flossie and Fancy trotting along at my side. Stardust greeted us at the back door and I picked her up for a cuddle. She purred and buried her soft head against my neck.

'You're such a sweetheart,' I told her as I sat down in the nearest chair so she could curl up on my lap. While we had a snuggle session, I checked my phone. Roxy had texted me minutes earlier, probably as soon as she finished her final class for the day.

Schmidt @ math club. She inserted a nauseated emoji before adding, **I'm gng sleuthing.**

Alarm shot through me when I read the message.

No! I wrote back as quickly as my thumbs would let me.

Not arrested so need more evidence, her next message said.

I quickly put a call through to Roxy. Each ring seemed to go on forever and I worried that she wouldn't answer my call, only wanting to communicate by text. Thankfully, she picked up after the third ring.

'Roxy, you need to stay away from Miles's house,' I said, skipping any form of greeting.

'He's getting away with murder!' she protested. 'Literally!'

'We don't know for sure that he's the killer,' I pointed out.

'But he could be,' she countered. 'I'm going over there.'

I could tell by the tone of her voice that there was nothing I could say to dissuade her.

I figured that gave me just one option.

'Fine,' I said. 'But I'm coming with you.'

TWENTY-SIX

Ten minutes later, I picked up Roxy at Twilight Cove's one and only high school.

'I'm not sure this is a good idea,' I said as soon as she'd dropped into the passenger seat of my car. 'What if math club doesn't last long?'

Unconcerned, Roxy fastened her seatbelt. 'I asked one of the members – casually – how long it goes. It's usually an hour and a half, and they're only a few minutes in.'

'What if Miles decides to end it early today?' I asked, anxiety swirling in my stomach as I drove away from the school.

Roxy still showed no sign of nerves or second thoughts. 'You worry too much, you know that?'

Fancy voiced her agreement with an 'a-woo' from the back seat.

'You're not the first person to say so.' Worrying and overthinking were my specialties and, in this case, I didn't think they were unwarranted.

'After you called, I peeked into the room and the club was deep into calculus or something like that,' Roxy said. 'We've got time.' She looked over her shoulder at Flossie and Fancy and gave them a smile. 'Besides, we've got two lookouts right here.'

Fancy let out an excited 'woo' and Flossie gave a little yip.

'See?' Roxy said. 'They're on board.'

I gave in, against my better judgment. 'OK, but we're in and out. No lingering.'

She gave a dramatic shudder. 'I wouldn't want to linger in a murderer's house.'

'Yard,' I corrected. 'We're not breaking into his house.'

Roxy said nothing in response. That only added to my unease.

Two minutes later, I parked half a block away from Miles's house. We walked around the corner with the dogs and into the patch of woods at the back of the line of properties. Birds twittered in the trees and twigs and leaves cracked and crunched beneath our feet, but otherwise all was quiet. When I thought we'd walked far enough, we crept closer to the edge of the woods and found a split-rail fence running along the back of Miles's spacious yard. He had about an acre of land and – fortunately for us – tall trees hid the neighboring houses from view. Hopefully that meant no one would notice us sneaking around.

Somewhat belatedly, I wondered if I'd erroneously assumed that Miles lived alone. I figured he was single, since he'd recently been dumped by Genevieve, but it was possible he had a family member or roommate living with him. I cast my mind back to the visit Callum and I had paid to Miles. I didn't remember seeing any signs that anyone other than him lived in his house. That brought me a modicum of relief.

I paused by the fence, wondering why the heck I ever fancied myself an amateur sleuth when the mere thought of trespassing made my palms sweat and my heart race. I didn't feel brave enough for this sort of escapade. My happy place was sitting at home, writing fictional adventures, but this was for Tessa, so even if I didn't feel brave, I'd just have to pretend to be courageous.

'OK, let's make this quick,' I said.

Roxy was already climbing the fence and Fancy and Flossie had ducked beneath the bottom rail. I clambered over the barrier and picked up Flossie's leash while Roxy took Fancy's. We were in the back corner of the spacious yard, so we skirted along the side border of trees and hurried over to the house. Roxy led the way and approached a basement window. She crouched down and cupped her hands around her eyes so she could see inside.

I joined her there and shaded my eyes in the same way while Flossie and Fancy pressed their noses up against the glass.

'A workshop,' Roxy observed.

Sure enough, I saw a long room with a workbench running down one side. The bench was strewn with tools and the floor was covered in sawdust. I also spotted a table saw.

Roxy darted around the back porch to another basement window. I quickly wiped away the dogs' potentially incriminating nose marks with my sleeve and then hurried after her.

'That's the room Callum and I were in the other day,' I said when I peered in through the next window and saw the pool table. 'There's nothing suspicious in there.'

Again, I made sure to wipe the spaniels' nose prints from the glass. I didn't want Miles to even suspect that anyone had been on his property while he was away.

Roxy peeked under the porch next. A quick glance told me that Miles had some lumber and an old lawnmower stowed there. Flossie tugged on her leash and it slipped out of my loose hold. She bounded up the steps to the back porch, her leash trailing behind her, and touched a paw to the door.

'Flossie,' I said in warning when I heard a click.

I knew she'd just unlocked the door and I was afraid she might use her telekinetic powers to open it next.

Roxy brushed past me and jogged up the steps.

'I don't suppose we'd be so lucky . . .' She trailed off as she joined Flossie by the door and tried the knob. It turned easily in her hand and the door opened. 'Who leaves their door unlocked?' Roxy answered her own question. 'People who aren't scared of murderers because *they're* a murderer. That's who.'

I suspected that quite a few people in small towns like Twilight Cove had a habit of leaving their doors unlocked, even though I didn't think that wise. Having lived in Los Angeles and several other cities before that, I preferred to keep my house locked up tight whenever I left the farm. Regardless, I was pretty sure Miles had locked his door, but I wasn't about to say that out loud.

'Roxy.' I used the same warning tone that I'd just used on Flossie. She unclipped Fancy's leash. 'It's not breaking and entering if we didn't have to break in.'

'Roxy!' I hissed as she and Flossie disappeared into the house.

Fancy wasted no time following them inside.

'We're so going to jail,' I muttered under my breath as I hurried after them. 'Two minutes,' I warned when I found Roxy and the dogs in the kitchen. 'Then we're out of here.'

'No body parts,' Roxy said with disappointment as she opened the freezer and studied its contents. She closed the freezer door and moved on to the dining room.

As much as I wanted to stick close to her to make sure she didn't get into any deeper trouble, I decided we'd get out of the house faster if we split up. I called to Flossie and unclipped her leash before taking the other door out of the kitchen. I peeked through one door and discovered a small bathroom. Another led to a closet. I bypassed the door that led to the basement, since I'd already been down there. Maybe there was another room on that level that I hadn't seen, but for the moment I wanted to focus on the rest of the house, partly because basements had a tendency to creep me out, especially when they belonged to a potential murderer.

We didn't find anything on the main floor so we crept upstairs next. Well, I crept. Roxy jogged. She didn't seem to harbor any of the misgivings that I did.

'You have to look in his bedroom,' she told me when we reached the top of the stairs. 'He's my teacher so I do *not* need to see any of that.'

Even though Miles wasn't my teacher, I still wasn't keen to violate his privacy by looking in his bedroom. I took a peek through the door and saw nothing unusual, so I quickly ducked out again. I gave the upstairs bathroom a look while Roxy checked out the other two rooms.

'Nothing,' she said with disappointment when we met in the hall again.

'Let's get out of here.' I was already leading the way down the stairs. 'And let's not make a habit of breaking into people's houses.'

'We didn't break in.'

'It's still illegal. And landing ourselves in jail won't help Tessa.'

I could practically hear Roxy roll her eyes behind me, but she followed me out of the house. Once out on the back porch again, I shut the door behind us. As Roxy headed down the porch stairs, I gave Flossie a pointed look. She touched her paw to the door and I heard a faint click as the lock engaged.

We scurried after Roxy and Fancy. I was about to suggest we get back to my car, but I didn't get a chance because Fancy took off at a gallop. Flossie shot after her sister before I realized what was happening.

'I bet they're on to something!' Roxy ran after the dogs.

With a groan, I broke into a jog and followed.

The spaniels charged straight to the split-rail fence at the back of the property. They ducked under the lowest rail and sniffed around. Roxy had already climbed the fence by the time I caught up. We were farther along the back border of the property from where we'd originally entered the yard.

'Check this out.' With her sleeves covering her hands, Roxy picked up a couple of tin cans with bullet holes in them.

'Target practice,' I surmised. 'That doesn't make Miles a killer. Besides, Genevieve was poisoned, not shot.'

'Sure,' Roxy said. 'But you have to admit, this is *really freaking creepy*.'

She held up two more tin cans, both with bullet holes and both taped to sketches of Genevieve's face.

TWENTY-SEVEN

Roxy snapped a photo of the sketch-and-can combinations and then, finally, she agreed to leave Miles's property.

'He's totally the killer,' she said when we climbed back into my car.

'He does seem like a good candidate,' I agreed. 'But how are we going to convince the police that he's the culprit? We can't admit that we snooped around his house and yard. That will only get us into trouble.'

'Then we'll have to find another way to nudge the cops in the right direction.'

Neither of us came up with a solid way to do that during the drive to Roxy's house. We'd have to hope that the information we'd already passed on to the police would be enough to get them to investigate him more closely. Then maybe they'd find the cans and sketches all on their own.

Before dropping Roxy off, I made her promise once again to not do any sleuthing on her own. That got me another eye roll, but she did accede to my request.

Robbie and his friends were out in his front yard, playing a game of catch, when we pulled up to the curb. After Roxy got out of my car, she marched over to them. Although I lowered the passenger-side window, I didn't catch any of their conversation as I drove past. By the time I reached the end of the street and glanced back, Roxy had left the boys and was entering her house.

'I could use a bite to eat,' I said as I turned on to Larkspur Lane a few minutes later. 'Now that I'm not worried about getting caught breaking the law, I'm starving.'

Fancy bayed and Flossie licked my ear.

I laughed. 'OK, message received. I'll get you something as soon as we're home.'

True to my word, I gave each dog a treat once we returned to the farmhouse. Stardust didn't want to be left out, so I shook a few tuna snacks out of a package for her. She gobbled them up and then tore around the main floor of the house, leaping on and off the furniture and skidding across the floors. The dogs joined in the fun, chasing the kitten with their tails wagging.

Shortly after bringing Stardust home to live with us, I'd moved a lamp with an antique leaded-glass shade up to the attic for safekeeping. Two precious vases had gone over to the carriage house for Auntie O to use. If I'd left any of those items on the main floor of the farmhouse, they'd no doubt be shattered by now.

While the animals played, I started chopping up vegetables for a pot of homemade soup. I planned to serve it with slices of sourdough bread from the local bakery, since my attempt at making bread had failed.

I texted my aunt, inviting her to join Callum and me for dinner. It turned out she already had other plans, so it would be just me and Callum that evening. In recent weeks, the two of us had started having dinner together every evening. Sometimes I cooked and sometimes he did. Other times we prepared the meal together. Cooking or eating, I loved spending time with him. I loved *him*. Just thinking those words lit a happy glow inside of me. Knowing that he loved me back made that glow bright enough to rival the sun.

While the soup simmered on low heat, I took Stardust and the dogs out to the barn and tackled my evening farm chores. Twiggy's eye infection had cleared up and Tootsie's sores were well on the way to healing. Her hair had even started to grow back in the places she'd rubbed raw. Best of all, the spirits of the two donkeys were so much brighter.

Callum and I finished up our farm work around the same time. He made a trip to his cabin for a quick shower while I finished getting our dinner ready at the farmhouse.

'I just talked to my parents on the way over here,' Callum said once we were sitting at the kitchen table with soup and slices of bread in front of us. 'They're leaving in a couple of days, and they're aiming to be here on November first. They haven't booked a place to stay yet. I told them I'd take care of it so they can hit the road tomorrow without worrying about that.'

'I thought they were going to stay at the Twilight Inn,' I said with surprise.

'They had a room reserved there when they originally planned to come in September, but the inn's all booked up for the next week.'

I thought about that for a moment as I enjoyed a spoonful of soup. 'Why don't they stay here on the farm?'

Callum buttered a slice of bread. 'They don't want to be an inconvenience. There are other places to stay in town. I don't think it'll take long for me to find them something.'

'If you stayed here with me, they could have your cabin.'

He set down his knife and met my gaze. 'Are you sure about that?'

'Unless you'd rather not have them quite so close while they're in town.'

'That's not an issue,' he assured me. 'I love having them around. You wouldn't mind me staying here at the farmhouse for several days?'

'Hmm.' I pretended to think about it. 'Let's see. Spending every night with you, waking up next to you in the morning . . . I'm pretty sure I can handle that.'

Leaving his dinner, he got up and came around the table, taking my hand and pulling me up to my feet. 'Every night with you sounds like paradise, Georgie.'

I smiled and wrapped my arms loosely around his neck. 'There's just one problem. I might not get much writing done. You're too distracting.'

He leaned in close to whisper in my ear. 'I'll be quiet.'

His breath against my neck sent a shiver down my back.

'Even when you're quiet, you're distracting.'

'Oh?' The slow grin that I loved so much took shape on his face.

'It's those green eyes of yours,' I said. 'Plus, your blond hair.' I swept a curl of that hair off his forehead and then traced a finger down the side of his face. 'Your strong jaw.' My finger tracked down until I could press my hand against his chest. 'And all those muscles.'

'Hmm.' Humor danced in his eyes. 'I could make myself scarce, if that would help. You could even banish me to one of the guest bedrooms.'

'Never.' I pressed my lips to his and then met his gaze. 'I like being distracted by you.'

'Right back at you.'

We lost ourselves in the kiss that followed, so much so that our soup had nearly gone cold by the time we sat back down at the table. I ended up putting our bowls in the microwave for a minute so we could enjoy our meal the way it was meant to be eaten.

'Are we ready to head out?' I asked once we'd rinsed our dishes and put them in the dishwasher.

Callum grabbed our coats from the hooks by the door. 'Let's do it.'

Praise had sent out another email to the Pumpkin Glow volunteers the day before. The competitors had started building their sculptures yesterday and would have until dusk tomorrow to finish. Then judging would take place before the display was opened to the public. Tonight, Praise needed an army of volunteers to help set up all the decorative jack-o'-lanterns that hadn't already been put in place. Callum and I had offered to help out, so Griffin Park was our destination.

If I'd planned this volunteer shift earlier, I wouldn't have bothered taking our carved pumpkins to Praise's house and instead would have taken them to the park with us this evening. I didn't regret that extra trip, though, because it had allowed Euclid to lead me to Linette's house, where I'd overheard her conversation with Barclay about Genevieve's will.

We left Flossie, Fancy, and Stardust at the carriage house with Auntie O, who'd returned from dinner with friends and now planned to spend a quiet evening reading and watching television. Callum and I headed to the park in his truck and found Praise and five other volunteers gathered at the pavilion. Praise explained that she wanted the decorative jack-o'-lanterns to fill in the gaps between the sculptures and to line the pathways. Small carved pumpkins needed to be affixed to all the stakes on the archway Callum and I had set up previously, to create the jack-o'-lantern tunnel. Those pumpkins would be lit with battery-operated LED candles. We didn't need any real candles falling out and landing on someone's head or clothes.

All of us, including Praise, got to work moving pumpkins from the beds of two volunteers' pickup trucks. Once we'd emptied each truck, the drivers then returned to Praise's house to pick up another load. Apparently, many more volunteers had dropped off jack-o'-lanterns since I'd left the ones that Callum, Tessa, Roxy, and I had completed. According to Praise, there were close to two hundred donated jack-o'-lanterns. Since they all had to be set out and fitted with candles, we had our work cut out for us. Fortunately, we had the use of four large wheelbarrows.

As we worked, transporting pumpkins and arranging them in an aesthetically pleasing way, we chatted and generally had a good time. At one point, I returned to the trucks to get another load of jack-o'-lanterns and my gaze drifted across the street. Since my last trip to the trucks, the owners of a beautiful Victorian house had lit up the jack-o'-lanterns decorating their front porch.

I knew the homeowners operated a bed-and-breakfast out of the Victorian. If we hadn't already decided to offer Callum's cabin to his parents, the bed-and-breakfast might have been an option for them. I was about to turn back to my work when the front door of the bed-and-breakfast opened and a man hobbled out on crutches. He made his way to a seating area at one end of the porch and eased himself into a chair. Someone else came out of the house, carrying a mug, which they set on the outdoor coffee table before returning indoors.

It was nearly dark now and the man was all the way across the street, but I was fairly certain he was Enrique Ramos, the trespasser who'd broken his leg when Hattie and I had caught him trying to break into Genevieve's house.

All the other volunteers were busy elsewhere in the park, so I decided to take a short break. I jogged across the street and then slowed my pace as I approached the Victorian.

'Mr Ramos?' I called out as I started up the steps to the porch.

The candles inside the grinning jack-o'-lanterns danced and flickered as he sat forward to peer at me through the semidarkness. 'Who's that?' When I entered the pool of light cast by the bulb by the front door, he frowned. 'I don't think I know you.'

'My name's Georgie Johansen,' I said. 'You don't recognize me?'

'Should I? I don't know much of anyone in this town.'

I stayed standing at the top of the steps. 'You tried to attack me when you were attempting to break into Genevieve Newmont's house.'

Enrique reached for his crutches but didn't try to get up. His face had taken on a guarded expression. 'Why are you here? I never touched you, so you can leave me alone.'

I moved closer and sat in a chair that faced him, the coffee table between us. I was pretty sure he would have struck me if he hadn't fallen and broken his leg, but I decided not to mention that. 'I'm not here to harass you. I just wanted to make sure that you're all right after your accident.'

He regarded me with suspicion, understandably so. 'If you think I was trying to attack you, why do you care?'

That was a fair question.

'I get that you reacted in the heat of the moment,' I said, hoping to put him at ease. 'I don't think it was personal.'

'Of course it wasn't personal,' he grumbled. 'I don't even know you.'

'But you knew Genevieve.'

'So?' His suspicion intensified.

I wasn't sure I'd get any useful information out of him, but I decided to keep trying.

'I didn't know Genevieve for long, but she was a real piece of work,' I said.

He relaxed slightly and released his grip on his crutches. 'That's an understatement.'

He offered nothing further so I tried a slightly different approach.

'I hear you came to Twilight Cove on vacation. Did you choose this destination because you knew Genevieve was here?'

'It's not really a vacation. I just said that to nosy people who were asking why I was in town. I'm still here because I can't drive with this broken leg and my daughter can't come pick me up until the weekend.'

'So you really just came here to see Genevieve?'

'Not that it did any good.' He was back to grumbling. 'That woman was as cold as ice. Didn't care about anyone but herself.'

'I don't suppose you know of anyone who might have wanted to kill her?' I asked.

He narrowed his eyes at me. 'Why are you asking me that?'

I decided to be honest and hoped that would win his trust. 'A friend of mine is one of the suspects, but she didn't do it. I'm hoping the police will catch the real culprit soon so my friend is no longer under suspicion.'

'It wouldn't surprise me if half this town wanted to kill Genevieve,' Enrique said. 'She made enemies everywhere she went. But, like I said, I don't know people here.'

'Maybe someone came from Portland to kill her,' I suggested.

'What?' he challenged. 'Like me?'

A shadow seemed to pass across his face and the belligerence drained out of him. His shoulders sagged and he leaned back in his chair, his face etched with weariness.

'With Genevieve dead, I have no chance of getting compensation. Not that I had any chance when she was alive.' He stared out into the deepening darkness. 'You're not the only one who thinks I make a good suspect. The police have questioned me too.'

'I didn't mean to suggest—'

He cut me off. 'Sure you did. And if I were you, I'd suspect me too. Yes, I wanted to steal those antique watches so I'd have some restitution, but I didn't kill the woman and I don't know who did. I wish I had an alibi, but I heard that the poison that killed her was in a dessert or something, and the police don't know when she got hold of the food. But alibi or not, I'd never commit murder. I may be broke, thanks to Genevieve, but I'm not about to give up being around for my grandchildren. They're everything to me.'

The sadness and weariness on his face tugged at my heart. Maybe he was lying to me, but I didn't think so.

'I'm sorry she treated you so poorly,' I said as I got to my feet. 'And I hope your recovery goes well. Thanks for talking with me.'

I left him there on the porch and returned to my volunteer work. I loaded up a wheelbarrow and navigated the winding paved pathway until I reached the farthest two jack-o'-lantern sculptures. It was hard to tell if the pumpkin sculptures were finished, since they weren't currently lit up and that made it difficult to see exactly what they were meant to be. Complete or not, the competitors weren't working on them at the moment so the area was quiet. Although the orange twinkle lights glowed in the trees, that was the only illumination in the middle of the park where I now worked.

A cold breeze whispered against my skin and I shivered. It was spooky out here on my own. All the other volunteers seemed to be elsewhere at the moment. I decided to move quickly, wanting to get back closer to the pavilion.

Moving as fast as I could, I unloaded the wheelbarrow, setting out the jack-o'-lanterns between the unlit sculptures. When I set down the final pumpkin, next to what I thought was a sculpture of a Tyrannosaurus rex, a leaf crunched somewhere close by.

I froze, staring into the darkness beyond the sculptures. Tree branches swayed in the breeze, but otherwise nothing moved. I strained to hear any further noises, but all was quiet.

It was probably just a raccoon or other small animal, I decided. Nothing to worry about. Nevertheless, I wanted to get back to the brightly lit pavilion, where I'd hopefully find Callum.

As I took a step toward the wheelbarrow, I heard a rustle of movement off to my right.

My gaze snapped to the Tyrannosaurus rex.

A flash of movement drew my gaze upward.

Just in time to see the artfully stacked jack-o'-lanterns tumble down toward me.

TWENTY-EIGHT

I crashed to the ground as pumpkin after pumpkin hit me like a hailstorm of bowling balls. When the bombardment finally stopped, I was face down on the grass, buried beneath a heavy pile of jack-o'-lanterns. I gasped, trying not to panic. My hands grabbed at the grass when I heard footsteps close by.

Somehow, I knew they didn't belong to someone friendly.

'Mind your own business,' a deep voice growled. 'This is your only warning.'

Footsteps sounded again, this time running away from me, first on the grass and then on the paved pathway. I gulped in a breath and took stock of my situation. I didn't feel like I was injured and I thought I might be able to get the pumpkins off my back. As I raised myself up on to my elbows, some of the jack-o'-lanterns shifted and rolled off of me. The load on my back immediately lightened.

I heard running footsteps again, coming my way. I froze, my heart nearly stuttering to a stop.

'Georgie?' Callum called out.

I nearly cried with relief when I heard his voice.

'Under here!' I yelled.

He called to someone else and more footsteps came in my direction. Within seconds, people began lifting the pumpkins off of me. As soon as there was a big enough gap, Callum grabbed my hand and pulled me out from under the rest of the jack-o'-lanterns. They rolled away and I clambered to my feet.

'Are you OK?' Callum asked, his eyes full of concern as they searched me for any obvious signs of injury.

'I think so,' I replied, not liking the slight tremor in my voice.

'What on earth happened?' Praise asked.

She and one of the volunteers had helped Callum shift the pumpkins off of me. The other volunteers came jogging down the path toward us.

I didn't want anyone to see how shaken up I was, but my body betrayed me by trembling. Callum pulled me into his arms and I leaned against him, grateful for his warmth and solidity. Most of all, I was grateful for how safe he made me feel.

'Someone ambushed me,' I explained to the small crowd that stood waiting for an explanation. 'They pushed the dinosaur sculpture over on top of me.'

That garnered several shocked and indignant exclamations.

'Why would anyone do that?' Praise asked.

'Just a stupid prank, maybe,' I said, although I didn't believe that for a second.

When I looked into Callum's eyes, I could see that he too suspected there was far more to it than a simple prank. I wanted to tell him everything, but not with all the others listening in.

'We'll have to get in touch with the team that built the sculpture,' somebody said to Praise as everyone assessed the damage.

The entire dinosaur would need to be put back together. Fortunately, as far as I could tell in the semidarkness, only a few pumpkins had broken. Hopefully all the others could be salvaged.

'I feel terrible that they'll have to build it again,' I said.

'It's not your fault,' Praise assured me. 'Whoever pushed it over is the one responsible. I think the team will be able to rebuild it in time for judging. I'm just glad you weren't badly hurt.' She turned her focus from the destroyed sculpture to all of us standing around her. 'Let's call it a night. I'll text the team that built this sculpture and make sure they get the time they need to fix it. Other than that, there's nothing else for us to do here.'

We began walking back toward the pavilion as a group, but Callum and I soon fell behind the others. I leaned into him as we walked, his arm around my shoulders.

'Are you sure you're OK?' he asked with obvious worry.

'Just a little shaken up. That's all.' I told him about the threat that my ambusher had growled at me. I could feel tension creeping into Callum's body as he listened.

'We need to tell the police,' he said.

I sighed, knowing he was right, but wishing I could go straight home. Callum drove me to the police station and sat next to me, holding my hand, as we waited to speak with an officer. Brody wasn't on duty that night, so I ended up talking to Officer Jenna Blanchet. I'd seen her around before, but this was my first time meeting her.

When I told her about the threat, I explained that I'd spoken to a few people about Genevieve's murder. I didn't admit to conducting my own investigation, though. Instead, I made it sound like I'd simply been gossiping like any other local.

Officer Blanchet filed a report, but there wasn't much else she could do. I had no description to provide and I couldn't even be sure if my assailant had been a man or a woman. Although the voice had been deep and grumbly, it didn't sound natural. Whoever it was had likely disguised their voice. It sounded more like a man, but I couldn't rule out the possibility that a woman was behind the incident.

By the time we made it home and stood on the back porch of the farmhouse, weariness had seeped deep into my bones. Auntie O had brought the animals back to the house before turning in for the night, so they greeted us with exuberant enthusiasm when I opened the back door.

I scooped Stardust into my arms and held her to my chest as Flossie and Fancy bounded down the steps for their final outing of the night. Callum moved in close, cupping my face with one hand while Stardust purred between us.

'Is it all right if I stay tonight?' he asked. 'I don't want to leave you.'

'It's more than all right,' I said. 'I want you here with me.'

Always.

The word popped into my head, unbidden. It was too soon to be thinking such thoughts, but that silent declaration had come from my heart, honest and unfiltered.

One day, I would say it out loud.

TWENTY-NINE

In the light of day, the pumpkin incident felt no less scary, but it stirred up sparks of anger that threatened to ignite a fire inside of me. In our group chat, I let Tessa and Roxy know what had happened to me at the park, making sure to add that I was fine. I also mentioned that I was more determined than ever to clear Tessa's name and identify the real killer. She wrote back to say that the police hadn't questioned her any further and that she regretted asking me to help her. She wanted me to give up the investigation so I wouldn't end up in danger again. Even though I was relieved by the news that the police hadn't been hounding her, I knew it didn't necessarily mean she was off the hook. I wasn't going to give up until Tessa was cleared of suspicion, and I told her that. Roxy supported my position and Tessa eventually backed down, expressing her gratitude with lots of heart emojis.

After completing my morning farm work, I tried to spend a few hours writing. I lasted only one. As much as I enjoyed writing the thriller I was working on, I was too distracted. I kept remembering my assailant's threat and the fear I'd felt as the pumpkins tumbled down on me. I also wondered if it meant that the killer thought I was getting too close to the truth.

When I realized I'd been staring at the blinking cursor on my screen for ten minutes straight, I looked to Flossie and Fancy.

'What do you think, girls? Should I call it quits for the day?'

The spaniels responded with enthusiastic barks, which I took as support for the suggestion. Stardust, too, got excited and scampered around the kitchen before pouncing on a catnip toy she'd left on the floor.

I scooped her into my arms and nuzzled my face against her furry cheek. 'Enablers, all of you. I really should be writing.'

Fancy pointed her nose toward the ceiling and let out a long 'woo-woo'.

'I know,' I said. 'I'll be more productive with my writing once Tessa's name is cleared.'

Flossie agreed with a woof and Stardust added a tiny meow.

'Let's see what I can find online.'

After setting Stardust on the floor, I pulled on a blue hoodie that Callum had left at the house. It was comfy and smelled faintly of him. Wearing it not only warmed me up, but also made me feel safe, just like Callum did. Although the pumpkin incident had fired me up, leaving me all the more determined to identify Genevieve's killer, it had also shaken me up more than I liked to admit. I'd slept well during the night, but probably only because Callum had his arms around me and the dogs and Stardust were sleeping nearby. Now, although Callum was busy checking the farm's fences and tending to the animals, wearing his hoodie made me feel close to him.

Flossie, Fancy, and Stardust accompanied me out on to the back porch, where I sat in a comfy wicker chair with my laptop on my knees. I did a quick search for information on cyanide poisoning from apricot kernels. Most of the information I found was fairly basic and didn't go beyond what I already knew, thanks to Valentina's information and facts I'd learned about cyanide poisoning while writing thrillers. However, when I scrolled farther down the search results, I came across an article about a man who'd eaten apricot kernels as a snack, thinking they weren't much different than almonds. Thanks to a friend telling him that the kernels were poisonous, the man survived. If he hadn't gone straight to the hospital after his friend's intervention, he would have died of cyanide poisoning, just like Genevieve had.

The story, while interesting, didn't help my investigation. The same was true of every other site I looked at. With a sigh, I shut my laptop and took it indoors. Looking around online wasn't getting me anywhere.

Eager to stretch my legs, I walked across the lawn to the carriage house, with the spaniels and Stardust trotting along behind me. When we were halfway to our destination, Stardust put on a burst of speed and scurried past me. She pounced on something – a bug, probably – but she had so much momentum that she ended up doing a somersault. She bounced back to her feet, her eyes so wide and surprised that she looked like a cartoon character.

I laughed and Fancy let out a 'woo'. Stardust ran around me and then leaped clear over Flossie's back. She kept running and the dogs chased after her. She zoomed right up to the carriage house and jumped up into one of the window boxes that was currently bursting with chrysanthemums and ornamental grasses.

Tails from the Crypt 157

I swept the kitten into my arms before she could trample any of the pretty flowers. She and the dogs calmed down once we entered the carriage house to visit with Auntie O. I chatted with my aunt about the Trail of Terror and we hashed out some final details. The rehearsal would take place the following evening and the main event would be the night after that.

Auntie O and I decided to supply treats for the volunteers during the rehearsal. She planned to bake a couple of pumpkin pies to serve and I offered to get an assortment of cupcakes from the local bakery. Instead of calling the bakery to place the order, I decided to do that in person.

I wasn't entirely sure what my next investigative step should be, but I was hoping for a chance to speak with Praise. I hadn't questioned her at the park the night before because there were always other people nearby and I didn't want to ask her any probing questions with anyone other than Callum, Tessa, or Roxy around. At the same time, I wanted to be careful, and I'd promised my aunt and Brody that I would be. So stopping by Praise's house to chat while I was on my own probably wasn't a good idea.

I didn't think Praise could have been the one who threatened me at the park, but Callum couldn't say for sure where she'd been before showing up to help me out from under the pile of pumpkins, so I couldn't yet rule her out entirely. That meant I still needed to be cautious around her.

Stardust stayed at the carriage house with Auntie O, who was prepping lunch for herself and a few friends who would soon be joining her for an afternoon of card games. I drove with the dogs into the center of town and I tied their leashes to a bench that sat outside the bakery. The shop had two large picture windows, so I'd be able to keep an eye on the dogs while I was inside.

When I entered the bakery, one customer stood at the counter, purchasing loaves of bread and a box of donuts. While I waited, I studied the contents of the display case. My mouth watered at the sight of a chocolate cake, apple fritters, chocolate croissants, and blondies. My stomach grumbled with hunger, but I barely noticed because I'd spotted almond tarts. According to the small sign in front of the tarts, they were filled with blackberry jelly.

As the customer ahead of me left the bakery, Stacey – the owner – smiled at me from behind the counter.

'How can I help you today, Georgie?'

I asked her about placing an order for two dozen cupcakes and she assured me that she could have them ready the next day. I decided on one dozen pumpkin cupcakes and vanilla cupcakes for the other half of the order. Since my stomach was still rumbling, I also purchased two croissant sandwiches. As Stacey prepared them, my gaze strayed back to the tarts.

'Those almond tarts look delicious,' I said. 'Do you ever fill them with apricot jam?'

'I've only made them with blackberry, cherry, and grape jelly,' Stacey replied as she layered cheese, avocado, tomato, and lettuce on croissant halves. 'And I'm really glad of that now.'

'What do you mean?' I asked.

Even though we were alone, Stacey lowered her voice a notch. 'The police asked me the same thing. You know that lady who died? I heard she was poisoned. Judging by the questions the police asked me, I'm guessing the poison was in tarts filled with apricot jam, or some sort of similar dessert.'

I didn't let on that I thought she was right about that.

'Imagine if word got out that it was apricot tarts that killed her,' Stacey continued. 'If I sold them, it wouldn't matter if the killer got them here or not. Nobody would want to buy mine. They might not even want to buy *anything* from my bakery.'

'I see what you mean,' I said. 'Even a hint of suspicion can be bad for business.'

'Exactly.'

Two more customers entered the bakery. After calling out a greeting to them, Stacey changed the topic of our conversation to the upcoming Trail of Terror, which she planned to attend. A few minutes later, I left the bakery with the sandwiches in a paper bag. Flossie and Fancy sniffed at the bag and then sat in front of me, looking up at me with pleading brown eyes.

'Sorry, but these are for humans only.'

Fancy lay down, letting out a sad whine as she rested her chin on her paws. She raised her eyes again, looking pitiful now. Flossie copied her sister and the combined assault proved too much for me.

'We'll compromise,' I said, giving in. 'I'll get you each a treat at the Pet Palace.'

The dogs jumped to their feet and Fancy gave a 'woo' of happiness. I untied their leashes from the bench and they led the way to their favorite store, their tails wagging. Once I'd bought them each a special dog cookie, we stepped back out on to the sidewalk. I was about to start walking up the hill, toward my car, when I heard a familiar 'hoo-hoo' close by.

Flossie barked and she and Fancy looked up at the nearest old-fashioned streetlamp. Euclid sat perched at the top. As soon as we made eye contact, he took off and flew to the next streetlamp, in the opposite direction from where I'd parked my car. Then he flew to the next one.

'OK, Euclid,' I said quietly. 'We're coming.'

As the dogs and I walked down the hill, in the direction of the ocean, Euclid took flight, disappearing over the rooftops. I'd barely had a chance to wonder why the owl had sent me this way when I noticed Barclay standing on the next corner, his cell phone to his ear. He paced back and forth, not noticing me as the dogs and I drew closer.

'I'm hoping to be there within the week,' I heard him say into his phone. After a pause, he added, 'Yeah, yeah, but those goons won't find me in this town. It's barely big enough to be on a map.' He laughed at that, the sound abrasive and unpleasant to my ears. 'Besides, I've got a plan. I'll be able to pay them back and join you in Mexico.'

His gaze flicked my way and he hurriedly ended the call with a few more words.

'Afternoon,' I greeted, as the dogs and I reached the corner.

Barclay mumbled something in response.

'Are you staying in Twilight Cove for a while?' I asked, pretending I hadn't overheard his plans to leave the country.

He shrugged and stuffed his phone into the back pocket of his jeans. 'My aunt died here,' he said as if I needed to be reminded.

I didn't fail to notice that he didn't answer the question.

I gave him what I hoped was a sympathetic nod. 'I'm sorry for your loss. The funeral's going to be in Portland, right?'

He narrowed suspicious eyes at me. 'What do you care?'

'I was just making conversation.'

'Well, don't,' he grumbled.

With that, he strode off across the street, forcing an oncoming car to come to a quick stop.

Flossie let out a low growl as she watched him leave.

'I know,' I said to her. 'I don't like him either. And it sounds like he owes someone money, maybe someone dangerous. That means his financial situation is even more precarious than we realized.'

I paused before adding, 'And *that* means his motive for murder is stronger than ever.'

THIRTY

It turned out that I wouldn't have found Praise at home even if I'd decided to stop by her place before returning to the farm. When I arrived at the carriage house to check on Stardust, I discovered that Praise was one of the friends Auntie O had invited over to play cards. They were enjoying a light lunch before starting their card games and they invited me to join them. I declined, since I had croissant sandwiches to share with Callum, but I stayed to chat for a few minutes while the spaniels enthusiastically accepted attention from the ladies.

I was about to leave when Auntie O and her friends started clearing the table of their dishes. After sharing a glance with the dogs, I decided I shouldn't pass up the opportunity to speak to Praise.

'I was admiring your green coat the other night when you were here for the Gins and Needles meeting,' I said to her as she passed me on her way back from taking her plate to the sink.

'Oh, thank you,' she said with a smile. 'It's one of my favorites.'

'I think I saw you wearing it at Griffin Park.'

She looked puzzled. 'Last night? I'm so glad you weren't hurt by that prankster, by the way.' I thanked her and she continued. 'But I was wearing a different coat yesterday. The green one is too long for working in.'

'No, before last night,' I said. 'The evening Genevieve died, maybe?'

An expression of sheer panic passed across her face, gone so quickly that I would have missed it if I'd blinked. A forced smile moved in swiftly to replace it, although I thought I could still detect a hint of fear in her eyes.

'You must be thinking of another time. I wasn't at Griffin Park that night.' She practically lunged for the salad bowl sitting on the kitchen table. 'I'd better help clean up.' Hugging the bowl to her chest, she gave me another forced smile. 'Nice to see you again, Georgie.'

She joined in the chatter of the other ladies, so I waved at my aunt and left the carriage house with Stardust riding on my shoulder and the dogs on either side of me. A heavy weight settled in my stomach, silencing my rumbles of hunger.

I liked Praise and I didn't want her to be guilty of anything nefarious, but I had no doubt in my mind that she'd just lied to me.

My appetite returned in time to enjoy the croissant sandwiches with Callum on the back porch of the farmhouse. As we finished eating, Dr Mahika Sharma pulled up in her truck for a visit we'd scheduled a few days earlier. She was going to check up on Tootsie and Twiggy to see how they were recuperating. I felt optimistic that she'd be pleased with their progress, and that turned out to be the case. When she finished examining Twiggy and Tootsie, she declared them ready to join the other donkeys.

That good news helped to ease the worry that had settled inside me after speaking with Praise. Callum suggested we take things slow by first putting Tootsie and Twiggy in a pasture next to the one where the other donkeys were grazing. That way the two groups could get to know each other while still having their own space. Hopefully it wouldn't be long before the newcomers were fully integrated into the herd.

'You two are the cutest,' I said as I gave each of Twiggy and Tootsie a kiss on the nose.

From outside the pasture, Fancy let out a 'woo' of protest.

'The cutest new donkeys at the sanctuary,' I amended, not wanting to upset the other donkeys either. 'You and Flossie are definitely the cutest dogs in the world,' I said to Fancy.

This time her 'woo-woo' sounded like one of agreement.

Grinning, Callum ran a hand along Tootsie's back and shook his head. 'I swear those dogs understand everything.'

Fortunately, he didn't seem to be expecting any form of response from me.

We moved Tootsie and Twiggy to their new pasture and spent a while watching as the donkeys on the other side of the fence eyed the newcomers with curiosity. Charlie, one of the most outgoing of the donkeys who'd been living at the farm for a while, walked right up to the fence and peered at his new neighbors. Eventually, Twiggy ventured close enough to sniff at Charlie. When they touched noses and seemed to make friends, I couldn't help but smile. Glancing over at Callum, I saw a grin on his face too.

I couldn't *not* kiss him in that moment.

'What was that for?' he asked when I pulled back, his green eyes alight with happiness and a little heat.

'Just because I love you.'

It felt so good to say those words out loud. It was as if I'd had caged birds inside my heart, longing for freedom. The first time I'd told Callum I loved him, those birds had taken flight. The man still gave me butterflies, though, and I hoped those would never go away.

'I love you too, Georgie.'

We kissed again, until Twiggy pushed her nose between us, wanting our attention. We laughed and fussed over the donkeys some more. A little later, we made a quick trip to the pumpkin patch, this time to pick out pumpkins to decorate the farmhouse. I had a few small ones on the front and back porches already, but I wanted to buy some larger ones to carve and light up.

Auntie O had warned me that we wouldn't get any trick-or-treaters, other than the four kids who lived two properties away. They always stopped on their way into the center of town, where the distance between each house was far shorter. Nevertheless, we would have plenty of visitors at the farm on the night of the Trail of Terror, and I wanted the house to look festive. Besides, I loved pumpkins, jack-o'-lanterns, and all things autumnal. Even if no one else saw the house, I'd still want to decorate it for my own enjoyment.

During the drive to the pumpkin patch, I shared my concerns about Praise with Callum. He encouraged me to listen to my instincts and gut feelings, and to be careful around Praise and everyone else on my suspect list. That evening, when Tessa came over to carve pumpkins with us again, she echoed Callum's sentiments.

While we cut faces into our hollowed-out pumpkins, I told them about my encounter with Barclay that morning.

'I've never met the guy, but I don't like him.' Callum looked so serious and concerned that I felt a tug on my heart.

I reached over and gave his hand a squeeze, not caring that I ended up with some pumpkin guts on my fingers. 'Neither do I.'

He entwined his fingers with mine. The little line between his eyebrows hadn't disappeared. 'Please stay away from him if you can.'

'I will,' I assured him. 'I don't think there's much point in trying to talk to him again anyway. He's not about to be open with me.'

'And it sounds like he could have some dodgy characters coming after him for money,' Tessa said. 'Didn't you say that he likes to gamble?'

I'd mentioned that in our group chat. 'That's what I overheard Linette and his friends say.'

'It would be best for all of us to steer clear of him,' Callum said. 'Killer or not, he sounds like he's nothing but trouble.'

I sized up my pumpkin, deciding where the nose should go. 'Hopefully I've seen the last of him. I wouldn't mind if he left town, except for the fact that the police might have a harder time arresting him if he's the poisoner.'

By the time I moved on to scraping out my second pumpkin of the evening, the conversation had turned away from Genevieve's murder.

'I think volunteering here at the sanctuary has done Roxy a world of good,' Tessa said as she carved intricate eyes into her pumpkin. She had far more artistic talent than I did.

'That's good to hear.' Callum picked up a knife, ready to work on his second jack-o'-lantern of the night.

He had even less artistic talent than I did, but I still thought his clumsily carved pumpkins had a certain goofy charm about them. Maybe it was ridiculous, but seeing him take on the task – even though he knew it wasn't something he was good at – warmed my heart.

Wow. I really had it bad. But that wasn't news to me.

'Have you noticed a difference with Roxy at school?' I asked Tessa, trying to keep my mind on track.

'Definitely,' she replied. 'She's more confident and she just seems like a happier kid. Having her dad back in her life has probably helped with that, but I'm sure working here at the sanctuary is part of it too. It's early in the school year, but I think she's applying herself more in her classes.'

'I'm glad it's helping her,' I said, my heart happy. I'd grown fond of Roxy over the past several months and wanted to see her thrive. 'I think Callum's been a good role model for her.'

He glanced at me with surprise as he carved a triangular nose into his pumpkin. 'I think *you've* been a good role model.'

I shrugged. 'Showing her the ropes on the farm, giving her free riding lessons . . . you've done a lot for her.'

'I think you're both great role models for her,' Tessa said. 'And inviting her to join us for our baseball practices was a great idea. She really enjoys it.'

Back in the summer, we'd started getting together with some of our friends to play baseball. Callum was hoping we'd form a team and join the local adult fun league next spring. I loved learning how to play the sport that was so much a part of Callum, but I hadn't yet committed to joining the team. I definitely needed more practice first. And hopefully plenty of private lessons with Callum.

He nodded in response to what Tessa had said. 'Roxy's got talent. I'm hoping she'll have a chance to build on it and see her potential. If she could actually believe that she's good at something . . . that would be a big deal for her.'

Tessa sighed and stopped carving for a moment. 'Too bad there's no softball team for girls her age in Twilight Cove.'

'Not even at the high school?' I asked with surprise.

She shook her head. 'The teacher who coached the girls' softball team retired a few years ago and Coach Branstad – who's in charge of the boys' baseball team – didn't want to take on the extra work, so there hasn't been a girls' team for ages.'

'About that . . .' Callum said. When we both looked to him, he continued, 'I'm thinking of having a chat with the school principal. Tessa, I was going to ask if you could introduce me sometime soon.'

I set down the knife I was using. 'Are you thinking of coaching at the high school?'

'If they'll have me. Just the girls' team, though. I don't want to step on Coach Branstad's toes.'

'Oh my gosh!' Tessa exclaimed with delight. '*If* they'll have you? A former MLB player? They'd be nuts to turn you down!'

I threw my arms around Callum and gave him a hug, not caring if we got pumpkin guts on each other. 'That's amazing!'

He looked into my eyes. 'You think so?'

I beamed at him. 'Absolutely. Especially if Roxy can be on the team.'

'As far as I'm concerned, she's got a place if she wants it,' Callum said, 'but I'm not going to mention it to her until I know if it's going to happen.'

'Good idea,' Tessa agreed. 'We don't want her getting her hopes up just to have them crushed.'

'I'm keeping my fingers crossed,' I said. 'It would be amazing for Roxy and for you too, Callum. I know how much you love baseball.'

'How come you didn't go into coaching when you retired?' Tessa asked as she got back to carving her pumpkin, now adding a nose with flames spurting out of the nostrils.

'I had a couple of offers at the time,' Callum said, telling Tessa what he'd already shared with me in the past. 'But I grew up on a ranch and I missed working on the land, tending to animals. Baseball is in my blood, but so is farming. It just seemed like the right move at this point in my life.'

'Makes sense.' Tessa removed a chunk of pumpkin, revealing more of the face that was taking shape. 'I'm glad you moved here and I know Georgie's *really* glad you did.' She gave me a sidelong glance and a smile.

Callum held my gaze as he said, 'It's one of the best decisions I've ever made.'

'Ooh!' Tessa exclaimed with delight. 'You two are so cute!'

Callum laughed and I felt my cheeks flush, though I also couldn't help but smile. Across the room, my phone buzzed on the kitchen counter. I washed and dried my hands before opening the text message I'd received.

'It's from Roxy,' I told the others as I accessed the message.

Ghost lights at vic's house, she'd written. **Meet me?**

'Is something wrong?' Tessa asked, probably noticing the worry on my face.

'I'm not sure,' I replied. 'But I think we'd better go ghost hunting.'

THIRTY-ONE

'I should have made Roxy explicitly promise that she wouldn't do any investigating on her own,' I said as Callum drove us to Genevieve's house.

Anxiety coiled inside me like a tightly wound spring. The fact that Roxy was poking around Genevieve's house after dark was bad enough. If she decided we were taking too long to meet her and tried to get a closer look at the so-called ghost lights, she could end up in real trouble. Maybe even in danger.

I'd texted her a reply right away, telling her that we were on our way and not to do anything until we got there, but Roxy could be reckless and impulsive. I didn't feel entirely confident that she'd follow my instructions.

'It's probably just those kids filming their horror movie again,' Tessa said from the back seat, where she sat with Fancy and Flossie on either side of her.

I bounced my knee up and down, needing a release for my nervous energy. 'I hope so.'

I directed Callum to Genevieve's street and he pulled into a free parking spot in front of her dark house. The truck had barely stopped when I jumped out of the cab. I couldn't see any lights in or around Genevieve's house, and I couldn't see anyone out on the street either. Then a shape melted out from behind a tree and I nearly jumped out of my skin.

'Roxy.' I pressed a hand to my chest. 'You nearly gave me a heart attack.'

She wore black cargo pants and a black sweatshirt with the hood pulled up. She blended in with the shadows and I hoped that wasn't because she had plans for breaking and entering.

She swept the hood off her head as Flossie and Fancy ran up to greet her.

'Please tell me you didn't come here to break into Genevieve's house,' I said.

She crouched down to hug the spaniels. 'Of course not,' she said as if it were silly of me to even think that.

I, however, didn't think my suspicion was entirely unfounded.

'I'm only here because Robbie and his friends came running home and told me they'd seen ghost lights at the murder victim's house.'

'What were they doing here?' Callum asked.

'Filming their stupid movie again,' Roxy replied. 'The cops told them not to come back here, but they didn't listen. They sure high-tailed it home when they saw the lights, though.'

'Ghost lights,' Tessa said with more than just a hint of skepticism.

'Supposedly.' Roxy gave the dogs a final pat each and stood up. 'I don't believe in ghosts. I bet it's someone who's very much alive.'

'Then we should call the police,' Callum said. 'Do you know how long it's been since the kids saw the lights?'

Roxy shrugged. 'I saw a light right before I texted Georgie. And again two minutes ago.'

We all turned to stare at the house with its dark, blank windows. At first, we didn't see anything, but then a beam of light flashed in an upstairs room.

Callum pulled his phone from his pocket and called 911.

'The killer probably wants something of Genevieve's,' Roxy said. 'Maybe that's even why he killed her.'

'The killer could be a woman,' Tessa interjected.

'Maybe,' Roxy said, sounding thoroughly unconvinced, 'but I'm betting it's Mr Schmidt. He was obsessed with Genevieve and he's, like, crazy for math.' She said that as if those two things clearly proved him to be a killer.

'Hey, I like math,' Callum protested as he ended his call.

'Yeah, but he's nuts about it.' Roxy shrugged one shoulder. 'Plus, you like baseball so that's cool.'

That got a half-grin out of Callum before he said, 'There's a patrol car on the way.'

'Let's not jump to any conclusions,' I advised Roxy as I returned my attention to the house.

The light we'd seen in the upstairs room had disappeared, leaving the place entirely dark again.

Beside me, Flossie gave a sudden bark, making my heart jump in my chest. Before I had a chance to give her head a reassuring pat, she and Fancy took off toward the house.

'Flossie!' I whisper-shouted. 'Fancy!'

The spaniels disappeared around the back.

'They're going to catch the killer!' Roxy said with excitement. Then she chased after the spaniels.

'Roxy!' Callum called out, not quite shouting but definitely not whispering.

She, too, disappeared around the side of the house.

Callum broke into a run and Tessa and I hurried to follow him. We had to slow down after we passed through the open gate at the side of the house. Without any light from the streetlamps, the darkness was deeper there and I didn't want to trip and break my leg like Enrique had.

'Hey!' I heard Roxy yell just before we made it around to the back of the house.

Flossie and Fancy barked frantically as they jumped at a shadowy figure that was clambering over the back fence. Fancy leaped higher and grabbed on to the person's shirt. There was a ripping sound and a grunt from the figure, but then the prowler disappeared over the fence and into the alley. Pounding footsteps suggested that they were making a quick getaway.

Roxy ran to the back gate and was about to open the latch when Callum yelled out, 'Roxy, stop!'

'They're getting away!' she protested, but she stayed put.

We reached her side and stopped, out of breath. Well, I was out of breath, but Callum and Tessa didn't seem to be. I was in decent shape, but fear and worry were constricting my chest, making it hard to draw air into my lungs. Callum must have noticed, because he rested a comforting hand on my lower back. As if his touch were magic, the pressure on my chest instantly eased.

'If you open the gate, the dogs will take off again,' I warned Roxy. 'We don't know what that person would be willing to do to them.'

That gave her pause. She dropped her hand from the latch and turned on her phone's flashlight app. 'Hey,' she said crouching down in front of Fancy. 'What's that you've got, girl?'

Fancy proudly dropped a scrap of dark green fabric into Roxy's hands. The spaniel sat next to her sister, looking pleased with herself, while Roxy straightened up and held the fabric between her thumb and forefinger.

'Way to go, Fancy!' she praised.

Fancy let out a proud 'a-woo' and wagged her tail.

'At least we got a clue,' Roxy said.

'We should give it to the police,' I advised. 'They'll be here any minute.'

'And we don't want them mistaking us for prowlers,' Callum added.

The four of us hustled to the front yard with Flossie and Fancy bounding ahead of us. They seemed to be having a great time, but my nerves were frazzled.

We made it to the front yard just in time to see a police cruiser pull in behind Callum's truck.

'It's Brody,' Tessa said when the driver climbed out of the vehicle.

Her voice held a mixture of relief and wariness, and I thought I knew why. It was nice to deal with a friend, but I didn't think she and Brody had talked at all since she'd become a suspect in the murder investigation.

Brody joined us on the front lawn and we quickly explained what had happened. Roxy handed over the scrap of fabric, which Brody placed in a plastic evidence bag. Then he had us wait out front while he took a quick look around the back.

'There's no sign of forced entry, but the back door was unlocked,' he reported when he returned.

'Was it left that way or did the burglar have a key?' I wondered out loud.

'I'll check with the officers who responded to the last incident here,' Brody said. 'They probably checked the doors before they left the scene, but I'd like to be sure.'

'The door must have been locked,' I said, still thinking out loud, 'because Enrique was trying to break in. He would have tried the door before he started jimmying the lock.'

'If it *was* locked and there's no sign of forced entry, that means the burglar had a key,' Roxy added.

Callum spoke up next. 'Genevieve's nephew might have a key.' I'd been about to say the same thing.

Brody held up a hand. 'I'm going to stop you there. You don't need to theorize. My colleagues and I will take care of it.'

Suitably chastised, we fell quiet.

'You can all head home now,' Brody said. 'There's another officer on his way. When he gets here, we're going to take a look inside to see if anything's been disturbed.' He paused before adding, 'Tessa, can I have a word?'

She glanced at the rest of us and then nodded.

I herded the dogs into the truck and Roxy climbed into the back seat with them. Then Callum and I got into the front and shut the doors, giving Brody and Tessa some privacy.

It was too dark for me to see Tessa's expression clearly, but I could tell that Brody was doing most of the talking. After a moment, he touched a hand to her arm and she nodded. Then she came over and opened the passenger door. I slid along the bench seat, closer to Callum, so she could sit next to me.

We waved to Brody as Callum pulled away from the curb.

'You OK?' I asked Tessa quietly.

She nodded, but she seemed subdued.

'All we have to do is find the owner of the ripped shirt and then we'll know who the burglar is,' Roxy said, leaning forward from the back seat. 'And there's a good chance that the burglar and the killer are the same person, so Fancy's clue could crack the entire case.'

The dog in question threw her head back and let out a long 'woo' of pride.

'Don't let it go to your head,' I warned her, looking over my shoulder. 'After all, you shouldn't have gone running off like that.'

Fancy grumbled as she lay down on the seat, resting her chin on Roxy's lap.

'Don't worry,' Roxy whispered as she stroked Fancy's head. 'I think you and Flossie are heroes.'

Fancy bounced up to a sitting position and licked Roxy's face while Flossie let out a happy bark.

'I appreciate that you got the clue,' I said, shifting in my seat so I could look back at Fancy again. 'It just freaks me out when you run headlong into danger.' I turned my gaze to Roxy. 'That goes for you too.'

Callum glanced my way. 'And I could say the same about you.' He had a grin on his face, but I knew he wasn't entirely kidding.

'OK, so maybe I haven't set the best example in the past,' I conceded, 'but I do *try* not to put myself in danger.'

Callum took one hand off the steering wheel so he could squeeze my knee. 'I know you do. And, I have to admit, I kind of like being one of your sidekicks.'

Flossie let out a yip and Fancy followed it up with a 'woo-woo'.

'I think *all* of us humans are the sidekicks,' Roxy said. 'It's Flossie and Fancy who are really in charge.'

I laughed. 'I'm pretty sure you're right about that.'

This time Fancy's 'woo' lasted a good three seconds.

We all laughed, even Tessa, who seemed more like her usual self now.

'Sleuths or sidekicks,' I said after a moment, 'I think it's time to call it a night.'

THIRTY-TWO

I woke up slowly the next morning. With my eyes still shut, I reached for Callum, seeking the warmth and comfort of his solid body. My hand found nothing but blankets. I cracked open one eye and saw that his side of the bed was empty.

Disappointed, I closed my eyes and thought I would drift off to sleep again, but my mind had other ideas. What was it that the burglar wanted from Genevieve's house? How could I figure out who had a torn shirt that matched the scrap of fabric Fancy had ripped from the fleeing prowler?

Those questions and others circled in my head, making it impossible to fall back asleep. It also didn't help that I could sense the emptiness of the room around me. I was used to having Stardust and the dogs climbing all over me as I woke up. It also hadn't taken long for me to get used to waking up next to Callum each morning. Today, however, the room practically buzzed with the absence of my boyfriend and the animals.

Hearing footsteps in the hall, I rolled on to my back and rubbed my eyes. When I opened them, Callum was coming into the room, dressed in jeans and a T-shirt. His easy grin woke up the slumbering butterflies in my chest.

Would he ever stop having that effect on me? I hoped not.

'Did I sleep late?' I asked after letting out a yawn.

'No, I just woke up extra early.' He took a seat on the edge of the bed, causing the mattress to dip slightly. 'The dogs are outside and Stardust is playing with one of her toys in the kitchen.'

I sat up and brushed a wavy lock of hair off my forehead. Callum then tucked it behind my ear.

'Your parents' visit is getting close,' I said as my mind became more alert.

'They'll be here in three days. I'm excited to see them.' He took my hand and skimmed his thumb over my knuckles. 'Are you nervous?'

Instead of answering his question, I blurted out one of my own. 'Did they like your ex-wife?' Heat rushed to my cheeks, then to the rest of my face. 'I'm sorry,' I hurried to add. 'Forget I asked that. It's a stupid question.' I stared at my blanket-covered legs, my face burning.

'Hey.' Callum touched my arm. 'It's not a stupid question, Georgie. You can ask me anything, anytime.'

I kept staring at my lap. 'Still, you don't have to answer.'

'Georgie.'

When I kept my gaze firmly away from his, he put two fingers to my chin and turned my face gently in his direction. Even though his eyes held nothing but kindness and love, I still felt silly for asking about his ex-wife.

'I want to answer any question that's on your mind.' He clasped one of my hands with both of his. 'My parents liked Vanessa, but they never grew close to her. They never saw much of her, to be honest. Even so, right from the beginning, they sensed that we weren't a good match. They never said that to me at the time, and they always supported me, but after Vanessa and I separated, my parents admitted that they'd had reservations from the start.'

'Because you rushed into the marriage?'

I knew from past conversations that Callum and Vanessa Lee Raine – an actress – had married in a spontaneous ceremony in Vegas after a whirlwind romance of just a few weeks. Three years later, they'd divorced amicably. He'd offered up those details voluntarily and I'd never pressed for more. Until now.

'Partly because we rushed things, but mostly because my parents could see that our lives didn't fit together,' Callum replied. 'Vanessa is very much a city girl and always will be. She loves parties and an exciting nightlife. I've always preferred a quieter life. I enjoyed seeing different cities when I was playing baseball professionally, but I'll always be a country boy at heart. And Vanessa and I were just better off as friends. Officially, we were married for three years, but we separated after barely more than one year, and because of our schedules, we weren't together much during that time.'

'Do you think things would have turned out differently if you'd had more time together?' Now that I'd started asking questions, I couldn't seem to stop. Nerves danced in the center of my chest, stirred up by the thought that I might get an answer I didn't want to hear, but I knew it was best to know the truth, whatever it might be.

Callum considered the question before responding. 'I think the marriage would have ended even sooner. Sure, the whirlwind romance part was great, but when it came down to living in real life, we were such different people and we wanted such different futures. We both knew we'd made a mistake rushing into the marriage. We're good as friends, but not as spouses. It didn't take long to figure that out. It's not like we fought a lot or anything. I'm not sure we even drifted apart. It's more like we realized that we were never really that close to begin with.'

I let his words sink in, felt them slide smoothly over my heart and ease the worst of my nerves. Then a smile tugged at my lips. 'I never would have pegged you as a spontaneous-wedding-in-Vegas sort of guy.'

Callum laughed. 'That's because I'm not really. Certainly not anymore.' He shook his head as he thought things over. 'Back then, when I was twenty-seven, a lot of my friends and teammates were getting married, having kids, building families. Meanwhile, I was coming home to an empty apartment whenever we weren't on the road. I wanted what my buddies had. I think that's why I rushed into things with Vanessa. I'm more aware now – aware of what I really want and what I really need in my life.'

I hoped that meant that *I* was what he really wanted and needed in his life. I was, if the way he was looking at me right now was any indication.

I bit my bottom lip, unable to banish the last few worries and insecurities that were still living their best life inside my head that morning.

Callum brushed the back of one finger along my cheekbone. 'Georgie, you don't have anything to worry about. My parents know I've got my head on right this time. And you don't need to compare yourself to Vanessa. This is in no way a competition. Even if it were, you've already won because you're so right for me.'

His words made my heart sing, but those last pesky worries wouldn't leave me alone.

'Vanessa's an actress,' I pointed out. 'I'm just an introverted, totally-not-famous writer. Are you sure your parents don't want more than that for you?'

Callum shifted closer to me, still holding my hand. 'First of all, you're not *just* anything. You're *everything*. Everything I want and need. My parents know that. All you have to do is be yourself and they're going to love you. Like I said weeks ago, they're already fans of yours, just from hearing me talk about you all the time.'

That brought a smile to my face. To my relief, I realized that the last of my anxieties had quieted down. Maybe they hadn't gone away completely, but Callum's words – and the sincerity behind them – had left them greatly subdued.

I traced my finger along his collarbone before raising my eyes to meet his. 'Thank you.'

'I meant it when I said you can ask me anything.' Callum kissed the top of my head and ran a hand down my arm, leaving behind a trail of tingles. 'Now I've got a question for you: is it all right if I make us some pancakes?'

I smiled again. 'Of course. You don't have to ask.'

'It's your house. I don't want to impose or be presumptuous.'

'Mi casa es tu casa.' I put a hand to the side of his face and made sure he was looking into my eyes when I added, 'Really, Callum.'

The heat that flared in his green eyes warmed my skin. I happily fell back against my pillow as he kissed me. When our lips parted, he was leaning over me, propped up with a hand on either side of my head.

'On second thought,' he said, looking down at me with so much love that I thought my heart might burst, 'maybe the pancakes can wait.'

The questions that had haunted me upon waking that morning didn't leave me alone for long. By the time Callum and I had finished breakfast and had started in on the morning farm chores, Tessa's predicament and the unsolved mystery of Genevieve's murder were back to occupying much of my thoughts.

Unfortunately, I likely wouldn't have time for sleuthing that day. The volunteer actors for the Trail of Terror would show up at the farm that evening for a rehearsal. Tomorrow night, the main event would take place. That meant there wasn't much time left to take care of all the final preparations.

Although Auntie O and I had already mapped out the route that the event attendees would walk on Halloween night, we still needed to mark the path with battery-operated paper lanterns, and there were plenty of props and spooky decorations that had to be put in place. As soon as I'd finished tending the animals that morning I made a quick trip to the bakery, where I picked up our order of two dozen cupcakes. Then I stopped in at the hardware store. The owners of that business had donated the paper lanterns and LED lights we needed, and they helped me load the boxed donations into my car.

When I returned home, I got to work with Auntie O, decorating the farm's entrance. Later, we would prepare the path that led through the fields and the woods.

I was in the midst of setting up a display at the side of the driveway when Linette drove on to the farm. I finished stacking bales of straw and used them to prop up a large wooden sign declaring the farm to be the site of the Trail of Terror. Tessa had painted the sign a couple of weeks ago and decorated it with ghosts and other spooky creatures. I would add some pumpkins and two little spotlights to the display later, but for the moment I took a break and headed over to the carriage house, where Linette had parked. Auntie O had already come out to greet her and they stood chatting next to Linette's car.

Flossie and Fancy usually came to greet any new visitors to the farm, but they'd followed Callum off into one of the back fields earlier and had yet to return. Stardust had spent the first part of the morning hanging out in the barn, but now she was shut safely away in the farmhouse.

'As promised, I brought you some props from the Twilight Players' collection,' Linette was saying as I approached her and Auntie O.

'We can't thank you and the theater group enough for the loan,' my aunt said as Linette opened the trunk of her car.

I echoed her sentiments as I joined them.

Inside the trunk, we found two full-sized skeletons and a battery-operated witch with eyes that glowed red when she cackled. There was also a scary-looking scarecrow and, sitting in the front passenger seat, an animatronic man holding his detached head under one arm. Linette told us he had a motion sensor and would laugh and say creepy phrases whenever someone walked past him. In the back seat were several fake tombstones which I thought would look quite real at night. She'd also brought us three fog machines on loan from the theater group. Most of the props were left over from a haunted house event the Twilight Players had run two years ago.

'I wish I could stay and help you set up,' Linette said after we'd unloaded all of the items from her car. 'But I need to get home and make sure Genevieve's nephew hits the road.'

'He's leaving town?' I asked, even though that didn't come as a surprise to me, considering the conversation I'd overheard the previous day. I just worried he'd manage to evade the police if they discovered, after his departure, that he was guilty of killing his aunt.

'As terrible as it sounds, I hope so,' Linette confessed. 'I put him up for the last couple of nights since he ran out of money and couldn't afford a hotel. Or so he said, anyway. He still had enough money to stay out drinking. He came home at two a.m. last night and woke me up with all his stumbling about. He said he was leaving yesterday, but he didn't. I'm hoping the same thing doesn't happen again today.'

She and Auntie O chatted for another minute while I sorted through the props. Then Linette drove off, heading for home.

'We're going to need some fog machine fluid,' my aunt said as she checked over the machines on loan to us. 'There's half a jug here, but that won't be nearly enough.'

I made a couple of quick phone calls to find out where we could acquire the fluid. The only place nearby that had some in stock was a big box store on the highway a few miles outside of town.

'I can make a quick trip out there later,' I offered after tucking my phone back in my pocket. 'It shouldn't take long.'

'You'd better get a few jugs,' Auntie O advised. 'We want to test out the machines tonight and we'll be using them for a few hours tomorrow.'

'They told me they've got a fair bit in stock, so that shouldn't be a problem.'

A few hours later, after making good progress with the Trail of Terror preparations, I headed for my car. Flossie and Fancy had been hanging out with the goats, but they came racing toward me when they saw me getting ready to leave.

'You're just in time,' I told them as I gave them both pats on the head. 'We've got an errand to run. And,' I added more quietly as I opened the door of my car, 'maybe we can do a little bit of snooping on the way.'

THIRTY-THREE

I didn't know what I was hoping to find when I drove down Linette's street. I didn't think I could come up with a good excuse to knock on her door to see if Barclay was still around. Besides, I'd promised Callum I'd stay away from Genevieve's nephew. Even if I hadn't given him that assurance, I wouldn't have wanted to go near the guy on my own. Of course, if Barclay's sportscar was parked outside Linette's house, it would be obvious that he hadn't left Twilight Cove, but if his car wasn't there, I wouldn't know if he was gone for good or if he'd just left the house temporarily. Should I bother trying to find out?

That question flew from my mind when I saw Miles Schmidt approaching Linette's doorstep, a bouquet of flowers clutched in one hand. I pulled up to the curb one house away and sat there with the windows down. Even from this distance, the flowers caught my eye, highlighted as they were by a beam of late afternoon sunshine. The bouquet was made up of sunflowers and what looked like gerbera daisies in autumnal colors, with sprigs of greenery placed artfully here and there. The arrangement was wrapped in brown paper and tied with an orange ribbon that matched the color palate of the bouquet.

As I watched, Miles knocked on the door and stood waiting until Linette opened it. He said something I couldn't hear and then offered her the flowers. Linette didn't touch them. Instead, she stepped back and slammed the door in Miles's face.

My eyebrows hitched up in surprise. 'All is definitely not rosy there,' I said.

Fancy agreed with a 'woo' from the back seat.

I remembered that Linette had snubbed Miles when we'd had a Trail of Terror meeting at the farm. I wondered if she believed Miles capable of killing Genevieve. I wasn't about to ask her right then, if ever. She didn't look to be in the mood for visitors and I needed to get on with my errand.

Miles, his shoulders slumped, got into his car, taking the flowers with him. I waited until he'd driven away before I continued down the street, noting that Barclay's black car was parked at the curb. He hadn't left town, then. Maybe his continued presence had contributed to Linette's apparent bad mood. She definitely wanted rid of Genevieve's nephew, and I couldn't blame her.

Nevertheless, the fact that Barclay hadn't left town came as a relief to me. I didn't want anything to do with the guy, but if he'd killed Genevieve, then I wanted the police to catch him. That might be difficult if he got across the border into Mexico.

I decided to forget about Barclay for the time being. The Trail of Terror needed my attention for the rest of the day. Maybe in the morning a brilliant sleuthing plan would pop into my head. Unlikely, but I felt like I needed a bolt of inspiration if I was going to help Tessa, and I was even more anxious to do so in light of recent text messages I'd received from her. She'd noticed students eyeing her with suspicion and curiosity in recent days, and conversations often came to an abrupt halt whenever she entered the staff room at the high school.

The rumors and speculation were getting to her and I hated that she was suffering. Somehow, I had to find a way to banish every last molecule of the cloud of suspicion that was following her around.

For now, however, I focused on getting to my next destination.

I realized halfway to the big box store that I probably should have left the dogs at home. I was so used to doing my shopping in Twilight Cove, where I could either take the dogs in the shops or could see them easily when I left them outside the door. I'd never actually come to this strip mall outside of town before. Even though I was able to park close to the store's entrance, I decided that leaving the dogs in the car alone would be a last resort.

I didn't see any signs on the door saying that dogs weren't allowed, so I figured we would walk in and see what happened. Hopefully, we wouldn't get kicked out before I'd found what we needed.

Fortunately, it took me all of two minutes to find the jugs of fog machine fluid and take them to the checkout counter. The woman working the cash register was delighted to see Flossie and Fancy and even came out from behind the counter to pet them. We were out the door within five minutes of entering the store, and no one yelled at me for bringing the dogs along, so I counted the trip as a success.

I was loading the jugs of fluid into the trunk of my car when someone called my name. I looked in the direction of the voice to see Praise hurrying toward me.

'Georgie, I'm glad I ran into you here,' she said. 'This will save me a trip.'

'A trip?' I echoed, puzzled. Only then did I realize she was holding a small jar in one hand and a bouquet of flowers in the other.

Although I'd seen Miles's bouquet only from a distance, this one looked exactly the same. If the two arrangements had come from the same florist, that would explain the same brown paper and orange ribbon. However, the similarity of the flowers, right down to the orange sunflower in the middle, made me wonder if it was the same bouquet Miles had offered to Linette.

Praise presented the jar to me. 'I wanted to give each of the Pumpkin Glow volunteers a jar of my homemade jam or jelly. I remembered that you bought the grape jelly from the farmers' market, so I thought you might like that flavor again. But I've got other kinds in my car if you'd rather have something else.'

'No,' I said, tearing my gaze from the flowers and happily accepting the jar. 'I love the grape jelly. My boyfriend and I have been devouring it. Thank you so much.' I shut the trunk of my car, keeping hold of the jar. 'How's the Pumpkin Glow going?'

'It's all wonderful so far,' she replied with a bright smile. 'The sculpture that got damaged was rebuilt in time for the judging and tonight the park is open to the public.'

'I can't wait to see the sculptures all lit up,' I said. 'I plan to be there on Halloween.'

'I hope you'll enjoy it.'

I let my focus stray back to the bouquet.

'Those are beautiful flowers. Did you buy them locally?'

She smiled at the bouquet. 'They were a gift, actually. They are lovely, aren't they?' She took a step backward. 'I'm afraid I've got to run now, but thanks again for all your help.'

'My pleasure,' I called as she hurried over to her car, parked three stalls away.

I stowed the jar of grape jelly in the cupholder by my seat and drove back into Twilight Cove, wondering if Miles had given up on Linette and set his romantic sights on Praise.

* * *

By the time the actors arrived at the farm for the Trail of Terror rehearsal, we had the walking route lined with battery-operated tealight lanterns and the woods adorned with all manner of spooky decorations. The rehearsal went well, with only a few minor bumps that we soon ironed out. Everyone enjoyed the treats we supplied and we parted ways at the end of the evening with a shared excitement for the main event happening the following night.

The next day, I received an email from one of the producers I was working with, asking me to tweak two scenes in one of my screenplays. I spent much of the morning and early afternoon working on that project until it was done and ready to send back to the producer. Later on, I drove to the high school to pick up Roxy so she could help out with the sanctuary's animals and the preparations for the Trail of Terror. Once the event started, she'd be taking on one of the acting roles.

'No dogs?' Roxy said with disappointment when she got into my car and saw the empty back seat.

'Callum took them for a walk to the beach,' I explained as I pulled away from the curb. He'd done that for me so I'd have plenty of time to pick up Roxy and get ready for the fundraiser. 'But they'll be excited to see you when we get to the farm.'

Roxy looked at the car's clock. 'We have time for some investigating first.'

'I don't know *what* to investigate next,' I confessed. 'Normally, I'd want to know which of my suspects had alibis, but with such a hands-off murder, that's not going to work.'

'We should talk to Hattie,' Roxy decided. 'She's not just one of our suspects, you know; she lived right next door to Genevieve. Maybe she saw or heard something in the days leading up to the murder that would be helpful.'

'You're good at this,' I said with admiration, casting a glance her way as I continued to drive.

She shrugged, but looked pleased by the compliment.

'I guess there's no harm in swinging by Hattie's house,' I added, 'but I think we should make a stop on the way.'

I parked outside the Pet Palace and we made a quick trip inside to buy some cat treats. Hattie was a potential source of information, but she also had a beef with Genevieve and was one of my suspects. I didn't want her to know we were conducting an unofficial investigation into the murder, so I'd come up with an excuse to visit her.

Treats for her cats factored into that plan. However, I didn't leave the pet supply store without picking up treats for Stardust and the dogs as well. It didn't feel right to go to their favorite shop and not buy something for them.

'Georgie, what a nice surprise,' Hattie said a short while later when she opened her front door to find Roxy and me on her porch. 'What can I do for you today?'

'This is Roxy Russo,' I said, indicating the teenager at my side. 'She volunteers at the sanctuary and loves animals.'

'Georgie mentioned that you have cats and the most amazing catio,' Roxy piped up. She held up the package of cat snacks we'd just bought. 'I was wondering if I could see it and meet your cats. We brought treats.'

Hattie beamed at us. 'How thoughtful. Of course you can meet my fur babies. Come on in.'

She seemed so pleased by our visit that I felt a little guilty for having an ulterior motive. Nevertheless, I followed along when she and Roxy passed through the house to the backyard.

'Whoa,' Roxy said with awe when she saw the catio. 'That's so cool!'

Her reaction seemed genuine. There was probably no reason to act, since the catio really was a sight to behold. Roxy also didn't need to pretend to adore Hattie's cats, because that came naturally for her.

'You can go in the catio if you'd like to feed them the treats,' Hattie offered as she unlatched the door to the main enclosure. 'I just need to be careful that—'

She didn't even get to finish her sentence before Sylvester, the tuxedo cat, streaked past her, escaping into the yard.

'Sylvester!' Hattie quickly closed and re-latched the door so the other cats wouldn't get out.

The mischievous black-and-white cat had already disappeared among the bushes lining the back fence.

'Oh dear,' Hattie fretted. 'He always comes back eventually, but I get so nervous when he escapes. I don't want anything bad to happen to him while he's roaming. I bought a GPS tracker for him, but I haven't put it on his collar yet.'

'We'll help you catch him,' I offered. 'He hasn't gone over the fence yet, so maybe we still have a chance.'

'Thank you so much,' Hattie said gratefully.

The three of us spread out across the generous backyard, peeking into the bushes and calling, 'Here, kitty, kitty!'

A black-and-white streak flashed in my peripheral vision.

'He's over this way,' I called to the others as I headed toward the shed that stood in the back corner of the yard.

Roxy jogged over to help me search the area.

'This door is unlatched,' she said once she stood right in front of the shed. 'Maybe Sylvester got inside.'

'No!' Hattie yelled from a few feet away as Roxy opened the door.

Roxy stared into the shed, her eyes wide with surprise.

I moved to her side so I could see what had captured her attention.

My eyes widened too.

Hattie came up behind us. 'You weren't supposed to see that.'

THIRTY-FOUR

'It's not what you think,' Hattie said as Roxy and I stared at the Sasquatch costume lying in a heap on top of a lawnmower.

'Roxy, go wait in the car,' I instructed as I turned my back on the shed, wanting to keep my eyes on Hattie.

'No way,' she said. 'I'm not leaving you alone with a killer.'

'I didn't kill anyone!' Hattie protested.

Then she burst into tears. She stumbled her way over to a bench situated beneath an arbor. She practically collapsed on to the seat and dropped her head into her hands as she sobbed.

Sylvester slipped out from behind a rhododendron bush and padded over to Hattie. He rubbed up against her leg and she picked him up and hugged him, still crying.

I wanted to get Roxy away from Hattie in case she was dangerous, but I also didn't want to give the woman a chance to get rid of the Bigfoot costume before the police had a chance to see it there on her property.

I tried again to get Roxy to wait in the car, but she refused. We stayed a few feet away from Hattie, who continued to cry with Sylvester in her lap, while I called the police station. If I couldn't get through to Brody, I would call 911, but I hoped it wouldn't come to that.

Luck was with me, because Brody was at the station and came on the line within moments. I quickly explained where we were and what we'd discovered. He told me to take Roxy and lock ourselves in my car, and not to worry about the costume. Our safety was more important.

Roxy, however, still refused to budge, and I wasn't leaving without her.

I started the audio recording app on my phone and took a single step closer to Hattie.

'Why do you have the Bigfoot costume if you didn't hurt Genevieve?' I asked.

I hoped that, in her current emotional state, it would take only a bit of prodding for her to confess her crimes.

'I didn't kill Genevieve,' Hattie said, once again denying that offense. 'I just wanted to scare her.'

I didn't know the legalities surrounding an audio recording made by a civilian rather than a police officer, but I wanted the best confession possible, just in case it would be of use, so I tried a question that I hoped wasn't leading.

'What did you do?'

'I scared her off the road,' Hattie admitted through her tears. 'I didn't think she'd crash into a tree. I hoped she'd just end up in the ditch.'

Even that could have caused serious injuries, but I didn't bother saying so.

'But she didn't change her ways, even after the crash,' I said instead, hoping to keep Hattie talking.

'I didn't kill her,' she insisted again. 'I swear.'

Her sobs intensified, making it impossible to get any further coherent statements out of her.

The police arrived. Brody and Officer Blanchet jogged into the yard, heading straight for Hattie, though Brody did send me an unimpressed glance on his way.

Minutes later, while Officer Blanchet led a handcuffed Hattie to the police cruiser parked on the street, I told Brody about the recording I'd made.

'You were supposed to wait in the car,' he reminded me.

'That's my fault,' Roxy said in my defense. 'I wouldn't go and she wouldn't leave me here.'

'That wasn't smart,' he chastised. 'You need to take your safety more seriously.'

Roxy wisely stayed silent after that, as did I, at least until Brody had listened to the audio file.

'Do you believe her denial?' I asked when the recording came to an end.

Brody shrugged. 'We'll see if she has anything more to say at the station. For now, I need a statement from each of you.'

Another cruiser arrived on the scene at that moment. We waited in the front yard while Brody spoke with his colleagues, two of whom headed around to the back of Hattie's house. Meanwhile, Officer Blanchet drove off with Hattie.

Brody had a conversation on his radio, one we couldn't overhear. Finally, he had Roxy and I fill out witness statement forms and then we were free to go.

'But what about the cats?' Roxy asked Brody before we got in my car.

'They're in the house now,' Brody replied. 'Ms Beechwood has a sister in town who's going to look after them as needed.'

That information eased some tension out of my shoulders. Roxy, however, still appeared morose as we drove toward the farm.

'Are you still thinking about the cats?' I asked after a couple of minutes of heavy silence.

Roxy nodded, her shoulders slumped. 'Even if Hattie's sister looks after them, they won't understand why their human is gone.'

'I know,' I said with an ache in my heart. 'But if Hattie didn't kill Genevieve, she might not be gone for long.'

'Do you really think she's not the murderer?'

'I'm not sure what to think,' I admitted. 'She could have killed Genevieve when she scared her off the road, so it's not that far-fetched to think she might have tried another way to get rid of her when that one failed.'

'She probably did it,' Roxy said, her mood gloomy. 'I just wish the killer was someone who didn't have animals.'

'I know,' I said, sharing her sorrow. 'But they'll be well cared for. Let's hold on to that.'

After sharing the news about Hattie with Auntie O, Callum and Tessa – who arrived at the farm less than a minute after Roxy and I returned – we did our best to shake off our sadness. Although it came as a relief to Tessa that the police might have Genevieve's killer in custody, she too wished that the culprit was someone who didn't have animals who relied on them for love and care. We all threw ourselves into the final preparations for the Trail of Terror, wanting to forget about everything else, at least for a while.

That evening, as darkness fell over Twilight Cove and a hint of frost crept over the grass, the rest of the volunteers gathered on the farm. We all wore our costumes and Tessa and a couple of other artistically inclined volunteers applied spooky makeup for anyone not wearing a mask as part of their attire. That included me. I didn't have a role to play along the trail, but I was dressed as a witch, with black robes and a pointed hat, so I would blend in while moving here and there, making sure that everything ran smoothly. Tessa powdered my face to make my skin paler than usual and then painted my eyelids with shimmery green eyeshadow.

Beneath my eyes and at their outside corners she used black liner to draw spiderwebs.

She outlined my lips in black and painted them with dark green lipstick. If I'd tried creating the look myself I would have ended up resembling a clownish swamp monster, but thanks to Tessa's skill I was the very picture of a creepy witch.

Before we got our makeup on, Callum, Tessa, Roxy, and I had gone through the painstaking process of turning on all the battery-operated lanterns along the pathway through the woods. The effect was both magical and eerie, and I couldn't wait to see what the event attendees would think of the atmosphere we'd created.

As the first ticketholders arrived on the farm, everyone took their places. Roxy, dressed up like a ghost girl from a horror movie, with fake hair hanging like a curtain in front of her face, would spend much of the evening on the rope-and-plank swing that Callum had strung up just inside the woods. Small green spotlights stationed nearby gave her a ghastly and supernatural appearance, and when she half whispered, half hissed creepy phrases in different languages – which she'd learned thanks to an app on her phone – the result was so chilling that I had to remind myself that it was Roxy and not really a dead girl.

Callum had the role of a horseback-riding Grim Reaper. He wore a black cloak and had his face painted like a skull. He would wear the hood of the cloak pulled up over his head while he rode Sundance in a clearing in the woods. We'd set up one of the fog machines in that location. When I'd done a walk-through during the previous night's rehearsal, the clearing was a spooky sight to behold. Sundance had walked through the fog, steam rising off her body, as Callum sat on her back, holding a fake scythe and looking so much like the Grim Reaper that a cold tingle ran down my spine.

Other ghoulish characters were spread out through the woods and the fields, some of whom would pop out at those walking the trail or follow after them like hungry zombies. Auntie O was stationed near the barn, where she would divide the attendees into groups which would set out along the trail a few minutes apart.

Linette was the first actor the ticketholders came across, and she played her role perfectly. If I hadn't known it was her beneath the ghostly witch makeup and costume, I never would have guessed her true identity. She embraced the character of the spooky storyteller wholeheartedly, spinning a chilling tale for each group before they set off into the woods.

As the evening wore on, I heard plenty of screams and laughter. Everyone appeared to be having a great time, and when they reached the end of the trail, many hurried over to the small concession stand where Auntie O was now selling hot chocolate and hot apple cider.

'The last two groups are still out on the trail,' my aunt reported when I checked in with her late in the evening, 'but those are the last ones.'

'I'll walk the trail again and check for stragglers,' I said.

With a walkie-talkie in hand, I struck off toward the head of the trail. As I did so, I spoke into the device, letting the actors – who all wore earpieces – know that we were nearing the end of the event, but to keep up their roles for a little while longer until we were sure that everyone had finished the walk.

Since Roxy was the first character anyone would come across on the trail, stationed as she was just inside the tree line, I told her she could call it quits. She pumped her legs to make the swing go higher and then jumped off. When her feet hit the ground, she pulled off her wig and tucked it under one arm.

'Thanks for your help, Roxy,' I said. 'There's hot chocolate and apple cider at the concession. It's free for all volunteers.'

'I creeped out a lot of people tonight.' She sounded pleased.

'You creeped *me* out,' I said.

She laughed and set off across the field toward the hub of activity beyond the barn.

I continued on into the woods. I could hear screams followed by laughter, far off in the distance. I was happy people were having so much fun, and I was even happier that the tickets had sold like hotcakes. Even without the money earned from selling hot drinks, we'd raised an impressive amount for the sanctuary.

At first, I enjoyed the walk through the woods on my own, with the lanterns lighting my way. I met up with five more actors spread out through the woods and told them they were done for the night, making sure to thank them for their help. Then I climbed a small hill, knowing I wasn't far from the clearing where Callum was riding Sundance.

I'd taken only a few steps up the hill when I heard footsteps behind me. I swung around, but the pathway – or what I could see of it before it curved through the trees – was deserted. I stood still, listening carefully, but I heard nothing other than distant laughter and quiet strains of spooky music coming from near the concession stand.

'Who needs actors when you're perfectly good at scaring yourself?' I muttered as I continued on my way.

I took three more steps and stopped again. I could have sworn I'd heard someone moving through the woods, somewhere behind me. Again, I held still and listened, but there was no sign of anyone following me.

I gave my head a shake and quickened my pace. As I crested the small hill, a sudden cackle nearly made me jump out of my skin. I pressed a hand over my heart, which was galloping away in my chest. The animatronic man's eyes glowed red in the head he held under one arm.

'Pass at your own risk!' he said before cackling again.

As my heart began to settle, I started walking once more, my pace even faster now. Clearly, all the Trail of Terror spookiness was getting to me.

I started down the gentle slope, eager to meet up with Callum. Maybe he and Sundance could finish the walk with me. I wasn't too proud to admit to him that I was a scaredy-cat and desperately wanted his company.

I was about to round another bend in the path when the animatronic man let out another cackle. I froze. He only ever did that if something – or someone – set off his motion sensor.

I spun around.

A dark figure charged down the path toward me.

Was this for real or was it one of the actors playing a prank?

I got my answer when the figure – a man – tackled me to the ground.

I hit the hard-packed dirt with a painful thud that jarred my bones.

My attacker rolled me on to my stomach and pinned me to the ground. With my right cheek pressed against the dirt, I struggled beneath the weight pressing down on my back.

'Curiosity killed the cat,' the man growled in my ear. 'And it'll kill you too.'

I jammed an elbow back and made contact with him. He let out a grunt and I took advantage of his momentary surprise to push off from the ground and throw him off my back as I rolled over. I jumped to my feet, but he was already climbing to his as well.

I had only half a second to take in the sight of him – dressed all in black – before I broke into a run.

'Help!' I yelled into the night. 'Callum! Help!'

Footsteps pounded behind me.

I called for help again and ran as fast as I could, the lanterns lighting my way.

The footsteps drew nearer, closing in on me. I tried to run faster, but I could barely get any air into my lungs. My legs burned and my chest tightened. Still, I pushed harder.

Then a most welcome sound met my ears – thundering hooves. As I rounded a bend and broke into the clearing, the Grim Reaper charged toward me on his stately steed, his scythe pointed forward like a lance. I dove off to the side, landing in the tall grass. I heard a yell and a thud. The footsteps and the pounding of hooves both stopped.

'Georgie! Are you OK?' Callum was at my side by the time I got to my knees. He took my hand and pulled me to my feet.

'I'm all right,' I assured him.

Sundance let out a snort, her breath forming a white cloud in the chilly air. On the ground in front of the horse lay my attacker. At first, he looked like nothing more than a heap of black clothing, but then he climbed unsteadily to his feet.

Still grasping his scythe, Callum advanced toward him. He'd taken only two steps when my assailant turned and ran.

Callum adjusted the stirrups attached to Sundance's saddle. 'You ride and I'll walk,' he said. 'I don't want to chase after the guy in the darkness. There are too many tripping hazards, for us and for Sundance.'

'That's OK.' I leaned against Callum instead of climbing on to the horse's back. 'We don't have to chase him. I saw his face.'

He put an arm around me. 'You know who he is?'

I rested my cheek against Callum's shoulder, my trembling slowly starting to ease.

'Yes,' I replied. 'It was Genevieve's nephew, Barclay.'

THIRTY-FIVE

By the time a patrol car arrived at the farm, all of the actors had been called in and many of the event attendees had left without ever knowing anything was amiss. A few stragglers remained, sipping the last of their apple cider or hot chocolate as they wandered toward their cars. They sent curious glances in the direction of the two officers who climbed out of the cruiser, but they continued on their way and soon left the farm.

The actors huddled together, enjoying their drinks and the other treats Auntie O had set out for them. They, too, watched the police with curiosity, but they stayed clustered off to one side, chatting quietly. Meanwhile, Callum, Auntie O, Tessa, Roxy, and I met with the officers, one of whom was Jenna Blanchet.

I told them what had happened in the woods and how I'd identified my attacker as Barclay, Genevieve's nephew.

'He's staying with Linette Mears,' I said to finish.

Hearing her name, Linette broke away from the other actors and came over to join us. She confirmed what I'd said about Barclay staying at her house. She appeared both shocked and concerned when I repeated, briefly, what had happened in the woods.

'If he plans to skip town, he'll go back to my place to get his things,' Linette said after I'd assured her that I was unharmed. 'When I left home late this afternoon, he still had his belongings strewn all over the guest room.'

Officer Blanchet's partner spoke into his radio, asking for a patrol car to attend Linette's residence to look for Barclay. Then the officers took statements from Callum and me before leaving.

As soon as the cruiser turned off the driveway and on to Larkspur Lane, I headed for my car.

Callum easily caught up to me with his long strides and put a hand on my arm. 'Georgie, we should stay here.'

'I need to know if the police catch him.' I reached for my pocket before realizing I was wearing my costume and therefore didn't have my car keys on me. I altered my path and started toward the farmhouse. 'I won't be able to rest if he's still on the loose.'

Callum must have sensed that I wasn't about to change my mind. 'I'm coming with you, then.'

Tessa had kept pace with us as well. 'We can take my car.' She already had her keys out.

Changing my path once again, I hurried toward Tessa's vehicle, my friend and boyfriend accompanying me. Roxy, Flossie, and Fancy ran after us, not wanting to be left out.

'Let me know what happens,' Auntie O called after us as we piled into the car with the dogs.

I assured her that we would, and shut the door. As we pulled out of the driveway, I noticed Linette's car following behind us. Tessa pushed the speed limit and we reached our destination within minutes. When we turned on to Linette's street, we found red and blue police lights flashing in the darkness. Two cruisers sat in the middle of the road. Tessa parked near the corner and we jumped out of the car and jogged along the sidewalk with Flossie and Fancy on their leashes.

Barclay stood in the middle of Linette's front lawn, a suitcase on the ground next to him. Three uniformed police officers and a man in a suit – a detective from the state police, I figured – formed a semicircle before him.

Barclay looked our way as we jogged along the street. 'What is this?' he asked as we reached Linette's front lawn. 'Some kind of Halloween party?'

I realized then that Callum, Tessa, Roxy, and I were still wearing our costumes and makeup from the Trail of Terror.

Barclay stared at the police officers. 'Are you even real cops?'

'We're real cops, all right,' the man in the suit said. He flashed a badge at Barclay. 'Detective Cunningham of the Oregon State Police.' He addressed my friends and me next. 'What are you folks doing here?'

'I'm the one he attacked in the woods half an hour ago,' I said.

'I don't know what you're talking about,' Barclay grumbled.

Linette joined us on the lawn, slightly out of breath. 'Why are you leaving at this hour if you haven't got anything to hide?'

'I'm a night owl, and I'm supposed to meet some friends in Mexico. Nothing illegal about that.'

'Maybe not, but assault *is* a criminal offence,' the detective said. 'And that's why you're under arrest.'

One of the uniformed officers snapped handcuffs on Barclay's wrists while another read him his rights.

One of the leashes went taut in my hand and I noticed that Flossie had crept up close to the suitcase. She sniffed at it and then touched it with one paw. The little padlock holding the zippers together popped open. I glanced around, but no one else had noticed.

As I breathed a sigh of relief, Flossie backed away from the suitcase, keeping her eyes on it. I nearly panicked again when I realized that the zippers were opening, seemingly of their own accord. Fortunately, everyone else was so focused on Barclay that they weren't looking at the suitcase.

Until it fell over and the top popped open, spilling the contents on to the grass.

'Hey!' Barclay protested as Flossie and Fancy nosed around at the items now sitting in a pile on the lawn.

Each dog picked up something and brought it over to drop at my feet. I leaned down to look at the jewelry they left there. One piece was a locket on a gold chain and the other was a bracelet with a charm that matched the enamel rose locket.

I straightened up and looked at Barclay. 'This is Genevieve's jewelry.'

Linette came closer and checked out the rest of the suitcase's spilled contents, which I could now see contained many small valuables, including several watches. 'All of this is Genevieve's.' She glared at Barclay. 'You killed your own aunt?'

'I didn't kill anyone!' Barclay yelled.

'You broke into her house and stole all her valuables!'

'I didn't break in. She gave me a key.'

'You turned your key over to us,' the detective said.

'I made a copy as soon as I found out my aunt had died,' Barclay admitted. 'I just gave you the original.'

The detective's mouth formed a firm line. He inclined his head toward the nearest cruiser. 'Take him to the station.'

The uniformed officers nodded and two of them escorted Barclay to the vehicle.

Flossie fetched something from the spilled contents of the suitcase and dropped it on the grass in front of me. It was a rumpled, dark green shirt with a tear along the hem. I nudged it with the toe of my shoe.

'That's the shirt Fancy tore when the prowler ran from Genevieve's yard two nights ago,' Roxy said before patting my dogs on the head.

The remaining uniformed officer nodded, clearly aware of that incident.

'Get all of this bagged,' the detective said to the officer.

'He thought he was going to inherit,' Linette said, her arms wrapped around herself as she watched the cruiser drive off with Barclay in the back seat. 'He killed her for money, and when he realized she hadn't left him anything, he decided to steal from her estate.' Her voice trembled. 'How *could* he?' She blinked back tears. 'I'm going to call his parents. They need to know what's going on.' She turned and headed into her house.

The detective asked me a few questions about Barclay's assault on me and then he strongly suggested we head home.

I was more than ready to do that. My adrenaline had worn off and all I wanted to do was curl up in bed with Callum's arms around me.

THIRTY-SIX

'So did Barclay kill Genevieve, or did Hattie do it?' Tessa asked the next day when she joined me and Callum at the farmhouse.

It was late in the afternoon on Halloween and we were sitting out on the front porch with steaming mugs of hot apple cider. The dogs and Stardust chased each other out on the lawn while we waited for our one and only group of trick-or-treaters to arrive.

'I'm not sure.' I'd wondered the same thing for much of the night. 'Hattie clearly wasn't averse to harming Genevieve, and I experienced Barclay's violent streak firsthand.'

'Hopefully the police are putting the pieces together as we speak,' Callum said before taking a drink of his cider.

'I'm just glad they don't think I killed Genevieve anymore,' Tessa said. 'Brody called me this morning. The police are pretty sure the killer is either Hattie or Barclay.'

I reached over to squeeze her hand. 'I'm sorry you had to go through the stress of being a suspect, but I'm glad the police are getting closer to the truth.'

Tessa smiled at me. 'It wasn't a fun experience, but you had my back and that means the world to me.'

Callum's phone buzzed and he picked it up from where he'd left it on the porch railing.

'Your parents?' I guessed.

He nodded as he read a text message. 'They just arrived in Baker City. They'll spend the night there and take in the sights in the morning before driving to Twilight Cove. They should be here by late afternoon tomorrow.'

'So I'd better figure out what we want to serve them for dessert,' I said, selecting a recipe book from the pile I'd carried out to the porch with me.

'Is that why you made fresh bread?' Tessa asked. 'For tomorrow's dinner?'

She'd seen – and smelled – the gorgeous loaf of sourdough bread that was currently cooling on the kitchen counter.

'That's why *Callum* made fresh bread,' I said. 'I've discovered that breadmaking is not one of my skills.'

Callum leaned over to kiss my cheek. 'You just need practice.'

I wasn't entirely convinced of that, but I appreciated his confidence in me, no matter how misplaced it might be.

I had an assortment of Auntie O's recipe books on the small table in front of me so I could search for ideas for a dessert to serve when Callum's parents joined us for dinner at the farmhouse the following evening. At the moment, I was flipping through a book passed down to my aunt from her mother. It was filled with handwritten recipes.

Tessa asked Callum about the new donkeys and he filled her in on how well Twiggy and Tootsie were doing while I continued to look at recipes. I flipped the pages of the book and found a recipe for almond tarts. As I read the ingredients and instructions, I realized that the tarts sounded very similar to the ones I'd seen in the bakery's display case.

As delicious as the tarts had looked at the bakery, I wasn't about to add them to our dinner menu. They reminded me too much of Genevieve and her death by cyanide poisoning.

But before I turned the page, something drew me back to the list of ingredients. I read through them again.

'Everything OK, Georgie?' Callum asked a moment later, and I realized I was staring off into the distance.

'I'm not sure.' I grabbed my phone off the table and did a quick search on the internet.

'What is it?' Tessa asked, sensing that I was on to something.

I closed the browser on my phone. 'I think I might know how the police can find evidence of who killed Genevieve.'

It seemed fitting for the sun to send streaks of bright orange across the sky as it set over the Pacific Ocean on Halloween night. The trick-or-treaters from down the road had come and gone, and now Tessa, Callum, and I were heading for Griffin Park so we could see the jack-o'-lantern sculptures in all their glory. The spaniels came with us, but Stardust was back at the carriage house with Auntie O, where the kitten would safely await our return later that night.

By the time we reached the park, it was fully dark and the moon glowed from behind a thin veil of swiftly moving clouds. I caught the scent of woodsmoke on the air when I climbed out of the truck, and leaves crunched underfoot as we made our way down the street to the start of the path that would lead us through the Pumpkin Glow's display.

When we passed through the jack-o'-lantern tunnel, we had to stop and stare around us in wonder. Even the dogs seemed awed by the sight. It was magical having so many lit-up pumpkins arching over our heads. We snapped photo after photo, and I got a cute shot of Flossie and Fancy sitting just inside the tunnel.

When we finally had enough pictures of the glowing tunnel, we set off along the winding pathway that would take us among the various sculptures. We passed a grandfather clock – constructed mostly of carved mini pumpkins – three witches gathered around a cauldron, a fire-breathing dragon, a sea serpent, an Eiffel Tower, a giant turtle, and many other pumpkin statues. Ribbons had been attached to metal stakes that were stuck in the ground, declaring which entries had won prizes. The dragon had come in first, and the Eiffel Tower had captured second place. We hadn't yet come across the third-place sculpture.

We were deep within the park, nearing the end of the display, when we arrived at the Tyrannosaurus rex that had fallen on me the last time I'd visited the park. I knew now that Barclay was the person who'd pushed over the sculpture and threatened me. Our altercation during the Trail of Terror had been his second attempt to warn me off. When he first tackled me in the woods, he'd disguised his voice in the same way as he had at the park. That was evidence enough for me that he was behind both incidents.

'The team did a good job of putting this back together,' I remarked as I took in the sight of the dinosaur that loomed over us, glowing in the darkness. I noticed the third-place ribbon next to the sculpture. 'And they even won a prize, so I guess there was no real harm done.'

'This is so cool!' Tessa exclaimed, pausing to take a picture. 'I really wouldn't want to get buried under it, though. That's a lot of pumpkins! I'm glad you weren't hurt, Georgie.'

'Same,' I said, and Callum squeezed my hand, which he'd held for our stroll through the park.

Fancy let out an 'a-woo' of agreement.

As far as I knew, the police still had Barclay in custody, so I didn't have to worry about a repeat performance of the dinosaur incident. Not that there would be any point in coming after me now that the police knew just as much – if not more – than I did about Barclay's misdeeds.

Callum and I took some photos of our own and Flossie and Fancy reared up on their hind legs as if imitating the T-rex's pose. Laughing, I snapped a shot of their antics before they turned their attention to sniffing the ground around the pumpkins.

Pocketing my phone, I started to walk the length of the sculpture, from the head to the tail, impressed by how the team had put it all together. When I got to the end of the tail, a shadow flickered in my peripheral vision. I leaned around the end of the T-rex's tail and peeked behind the sculpture.

I nearly jumped with fright when I realized that someone was there.

'Linette?' I said with surprise, immediately on edge.

She was crouched behind the jack-o'-lantern dinosaur, her hair messy and her eyes wild.

'Linette, what are you doing?' Tessa asked as she appeared by my side.

I sensed rather than saw Callum move up behind my other shoulder.

Linette forced a laugh and stood up, brushing leaves and twigs from her clothes. 'It's silly of me, but I was just trying to avoid someone I don't get along with. I want to enjoy my evening, you know?'

She gave another laugh, this one sounding slightly crazed.

I took a step back and bumped into Callum's chest. He put his hands on my upper arms to steady me. When I took another step back, he moved with me, and Tessa copied us. I glanced over my shoulder and was relieved to see that Flossie and Fancy were staying behind us.

'We won't bother you, then,' I said, trying my best to smile naturally. 'See you around.'

Zorro suddenly appeared by the head of the dinosaur. Or someone dressed like Zorro, anyway.

'Linette? Everything all right?' Zorro asked.

As soon as he spoke, I realized he was actually Miles Schmidt. He wore a Zorro-style mask and a black outfit, and he had what looked like a real sword and dagger attached to his belt.

'I'm fine, Miles,' Linette replied, clearly annoyed by his presence.

There was a sudden rush of movement around us and several

police officers burst out from among the trees and from behind other sculptures.

Almost as one, Tessa, Callum, and I backed away from Linette. As Detective Cunningham joined the other officers, the annoyance disappeared from Linette's face, leaving her eyes wild again.

'Ms Mears,' the detective said in a loud voice, 'you're under arrest for the murder of Genevieve Newmont.'

THIRTY-SEVEN

In a flash, Linette turned and charged, crashing into Miles. He stumbled backward and by the time he regained his footing, Linette had his dagger. Even though she was shorter than Miles, she managed to wrap an arm around him and point the sharp blade at his throat.

'Don't come any closer!' she warned the police, who now formed a loose circle around her and the sculpture.

Fortunately, Callum, Tessa, the dogs, and I were outside of that circle. I would have liked to be even farther away, but I didn't dare move in case I startled Linette into cutting Miles with the dagger.

I settled for whispering, 'Flossie, Fancy, get back.'

They did as they were told, disappearing behind me.

While barely moving, Callum took hold of my hand and gave it a squeeze. I returned the pressure, my muscles tense as I watched the scene before us.

Detective Cunningham raised a placating hand. 'It's over, ma'am.' He'd ditched his suit jacket for a bulletproof vest. He appeared to be unarmed, but all of the uniformed officers present had their weapons drawn.

'Put down the knife,' Cunningham instructed in a calm but authoritative voice.

Linette shook her head with a deranged light in her eyes. 'You can't arrest me. I did everyone a favor by getting rid of Genevieve.'

'Murder is a crime, even when the victim is unlikable,' Cunningham said.

'No!' Linette shouted. 'Don't you see? I had to do it. She wanted to take everything from me. She wanted to ruin my life! It's always been like that, ever since we were kids. She pretended to be my friend, but she was wicked.'

'Why did you keep up the pretense of friendship with her if she was so terrible?' Miles asked, the steadiness of his voice impressing me.

'It was better than the alternative,' Linette said, her anger causing the dagger to tremble in her hand. 'You should have seen what she did to people who weren't on her side. She destroyed them.'

'But you said she tried to destroy you anyway,' Miles pointed out.

'She couldn't stand to see me happy. She couldn't stand to see me have *anything* good in my life. I moved here to get away from her and then she just followed me.' Linette adjusted her grip on the weapon, the point of the blade brushing against Miles's skin. 'Acting is my passion and she even wanted to take *that* from me. She wanted to join the Twilight Players! She was going to try to get the lead role in every play! She tried to get *my* role at the Trail of Terror!'

'Ma'am, why don't you put down the dagger and we can talk about this,' Cunningham implored.

'Maybe she was born already rotten,' Linette continued, ignoring the detective, 'but her parents made things worse. They spoiled her, told her she was the best. Her poor sister was always an afterthought, always in Genevieve's shadow, just like me. By the time we met in middle school, Genevieve was convinced she was so much better than everyone. But she wasn't. She was mean and cruel and petty and vindictive. But she always got what she wanted. Why do people like that always win?' Tears welled in Linette's eyes, but they subsided as she shook her head in anger. 'I won't let her take my freedom.'

She pressed the point of the dagger against Miles's throat. A line of blood trickled down his neck.

'You're going to let me leave,' she said to the police. 'I'm taking Miles with me.' When she spoke again, she was addressing her hostage. 'You dropped me like a hot potato as soon as Genevieve pretended that she was interested in you. And then you came crawling back to me when she dumped *you*.'

I suspected that he'd set his sights on Praise now, not spending much time wallowing over Linette's rejection. He did seem fickle, but I wasn't about to voice that thought.

'Is that what you think I deserve?' Linette asked, her eyes fierce. 'To be second best? A backup plan?'

Miles didn't respond. His body was tense, and the light of the nearby jack-o'-lanterns showed the fear in his eyes, but he didn't appear to be panicking.

'Ma'am, it's over now,' Cunningham said again. 'Put down the dagger.'

'Never!' she shrieked.

A low rumble sounded from nearby. The next second, the dinosaur sculpture collapsed, pumpkins rolling and toppling right on to Linette and Miles. They both got knocked to the ground and disappeared beneath the cascade of falling jack-o'-lanterns.

I stood frozen with Callum and Tessa, but the police jumped into action, closing in on the scene and tossing and rolling pumpkins aside until they uncovered Linette.

She seemed dazed, and when two officers pulled her to her feet, she no longer held the dagger. Within seconds, the officers had her handcuffed.

Other officers dug out Miles and helped him to his feet.

'I'm OK. I'm OK,' he assured them. He seemed a little unsteady, but he soon found his balance.

With her hands fastened behind her, Linette sobbed. 'She ruined everything! I just wanted my life to be my own!'

As the police led Linette away, Flossie and Fancy bounded over to me. I crouched down to hug them, relief that Genevieve's killer had been caught causing a wave of emotion to wash over me.

'That was you, wasn't it?' I whispered to the dogs. I was sure they were responsible for toppling the sculpture.

They wagged their tails, moonlight glinting in their brown eyes. Fancy bayed and Flossie barked.

'Yes,' I whispered, agreeing with what I thought they were saying, 'you really are heroes.'

THIRTY-EIGHT

The first day of November brought with it a hint of the approaching winter. Frost covered the grass in the morning, crunching beneath my feet as I trekked out to the barn in the semidarkness with Callum, Stardust, and the spaniels. The frost had disappeared by mid-morning, but the sun stayed hidden behind gray clouds and an icy wind swirled through the farmyard, sending dried leaves dancing and skittering, much to Stardust's delight. She played and cavorted about, the spaniels soon joining in the fun.

The wind and leaden sky didn't bother me in the least. I viewed the changing weather as a good excuse to wear cozy clothes and indulge in hot drinks.

As soon as the morning farm work was done, Callum met me in the kitchen to do some baking while Stardust and the spaniels settled in for a snooze, tuckered out from all their running and playing.

'Something smells good,' Brody remarked when he arrived at the farmhouse with Tessa in the middle of the day.

An apple pie – destined to be dessert that evening – was baking in the oven, filling the house with its tantalizing scent.

'I'm afraid I can't share that, even once it's baked, but Callum made brownies this morning.' I held up a plate of the chocolate-glazed squares.

Brody grinned. 'Even better.'

'He's always had a weakness for chocolate,' Tessa said with a smile. 'We've got that in common.'

She and Brody settled at the kitchen table while Callum and I brewed coffee and tea to go with our brownies. Tessa had texted me an hour earlier, letting me know that Brody had some information he could share that might help to appease my lingering curiosity about the murder case. Of course, I hadn't hesitated to invite them over.

Now, while Callum filled three mugs with coffee, I poured myself a cup of tea.

'Linette basically confessed at the park. Has she tried to take back what she said?' I asked as I joined the others at the table.

'Not at all, thankfully,' Brody said. 'Once she started talking, it's like she couldn't stop. She had a lifetime of grievances all bottled up, just waiting to spill out.'

'I don't get it,' Callum said from his seat next to mine. 'If Genevieve was so terrible to Linette, why did she stay friends with her for so long? I know she said it was easier to be friends with Genevieve in middle school than the alternative, but what about once they became adults?'

'I'm no psychologist,' Brody replied, 'but Linette definitely has some issues. I think she fed off of Genevieve's attention – when she gave it in a positive way – and by the time she might have been ready to move on, Genevieve wouldn't let her.'

'Like following her here to Twilight Cove,' I said.

Brody nodded. 'Maybe it was a rivalry or all about control, or some of both. Anything Linette achieved or added to her life, Genevieve found a way to take it away or one-up her.'

'That's really sick,' Tessa said.

'Linette and Genevieve both had their problems, that's for sure.' Brody paused to take a sip of his coffee. 'Apparently, Linette overheard Genevieve trying to take over her role for the Trail of Terror.'

I nodded, remembering that evening. 'I didn't realize she'd overheard the conversation, but Linette was definitely still here at the farm. Genevieve even tried to bribe her way into the role. She offered a big donation to the sanctuary, but Auntie O turned it down.'

'That's because Olivia's smart.' Tessa selected a brownie off the plate. 'That was really dirty of Genevieve.'

'She wanted to be queen of everything,' Brody said. 'Ultimately, that was her downfall. Maybe Linette was troubled from the start, or maybe she became poisoned by Genevieve's toxic influence. In the end, two lives were destroyed.'

'And here I thought her grief was genuine,' I said. 'I knew she was a skilled actress, right from the moment she auditioned for the Trail of Terror. I should have seen through her façade.'

'She had us all fooled,' Brody assured me.

That didn't give me much comfort.

'How did you even know that Linette was at the Pumpkin Glow that evening?' I asked as I nudged the plate of brownies closer to Brody.

He'd already eaten one, but he was eyeing the plate with obvious longing.

He took another brownie, but replied to my question before biting into it. 'We were out looking for her after we got the arrest warrant. An officer spotted her vehicle and called it in. We followed her to the park and planned to arrest her as she got out of her car, but she saw us coming and ran.'

'And hid behind the pumpkin dinosaur,' Tessa said to finish.

'Which turned out to be a good thing, in the end,' Callum added.

Fancy lifted her head and let out a soft 'a-woo', as if she were agreeing. Then she snuggled back in with Flossie and Stardust for another snooze.

Tessa nudged Brody with her elbow. 'Tell them what cracked the case.'

'I probably shouldn't encourage you, Georgie,' Brody said, 'but I have to admit that the investigation really started to move forward after you gave us that tip.'

'The one about the apricot kernels?' Callum asked.

Brody nodded. 'How did you make the connection?' he asked me before taking a bite of his brownie.

'I was looking at an almond tart recipe in a book passed down to Auntie O by her mother, and I realized that the tarts – made with almond flour – contained no gluten. Linette had told me that Genevieve wouldn't eat her baking because Linette used her grandmother's recipes from back when going gluten-free wasn't really on people's minds.'

'But almond tarts don't contain gluten to begin with,' Tessa added.

'Exactly,' I said. 'So Genevieve could have eaten them. I remembered a news story I'd read online, about a man who ate apricot kernels as a snack and ended up with cyanide poisoning. That prompted me to look up the web page for the Urban Moon, a store in Los Angeles where Linette told me she'd purchased some chocolate-covered blueberries. When I searched the online store, I discovered that the Urban Moon sells apricot kernels as a specialty snack food.'

Callum shook his head. 'I still can't believe something so poisonous is sold as a snack.'

'There's a warning on the package, but it's small,' Brody said. 'If an adult eats just one or two in a day, it's usually not a problem, but more than that can be deadly.'

'Crazy,' Tessa said.

'Anyway,' Brody continued after finishing off his second brownie, 'once we knew that Linette had been to the Urban Moon, we got in touch with the store. Linette paid for the apricot kernels with cash, but the shop had a record of the transaction and they still had the surveillance footage from that day. Sure enough, Linette was caught on camera, buying the kernels along with the chocolate-covered blueberries.'

I wrapped my hands around my cup of tea, letting the warmth seep into my skin. 'So she had the murder planned out well in advance.'

'Maybe she didn't know exactly when she was going to strike,' Brody said, 'but when she overheard Genevieve trying to take over her role for the Trail of Terror, Linette put her plan into action and baked the tarts.'

'But how could she be sure that Genevieve would eat them and not serve them to a guest or something?' Callum asked.

I'd wondered the same thing.

'We asked her about that,' Brody said. 'Linette gave Genevieve half a dozen tarts, filled with apricot jam – which Linette knew was her favorite. Apparently, although Genevieve claimed she never ate sweets, she would binge-eat them in private. Linette knew about that habit, and she also knew that Genevieve wouldn't be able to resist the jam-filled almond tarts. Sure enough, Genevieve must have eaten all of them. We found six foil tart tins in her recycling, but she must have washed them out because there wasn't even a crumb left on them.'

I thought that over as I drank more tea. 'Still, Linette took a risk. Genevieve could have shared the tarts with someone. Barclay, for example.'

Brody nodded his thanks as Callum refilled his coffee mug. 'I think Linette was so consumed by her anger and resentment that she wasn't too concerned about collateral damage.'

Tessa shuddered. 'I'm so glad she's behind bars now.'

'I think the whole town is relieved,' Callum said.

'I certainly am,' I agreed before asking, 'What about Hattie? Didn't she try to kill Genevieve too? How many people wanted the woman dead?'

'Hattie swears she never intended to harm Genevieve,' Brody replied. 'She admitted to sending anonymous threatening notes. She says she just wanted to scare Genevieve and make her look like a fool. Hattie thought if Genevieve claimed that Bigfoot had scared her off the road, people would think she was nuts, and – since reputation seemed important to Genevieve – she might decide to move back to Portland, especially if she feared someone was out to get her.'

'But Genevieve crashed her car because of that stunt,' Tessa pointed out. 'She could have been badly hurt, if not killed.'

'I think Hattie gets that now,' Brody said. 'She seems generally remorseful.'

'How did she even know that Genevieve would be driving along that road that night?' Callum asked.

I'd wondered that myself.

'She knew that Genevieve would be at a book club meeting that evening, and the route she'd likely take home,' Brody explained. 'Hattie bought a GPS tracker for one of her cats and decided to plant it in Genevieve's car. That way she knew when Genevieve was driving her way.'

'Do you think she'll end up in jail?' I asked, thinking of Sylvester and Hattie's other cats.

Brody tipped his head to one side as he considered the question. 'She's facing charges, but there's a good chance she won't do any jail time.'

We all fell silent for a moment as we soaked in the information.

'What? No more questions?' Brody asked with a grin.

I returned his smile. 'Give me a minute and I can probably come up with more.'

'I've no doubt.'

'In the meantime,' Callum said, 'I've got a question. Did the Bigfoot costume belong to Miles?'

'Oh, good one.' I smiled at him over the rim of my mug before taking a sip of my tea.

'Hattie stole it from Miles's house,' Brody explained. 'She was there one day, picking up donations for the charity shop where she volunteers. Miles left her alone in the basement to sort through what she thought the shop would want, and that's when she saw the costume. Apparently, that's also when she got the idea for the prank.' He took a sip of coffee before adding, 'Georgie, you were right about Praise's coat, by the way.'

He'd saved me from asking the question that was on the tip of my tongue. 'So she really was at the park on the night Genevieve died.'

'She admitted to it when we spoke to her several days ago,' Brody said. 'She was the first to find Genevieve, just seconds before you and Callum arrived on the scene. When she heard you coming, she panicked and ran. She thought Genevieve was already dead and she didn't want to end up as a suspect if there was foul play involved.'

Tessa nodded as she thought that over. 'Because everyone knew Praise had argued with Genevieve.'

'Exactly,' Brody confirmed.

I was glad that Praise wasn't the killer, especially considering her friendship with my aunt. I'd learned from Auntie O that Praise had received the bouquet of flowers from Miles as an apology gift and an attempt to woo her. He'd told her that he regretted having a hand in Praise losing her position as the head organizer for the Pumpkin Glow. She'd accepted the flowers, and the apology, but had firmly turned down his request for a date. I didn't think she needed to know that the flowers were likely the same ones that Miles had originally purchased for Linette.

I sat back in my chair, considering everything. 'What a mess. I'm glad it's over now, but Genevieve sure caused a lot of problems. Linette too.'

'Like for the guy who broke his leg,' Tessa said.

I nodded. 'Enrique Ramos.'

Brody drained the last of his coffee. 'Genevieve's sister arrived in town this morning. She didn't come sooner because her mother-in-law was in the hospital.'

'What was she like to deal with?' I asked. 'With a sister like Genevieve and a son like Barclay, I can't imagine she's Ms Congeniality.'

'She definitely thinks her son can do no wrong and swears that he never would have stolen anything from anyone, but despite that delusion, she hasn't been too difficult. So far, anyway. She even seems to know that Genevieve wasn't the nicest woman. When she heard Enrique's story, she said she was going to compensate him the way Genevieve should have done. She'll use some of the money she inherits from her sister to do that.'

That came as a surprise, but a pleasant one.

Tessa pushed back her chair. 'We should leave you to get ready for your dinner tonight.'

Callum and I walked her and Brody out to the driveway, where

Brody had left his truck. While the guys chatted, Tessa and I fell behind so we could talk privately.

'Are you nervous about tonight?' Tessa asked.

'And excited,' I said. 'I hope I'll be able to eat dinner. My stomach keeps swirling so much that I don't even have an appetite for Callum's brownies.'

Tessa put an arm around me. 'Try not to stress so much. Everything will be great.'

'I hope so. Callum says his parents are really laid back so . . .' The swirling in my stomach intensified.

'They'll love you.'

'That's what Callum keeps saying.'

Tessa gave me a squeeze. 'He's a smart man. You should listen to him.'

Fancy chimed in with an 'a-woo'.

I laughed. 'Overthinking is what I do best, but I'll try not to stress so much.'

We slowed to a stop and Tessa crouched down to fuss over the spaniels.

'How are things with you and Brody since the whole murder suspect thing?' I asked in a low voice.

She smiled as she stood up. 'We're good. He never suspected me for a second, and after we had that chat outside Genevieve's house, he kept checking in on me by text message, pretty much every day. He's a good friend.'

Brody and Callum had stopped by the driver's door of the truck, still chatting. Brody glanced over our way and his gaze settled on Tessa for a second or two. She must have noticed, because her cheeks turned a light shade of pink.

She always swore that Brody saw her as just a friend, but something in the way he looked at her in that moment made me wonder if that was changing.

Time would tell. For now, I kept those thoughts to myself.

Tessa hugged me and then got into the truck with Brody. Callum and I stood with the dogs, waving as they drove off.

As we wandered back to the house, Callum settled an arm across my shoulders. 'Time for us to start cooking dinner?'

'Yes,' I replied, smiling despite my nerves. 'Operation: Meet the Parents is officially underway.'

THIRTY-NINE

The spaniels alerted us to the arrival of Callum's parents later that afternoon. Flossie bounced around by the back door, barking with excitement, while Fancy howled. Startled by all the noise, Stardust skittered across the floor and disappeared upstairs in a blur of gray fur. I froze in the middle of the kitchen, suddenly finding it hard to breathe while my stomach performed a crazy acrobatic routine.

'They're here,' Callum said, looking out the window.

When I saw the big smile on his face, the tension in my body eased enough that I could draw air into my lungs. Even so, my anxiety must have shown on my face, because he took my hand and kissed my cheek.

'They'll love you, Georgie.'

His confidence in that regard warmed my heart even though it didn't erase my nerves.

The dogs were still making a racket and we could see through the window that a white crossover had come to a stop near the farmhouse, so Callum opened the back door. Flossie and Fancy shot out so fast that they sailed right over the porch steps and hit the lawn running.

Callum and I followed after them, though not at such a rapid pace. Flossie and Fancy were already over by the parked car, their tails wagging and their entire bodies wiggling with excitement. Even though they'd never met Callum's parents before, they seemed to sense that the visitors were welcome ones.

Both front doors of the crossover opened. Callum's dad unfolded himself from the driver's seat while his mom climbed out of the passenger side. Lachlan McQuade wasn't quite as tall as his son, but he still stood a little over six feet. He had gray hair and blue eyes and wore jeans with a polo shirt. Linda McQuade was at least a foot shorter than Callum, and her fair hair was straight rather than wavy, but she had the same green eyes as her son.

Fancy let out a long 'woo' while Flossie danced and bounced around the newcomers.

'This is quite the welcome,' Mr McQuade said with a grin as he leaned down to greet the dogs.

'Oh, they're adorable,' Callum's mom exclaimed as she came around the front of the car.

Flossie bounded over to greet her while Fancy continued to lap up attention from Callum's dad.

Within seconds, however, Mrs McQuade focused her attention on me and Callum. Tears welled in her eyes as she beamed at us.

'There's my boy.'

Callum stepped forward and hugged her. She returned the hug, giving him a good squeeze.

'It's good to see you, Mom,' Callum said as he released her.

She beamed at him again and then turned her eyes on me.

My stomach gave another nervous flip-flop, but then her smile grew even brighter and she wrapped her arms around me.

'Georgie, I'm so glad to finally meet you.'

My nerves melted away with the warmth of her hug. 'Same here.'

She pulled back and held me at arm's length. 'You're even more beautiful in person than you are in the photos Callum sent us.'

My cheeks heated at the compliment, but I couldn't help but smile as I thanked her.

Callum's dad hugged his son and then me next. Both of his parents exuded a warm and welcoming energy that made me feel far more at ease than I ever could have hoped I would.

'Dinner will be ready soon,' Callum said, 'but there's still time for you to get settled. How about we meet you at the cabin? Just drive past the barn and you'll see it up ahead. Georgie and I will walk over.'

Fancy let out a 'woo'.

'Flossie and Fancy will come too,' he added with a grin.

'I'm so glad to hear that,' Mrs McQuade said to the dogs.

They wagged their tails and looked up at her like they were already falling in love.

Callum's parents got back in their car and drove slowly across the farm while Flossie and Fancy walked with Callum and me.

'You doing OK so far?' Callum asked, taking my hand as we walked.

'I'm doing great,' I said with a smile. 'They're so nice.'

Callum laughed at the note of surprise in my voice. 'You didn't believe me when I told you that?'

'I believed you, but part of me was still worried they might not take to me.'

He shook his head, but his eyes were full of affection when he looked my way. 'That was never a possibility.'

I swung our joined hands as we walked, happy to no longer be riddled with anxiety.

'So you're not nervous anymore?' Callum checked.

I thought about the question for a second. 'I've gone from seventy-five percent nervous and twenty-five percent excited to one percent nervous and ninety-nine percent excited.'

'That's a good percentage, but that one percent of nerves will be gone soon.' He squeezed my hand. 'I promise.'

I smiled as happiness glowed inside me, because I knew he was right.

An hour later, Callum and I were seated at the farmhouse's dining room table along with his parents and Auntie O. We passed dishes around and loaded our plates with food while the dogs and Stardust – their stomachs already filled with their own dinners – slept beneath the table. The warmth and friendliness of Callum's parents made them easy to talk to, even for me, an introvert who sometimes suffered from bouts of shyness. It was like I'd known Lachlan and Linda for far longer than an hour, and we seemed to spend as much time laughing and smiling as we did chatting and eating.

After Callum and I had cleared the plates, I slipped back into the kitchen to get the coffee I'd put on to brew a short while earlier. The sun had set long ago, but the porch light was on. Through the kitchen window, I saw a flutter of wings, so I paused and looked out to find Euclid sitting on the porch railing. His gaze met mine and he blinked before spreading his wings and taking off into the night.

Smiling, I grabbed the coffee pot and set it on a tray with several mugs. On the way back to the dining room, I paused in the doorway – just for a second – and took in the sight of Auntie O laughing and talking with Callum and his parents.

The scene didn't just warm my heart; it also felt *right*.

Like it was meant to be.

Callum caught my eye as I continued into the room, and in that moment, I knew all was right in my world.

Acknowledgments

It's taken a village to bring the Magical Menagerie Mysteries to life, and I'm truly grateful to each and every person involved. Special thanks to Jessica Faust, Victoria Britton, Laurie Johnson, Piers Tilbury, Lianne Slavin, and the entire team at Severn House. Thanks also to Carina Chao, for planting the kernel that the idea for this story grew from. Thank you to my review crew, my readers, and everyone in the book community who helps to spread the word about cozy mysteries.